VARSITY HOUSE PET

BWWM Dark Hockey Romance

LAGUNA GROVE VIPERS
BOOK II

JAMILA JASPER

Get updates on my releases.

ISBN: 979-8-3303-3671-5

❋ Created with Vellum

SERIES TITLES

Laguna Grove Vipers Trilogy

Varsity Servant

Varsity House Pet

Varsity Property

AUTHOR'S NOTE

Makeba & Jayce's Story

This dark and spicy romance story is filled with triggers that will potentially disturb some readers including violence of all kinds, explicit language, and behavior portrayed that is downright criminal and morally depraved.

Jayce may disturb your sensibilities at first, so if you are sensitive to this type of content, proceed with caution. This book contains situations that are disturbing AF.

This is a work of fiction and Jamila Jasper does not endorse any illegal or unethical behavior IRL.

In my book universe… all bets are off.

Prepare yourself for triggers and behavior that will horrify most people.

Through the twists, the turns, the mess and the drama, I have a spicy, deliciously dark interracial romance story with wintery hockey themes, lots of heat between the sheets and a NO cheating guaranteed happily ever after ending.

DESCRIPTION

Only good girls get to sleep in my bed.
Getting laid before the big game should be easy.
Chicks at Laguna Grove dig hockey players…
Except the one woman Jayce wants.
His African American lab partner, Makeba Winston.

It's nothing he can't solve with tequila, a <u>thick leather leash</u>, and a pillow at the foot of his bed.

Makeba won't become his girlfriend right away, but a few days tied to the bed ought to change her mind…
Right?

BLACK CHICK IN PHYSICS CLASS

JAYCE CLUTTERBUCK

"Smoke some weed, Jayce. Do whatever it takes to calm your ass down. You're going to kill your chances at a career in this game if you don't pull back. I mean it."

Tuck's words of wisdom pulse through my head as I stare at Makeba's notebook. I only know her name because she writes it in cursive (who even writes cursive anymore) at the top of her notebook every day before class. *Makeba Winston–Physics 110.* Then she writes the date–which is the only reason I ever know what day of the week it is. I patiently wait for her to write the date before I grab her pen.

"Hey!" she hisses.

I nudge her with my elbow. "How much are you selling?"

"Excuse me?" she whispers back.

"I can buy an ounce after class, but only if it's under $350."

"Can you please give me my pen back?" she whispers.

Our professor, an old German dude named Lenny Marx, gives us a knowing stare and adjusts his glasses. It's old ass professor speak for "shut the fuck up and stop disrupting my physics class". This old dude doesn't get it. This is an emergency. I *need* to buy some weed. It's way more important than my dumb physics grade. Unfortunately, Makeba refuses to admit that somewhere on her person she has some dank ass kush.

"What's the matter? You don't sell to white boys?" I whisper. She gets all flustered the minute I talk to her. I like that. There's something about Makeba that's totally hilarious. I *love* tormenting her during class. This time, I actually need something. And she'd better deliver.

"Sell what?"

She's playing coy. I get it.

"*Reefer*."

Her eyes narrow. I wonder how much shit I would get for getting with a chick like her? Probably a lot. Not like she'd ever take the plunge. I've seen the classes she takes–classes with words like *supremacy* and *hegemony* in the title. That basically means she hates white people, and she definitely hates me based on her answer.

"I don't sell weed, period. Now give me my pen back."

I roll her pen across her notebook back in her general direction. I don't believe her, but maybe she's afraid of getting caught selling weed in class. I don't know what her problem is, but she definitely has a problem and it's not just the weed thing. Something's definitely wrong with Makeba today. Normally, she makes a different annoyed face when I'm bugging her. Today's annoyed face seems a little... I dunno... puffy? Man, she'd kill me if I called her puffy.

I mess with her all the time and normally she's totally chill, and she only makes that teeth kissing noise with her mouth and glares. She doesn't ignore me. I hate being ignored. My step-dad, my one and only shit-hole parent, ignored me my entire childhood. That changed when I hit the ice for the first time, but Makeba... she reminds me what it's like to be fucking invisible. What the hell is her problem?

I stare at her for clues (and hoping to piss her off). She's wearing this weird scarf around her neck. She *never* wears a scarf. It's not like I spend class looking at her neck or her collarbones, or her crazy long hair or anything, but the scarf is definitely blocking my view—especially of what she's got underneath that sweater. That's the best part of college. My step-dad sent me to Catholic School for high school. Zero tits for four painful years...

Boobs. It would be significantly easier to get good grades in this class if there weren't boobs right next to me every day. Makeba makes it impossible to focus. It's only fair I punish her for that. I pretend to listen to Marx for a little while longer, throwing Makeba off the trail.

She's taking notes on *magnetism* when I grab her pen away mid sentence.

"What the hell is wrong with you, white boy?" she whispers, pinching my thigh and trying to reach for the pen that I have under the table, dangling between my fingers and between my legs. I love our little games. Makeba gets so mad. It's pretty funny.

"I have a name and it isn't *white boy*. How would you like it if I called you *black chick?*"

She rolls her eyes. "Is your name *dumbass?*"

I lean over and whisper into her ear. "It's Jayce. You know that."

Getting close to her is a total mistake. That perfume is *incredible*. Fuck. This is so goddamn wrong. Dustin keeps trying to warn me I'll only get in trouble if I mess with the wrong chicks at this school. I'm not trying to mess with Makeba, I swear.

"That's what I said," she said. "Dumbass."

At least she's talking to me. I take my index finger and poke her in the side.

"What's with the scarf?"

"Mind your business," Makeba hisses, pulling her body away from mine. "And give me my damn pen back, you hooligan."

I flip the pen between my fingers and then stick it in my pocket. Makeba won't get away with blowing me off this easily.

"Where do you buy weed, then? Since you don't sell."

"I don't buy weed. Why would you assume I buy weed?"

"Because…" I whisper, trying not to sound offensive. "You're black."

Makeba smacks me across the face. Hard. Everyone in front of us turns around to look. Professor Marx ignores the smack, except for a small smile that crosses his face. Man, some professors have it out for athletes. They think just because we play sports we don't care about school or something. I care about college. It's just that I care about hockey more. *Way* more. That's why I need weed. According to Tuck, I need to chill and Dustin's dealer started charging him double after the incident with the Madagascar hissing cockroach.

I seethe quietly as Makeba writes her boring girl notes on *magnetism*. My cheek stings. Where the fuck did she learn to hit like that?

I can't believe she *smacked* me. Never in my entire life has any chick smacked the shit out of Jayce Clutterbuck. What the hell did I do wrong? Chicks are full of it. They say they want honesty, but they don't want it. At all. Next time she tries some shit like that, I'll make her pay… If only this class wasn't so fucking boring, maybe I could keep my mind off her. It's much easier for her to ignore me than the other way around. Maybe she can focus really well because of Adderall or something. I make a mental note to ask her at the end of class.

Towards the end of class, Makeba surprises me. She opens my notebook, which I haven't exactly looked at throughout class and she scribbles on a blank page...

I can get you weed. Let's talk after class.

Excellent. Murphy wants me to get a prescription, but I don't have time to sit around getting permission to smoke weed when this is a liberal arts college in Massachusetts. Practically everyone here smokes weed even if it's technically against the rules to do it on campus. Hey, it's legal. That's what counts. I can't wait to get Makeba's hook up. See? I knew the black chick in my class would have weed. Makeba just can't stand how secretly smart I am.

"Thanks, chica," I whisper.

"Shut up," she grumbles. "I'm trying to pay attention."

"Why?"

"Because I'm an A student."

"A what student?"

"An A student."

"I don't get it."

"How are you this dumb?" Makeba whispers to herself, as if just because she thinks I'm dumb, that means I can't hear or understand English. Whatever. I can ignore her attitude as long as I get whatever dope ass Jamaican weed

Makeba probably has access to. Physics couldn't end any faster. Professor Marx (technically Dr. Marx) hands back all the pop quizzes from last week and mine is the only one he hands back face down. Half the class snickers. Including Makeba. My cheeks feel warm, but I have to hold my head high.

I'm here to play hockey and without the hockey team, this school would be nothing. We have a shit basketball team, a worse football team, and the average weight of the guys on our baseball team is 105 lbs. Laguna Grove would be dead without hockey. Dead.

When our stupid class is finally over, Makeba tugs on my sleeve and points to a hallway with a bunch of empty classrooms. I sling my backpack over my shoulder as she dumps her stuff messily into her purse or whatever, and then I follow her.

"How much can you get me? I'm tight on cash for a while, so–

She interrupts me. "If I help you get weed, you have to do something for me."

"Like what?"

"Can I trust you, Jayce?"

"Probably not, since we don't really like each other."

Our eyes meet for a second, and Makeba scowls and then rolls her eyes. See? Chicks hate honesty.

"Right," she says. "We hate each other. But you're a crazy ass white boy who knows how to fight and I have basically unlimited weed."

"Unlimited weed?"

"Focus, Jayce."

I'm *trying*. "Right. Can you trust me?"

"Can I?" she repeats, suddenly sounding… scared. That freaks me out. I mean, it gets me interested because I don't know what the hell could scare a chick that just smacked me in the face like it was nothing. I'm a 6'4" mass of muscle. There are guys over six feet tall scared to skate near me. Not Makeba. So whatever is scaring her must be pretty bad.

"Are you scared or something?"

She folds her arms and bites her lower lip, like she's considering her options. She mustn't have many options if I'm the guy she's coming to. Like she said, we hate each other.

"Yes," she says finally, following up with a sigh.

No details follow. Why won't she just ask me to kick the guy's ass already?

"Okay…"

Maybe she's just a weird chick. I mean, I already knew she was a weird chick, but this is extra weird.

"Promise you won't make this weird," she says.

"Whatever."

Does this chick want to sell me weed or what? Makeba sighs and sets her bag on the ground. I can't look away from her and I don't want to. She's kinda tall for a chick, but not as tall as me. 5'10" maybe. She's skinny, but curvy in the right places – my favorite places.

She tugs at the scarf tied around her neck and she slowly unties the knot. Her body tenses, and her dark skin glows almost blue beneath the fluorescent light in the hallway. She won't look at me, but it's cool. I'm looking at her, taking in every bit of her. Fuck, I'm messed up, I know. I always talk shit about guys who go after black chicks. It's just a habit. Guy talk.

I'm pretty close to her, closer than I've been before, because this is supposed to be a secret drug deal or whatever and we need to be subtle. I don't stop watching her as she moves slowly, just in case this is a joke or something. I don't want her to mess with me or try to get me back.

Makeba won't meet my gaze as she moves the fabric away from her neck, sniffling as she loosens the knot. She unwraps the scarf and lets the fabric fall to the ground. I can already see parts of what she's covering up. Holy. Shit. She takes her sweater off, which almost gets me excited, but she's wearing a tank top underneath and what she shows me fades my excitement right away.

I don't feel very chill at all. I *feel...*

"What the fuck happened to you? Who did that?"

It burns. I don't expect my voice to sound so concerned. I clear my throat and try to play it cool, but it really burns. Someone hurt her. Makeba. She's just a chick who sits next to me in physics. She isn't popular. She doesn't look like the chicks who hang around the hockey house. No way. She's not a Pesthouse chick at all. But whatever happened to Makeba looks pretty fucking serious. I guess she messed with the wrong drug dealer or whatever.

"I got hurt," she says. "Duh."

She doesn't answer my question. She doesn't seem like the type of chick to get into a fight, but there are bruises everywhere. I feel like a dick for thinking about it, but I didn't realize bruises could show up on skin that dark. They're deep purple and black, but some of them have a greenish hue. Whatever happened to this chick, she took a serious beating. I want to kill whoever did this to her.

"Boyfriend problems?" I ask. The second I say it, I know it's a stupid fucking thing to say. I just want to lighten the mood and wipe that terrified look off her face. At least I'm successful with that mission, but her terror gives way to anger.

"That's not funny, Jayce."

I hate when she tells me off. Fuck, I always feel so dumb around this chick.

"What does this have to do with my weed, then?" I snap, turning toward impatience. Makeba's tone reminds me we aren't friends. That means I don't need to know who beat the shit out of her and I definitely don't need to care. But I can't help wondering about it. She's innocent. She's the type of chick who never leaves her room on the weekends, never goes to parties.

"If you want weed from me, I need help."

"What kind of help?"

"I need to learn how to fight, so I can get the person who did this to me."

"Don't you have a big black boyfriend who can kick his ass?"

"I don't have a boyfriend," she bristles, giving me a death stare like she wants to end my life. "Now, will you help me or not?"

Sheesh. Most people just want money for weed. I don't get what she wants from me.

"Why are you asking me this?"

"I'm Kya Ambrose's friend. I've been to all your hockey games this season. You spend half your time in the penalty box for kicking someone's ass. You're the only guy I know who can help me. And who can keep my secret."

"What makes you think I can keep your secret?"

"Because I'm too irrelevant to your life for you not to keep it," she snaps. "Now, will you just say yes? I want to take care of this before my friends find out."

2

DUMB AS DIRT

MAKEBA WINSTON

I know Jayce is as dumb as dirt, but does he have to be so impossible to talk to? I just want him to give me an honest answer. I'm already freezing my ass off without my scarf on and I'm nervous about the bruises. I don't want Kya or Raven to see. I don't want anyone to see. I don't know what B.J. will do to me if I tell, and I don't want my friends to know that I let some guy choke me out and kick me across the floor like a football. It's humiliating. I should have fought back.

All I did was crawl for the door as he landed another kick on my back and a punch in my ribs. I ran for my life back to my bedroom. The trauma screwed with my head. I just lay there for hours, still. In the morning, I couldn't bring myself to go to the health center, or to classes. I was just *so ashamed.* I looked it up online and this article said some people respond to trauma like this.

I never wanted to be that person. I should be a badass and I'm going to fix this. We only have one more night until spring break. I'll tell my friends before we leave just so they don't kill me for keeping it from them, but I at least want them to know that I have someone to teach me self-defense lined up.

It can't be any more humiliating than going to Jayce Clutterbuck for help, but he's the only person I can think of. I don't exactly know a lot of guys. They don't flock to me the way they flock to Kya. Even Raven, who openly prefers her book boyfriends, at least has guys online messaging her constantly. I'm the dark-skinned friend who gets overlooked. I think I look great, but guys don't seem to see it. I take care of myself, I eat right, I have a good sense of humor, I volunteer at a daycare, I have friends and hobbies and excellent grades. None of that matters to anyone at this stupid, shallow college. They just see my skin color and react. A lot of black women don't know what it's like to walk around with skin this dark and have so many people respond with... *revulsion.*

That's not how Jayce is looking at me now, I don't think. I have zero genuine experience with guys. I'm going to assume that guys outside of Raven's novels don't sit around giving you smoldering looks, so that can't be what's happening with Jayce.

The 6'4" hockey player's sorrel eyes fix on my neck and I can't help but think he's judging me or thinking something super racist because he takes forever to give me an answer. Then it's just one word that ignites hot shame through every inch of my skin.

"Sex," Jayce says, a smirk teasing across his face.

"I asked you to say *'yes'*," I remind him.

He's always hearing the wrong thing–especially in physics class.

It's unfortunate because if he weren't so dumb, he would be attractive. I mean, he's hot as hell. I'm not like Kya and Raven. I don't deny that I like white boys. That's never been my problem with white boys. What's not to like? Smooth skin that changes in all those exotic pink colors. Eyes that come in all these unnatural and alluring jewel tones. And that silky ass hair... It's so *weird* to touch, but I could run my hands through their hair all day.

White guys don't like *me*. That's more of the problem. I'm not some mixed girl with latte colored skin and bouncy prime-time TV approved curls. I'm definitely not like the white girls at Laguna Grove with identical blonde hair-styles and closets filled with bright pink designer clothes.

I'm invisible. And the last white boy I tried to date...

I bite my lip and avoid Jayce's gaze because I don't get why he just blurted that word out.

"Forget the weed. I'll teach you how to fight, but... I want sex."

Okay, he's crazy. Just like B.J. Maybe I need to make a new

rule that I never talk to any white man ever again because any time it happens, they're deranged.

"Why...? I can get you weed. Don't worry about it."

Yeah, I have no idea where to get weed. I can ask Raven, but she would just want to ask B.J. and I want to plan how to tell my friends so they know that I'm not a damsel in distress. Black women are supposed to be strong and my friends are some of the strongest I know. I'm just too ashamed of what happened to me to tell them without a plan.

"Because... I'm a guy."

Jayce seriously doesn't think anything through.

"So you would have sex with just about *anyone* because you're a guy?"

"Not anyone," Jayce answers, grinning and winking.

I wonder if he says that to all the girls he brings back to his room. It's not exactly a campus secret that Jayce Clutterbuck–and 90% of the hockey team–gets around.

"This isn't about sex," I snap, struggling to find my words through the warm, uncomfortable feeling of standing beneath Jayce's gaze. "I just need to learn how to throw a few punches and maybe... I don't know. Like a kick or something. I need to fuck someone up."

"Sex. I want sex in return," Jayce insists. That boy's head is 100% Egyptian cotton. No brain.

"Can you stop bringing up the sex thing? Look, I'll get you weed, I'll pay you, I'll do whatever you want, but I'm not going to have sex with you," I hiss, glancing around nervously in case anyone passes by.

How humiliating would it be if I traded my virginity just so I could kick B.J.'s ass? I think I've suffered enough. It's not like Jayce makes a compelling offer. He's one of those guys that's so attractive that you know he's never had to try hard in his life to please a woman. He probably wouldn't know the first thing about what to do with a woman in bed, especially not a black woman, considering his constant slew of cringe-worthy, racially inappropriate commentary.

And he's way more experienced than me. I wouldn't know what to do in bed with a guy like him except embarrass myself and maybe stare at his abs. No way. *No way.* Jayce is way too…

"Why not? I'm hot," Jayce says, clearly dumbfounded that a girl on the Laguna Grove campus would dare turn him down. He should take a walk in my shoes for a change.

"You're not hot," I snap, hoping that deflates his ego enough, so he lets the entire subject go. "You're a dick. Clearly I have a good reason why I need to learn how to fight and you won't even help me."

"It's only fair I get something in exchange."

"Screw you, Jayce. Coming to you was a total mistake."

I pick my things up and re-wrap my scarf. He's being super annoying and just standing there, watching me. Hello, I dismissed you?

"I'm leaving," I announce again, because it's still annoying that Jayce is leaning against the wall and staring at me in some type of weird white boy power move.

"Are you coming to Cole's party?" he asks.

"Why do you care?"

"No reason."

"I'm coming. But only to support Kya. You can just forget any of this happened."

I push past him and hurry down the halls away from him as fast as I can. Jayce doesn't care enough to follow me. Since the new semester started and I got my new room, I've been enjoying my alone time. Unfortunately, since the whole thing with B.J., I've turned into a recluse. I don't want Kya or Raven to know what happened. I barely want to admit to myself what happened.

It's been three days and the bruises haven't gone away. The only reason my friends haven't noticed that someone kicked the shit out of me is because it's winter in Massachusetts (isn't it always?) and I've been covering myself from head to toe. I want to tell them, but I don't know what B.J. could try next. Paralyzed. That's how I feel–and I hate it. I'm not exactly sheltered, but I'm not exactly experienced. I just have no idea what to do.

I'm scared. And until I can defend myself properly, I don't want to cross him. Still, I know he's the one who hacked Kya, so I know I can't keep this to myself forever. I want to tell them the truth at the party tonight after we've had a few drinks and had some fun before spring break. I don't want them to worry – especially not Kya. She should celebrate that things are all better with her and Cole now. I judged him at first, but when I saw the way he stood up for her... I just felt like I'd never have that. I just felt like I'd never be in love. I want her to have what I probably never will.

I wish the best for Kya. She's lucky. Not all of us girls can be.

I glance down at my phone to respond to the messages Kya and Raven sent me in the morning. They want to meet for lunch. Seeing them without telling them seems like it will be impossible. There's a part of me that still wants to get ready and prepare an exact speech or something.

I sigh and stare at my phone. Maybe I'll never be ready. My interaction with Jayce was a total fail. I'm just going to face this as myself–my boring black girl self.

Defenseless or not, I have to tell them. I shoot off a quick reply to the group chat. I know I have to trust my friends. And anyway, I could seriously luck out and they'll know exactly what to do about B.J. As soon as I enter the dining hall, I spot them. It's mostly Kya. Her hair is literally giant, and she's one of the few girls at Laguna Grove to rock her natural hair. I have nothing against my natural hair, but braids are easier and I can put beads on them and flip them in rude people's faces at lame ass Laguna Grove parties. So it's braids for me until my edges turn to dust.

Raven notices me first and waves. She has her reading glasses on and a new stack of romance novels. She's started reading these creepy romance stories lately about sexy stalkers, and I think she's going a little crazy because of her dating struggles. Online dating was a total bust for her. It's cool, though. I don't mind her crazy romance novels or Kya's sex stories. I'm a little crazy too.

"What's good, ladies?"

"Makeba! We haven't seen your ass in forever," Raven says. "I thought you died."

"I replied to the group chat!"

Kya shakes her head. "You disappeared since the War Hogs game."

"Aren't you hot in here with that scarf?" Raven says, wrinkling her nose. Damn. She's way too observant. I can't even postpone coming clean until I make myself a sandwich or something. At least I had snacks in physics class so I'm not famished.

"Yes, I'm hot with the scarf but... I have something to tell you guys and I don't know how you're going to react."

"What does that mean?" Kya says, dipping her raw broccoli in some ranch and then slowly nibbling at the florets.

"It's obvious," Raven says. "She and B.J. finally did it. She has a hickey."

"She does *not* have a hickey," Kya answers defensively. "And I think if Makeba lost her virginity, we would be the first to know. She wouldn't keep it from us"

"I broke up with B.J. anyway," I blurt out with more attitude than the situation warrants. Shit. My friends can't help it. It's not like they actually know what happened. I immediately feel bad for snapping. The fact that Raven doesn't already know that means B.J. didn't tell her.

"It was just a joke," Raven says. "Sorry."

"Sensitive topic," I mutter. "I didn't know how to tell you guys."

That's not all I have to tell them, but I want to break the news slowly. One step at a time, right?

"Breakups can be hard," Kya agrees. "Did you just want to be alone?"

Raven backs her up. "We missed you."

"It's not that. It's this…"

I slowly unravel my scarf and show my friends my bruises for the first time.

"Oh my God, Makeba! What happened?" Kya asks. I can tell she's ready to leap out of her seat and swing on whoever did that to me. Before I can tell them the truth, a pair of pale hands drag out the chair next to me, scraping it across the dining hall floor. I can smell the thick stench of pot and my throat tightens once I realize who it is. B.J.

"Hey ladies," he mutters, slamming his book bag on the ground and his plate on the table.

"B.J.!" Raven says. "We were just talking about you."

"We were?" Kya mutters. I don't think she's ever fully liked B.J. He turns to me and stares. It's so subtle that I'm the only one who notices how menacing his gaze is. If I talk, I'm dead. If I say anything about him, he'll hurt me.

"That's cool," B.J. says. "Makeba, how's it going? Long time no see…"

He smiles at me and then winks. My throat tightens. *I can't do this. I can't face him.*

"I'm sorry guys, I just remembered I have a peer tutoring meeting," I stammer out, hating myself for lying to them but too freaked out to do anything but escape. "I have to go."

I grab my things and I flee, my heart pounding in fear.

3

AIN'T NO PARTY LIKE A
PESTHOUSE PARTY

JAYCE

Kya, our teammate Cole's new girlfriend, has totally taken control of this party. It's awesome. We don't have to do anything but kick back, get drunk, smoke weed and let her handle all the chick stuff. Kya seems to disagree with our division of labor. Cole's little Hitler emerges with flared nostrils.

"Can you *assholes* stop lazing around smoking weed and get the keg from Dustin's truck? Do you *seriously* expect me to get it all by myself?" Kya complains.

Dustin grins. It's pretty easy to get under Kya's skin and almost always worth the future chewing out from Cole for messing with his girl.

"Aren't you a strong, empowered woman? Can't you lift it on your own?" Dustin complains, taking a huge toke and blowing a cloud of weed smoke all over Kya, who is totally unimpressed. She sucks in a huge breath of air so she can scream at us.

"It's a 160-lb keg, you lazy ass," Kya snaps. "Dustin, Jayce… *get up!*"

We exchange glances. Fine. Messing with her is fun enough, but if we accidentally get Cole's chica started on one of her feminist lectures, we could be here all night. Her lectures can seriously shrivel your dick right up. Dustin and I leave the couch and I hand Kya my half-finished joint, which she rudely crushes beneath her feet while she complains about how little we're helping. Geez. I thought she wanted this to be a nice chick-friendly party instead of a "grotesquely chauvinistic beer-ridden sausage fest" (her words). Whatever.

Dustin and I help her get the kegs in – we have five for the night when the formal party eventually turns into a crazy rager. Then Kya assigns all the dudes in Pesthouse all these little tasks and next thing you know, we're like her little servants and Cole's presiding over everything, making sure none of us talk smack.

This is his party to celebrate his new contract. Once the year's out, he'll play in Boston for three years, earning $10 million. It's one of the best rookie contracts a guy could hope for. Cole deserves it. I'm just a sophomore, so I have another year of playing before I try to get scouted. According to Tuck, if I don't clean up my act, I'll never make it. There's a part of me that wants to prove him wrong, but there's another part of me that just gets so angry…

I hear Kya chattering away on the other side of the room.

"Makeba and Raven are on their way down here, but she won't let Raven in the room while she's getting ready–"

Makeba. Hearing her name brings me back to physics class. I haven't been able to let go of it, but mostly because it was so weird. Everything about it was weird. She doesn't seem like the type of chick to get into fights and she definitely doesn't seem like the type of chick to ask an asshole like me for help. She must be desperate.

Not desperate enough to sleep with me.

Now that pisses me off. I mean… I've never struggled to get a chick to sleep with me. Ever. I normally have to ask once. But she said no. Worse, she said I wasn't even hot.

"Dustin, can we talk?"

"Anything to stop arranging stupid fucking cupcakes."

"I HEARD THAT!" Kya yells at him across the room. She would have made a great Nazi in another life. I should tell her that.

I drag Dustin by the arm and mutter some excuse about hockey, which I don't think Kya believes for a second.

"What's going on?" Dustin asks, reaching into his pocket for a strawberry flavored vape and taking a huge puff. Dustin's a fucking idiot.

"That chick Makeba's coming to the party."

"Who?"

"Kya's friend."

"The hot one or the dark one."

Dustin's my best friend, but he's definitely an idiot.

"The hot one is the dark one."

Dustin narrows his gaze and then shakes his head.

"No way. She's too skinny. And her boobs are too big."

There is no such thing as boobs that are too big. Write that down.

"Can you focus?"

"I thought we were talking about hot girls. I'm very focused. And you know… maybe I have a thing for black girls too. It's like… everyone's tasting them. I want to taste them. I'm on the hunt, brah."

"I don't have a thing for black girls," I snap at Dustin. I don't really want that sort of stuff getting out about me. It makes me seem like a weirdo. I mean… I like sex with chicks – all types of chicks. But a guy like me has a reputation to be cautious about, you know?

"Okay, so what's the question? You want to like… experiment?"

"No. I already asked her to hook up. She said no."

Dustin chuckles. "Wow. Are you serious?"

His caterpillar brows move a little more and he laughs a little harder than necessary.

"Yes, I'm fucking serious," I grumble.

"Does she have a boyfriend?"

"I don't know. Who cares? What chick in her right mind would say no to me?"

"What chick in her right mind would say yes…"

"Dustin… I'm serious. I need your help, dude. I need your tricks. I have to get this girl into bed."

"Why don't you ask Cole?"

"Cole!? He's going to tell me some pussy shit. Dude, no girl has ever said no to me. *Ever*. It's like… she's attracted to me, I know it. She has to be."

"Never? Never ever?"

I can tell Dustin doesn't believe me, and I may be a piece of shit, but I'm not a liar.

"*Never.*"

"Maybe she has a secret dick."

I swear I want to kill Dustin.

"She doesn't have a secret dick. And don't let Kya catch you saying shit like that."

We both glance over our shoulders and find ourselves mercifully safe from one of Kya's rants for the time being.

"No secret dick," Dustin whispers. "Fine. Maybe she doesn't like white guys."

"Don't be fucking stupid," I grumble, punching him in the shoulder.

"Who cares? She turned you down. I have… three chicks DTF tonight. Want one?"

"No. I want the one who said no."

Dustin laughs. "You're a sick fuck. I mean… she's coming tonight. Just get her upstairs."

"And do what? You can't just screw a girl who doesn't want to be screwed."

"Change her mind."

"How? She said… she said something so horrible when I asked. You wouldn't fucking believe it."

"Dude. What did she say? Wait… let me guess… she has four nipples? Four tits? Six tits?"

"No, dumbass," I grumble, my cheeks burning with humiliation. Dustin's totally going to give me shit for this. "She said I wasn't hot."

"Oh. Well, yeah. You're ugly as fuck, Jayce."

I can always count on Dustin in a hard time.

"Thanks."

"No problem… and no homo."

"Dumbass. Why do I talk to you?"

Dustin exhales another cloud of strawberry flavored vapor. "Because, motherfucker. I've got an idea."

"Another dumb Dustin idea. Great."

"Tequila. A thick leather leash. Your bed. Get her drunk. Tie her up. Get a humiliating video and blackmail her. Simple. Eventually, she'll get Oslo Syndrome and fuck you."

"You mean Stockholm syndrome?"

"No, dude. Oslo. Look it up. It's in Finland."

Dustin is a complete fucking idiot. But he may have a point about that tequila… Every frosh loves tequila and if Makeba doesn't love tequila, she'll learn to love it tonight. I'll shower her with attention, make a few stupid promises and then… *I'll win.* I'll prove to her once and for all that she was wrong. I'm hot and she *is* attracted to me. And she's wrong. I'm not a self-obsessed, egotistical bastard. I'm just a superior specimen of man. Simple.

When the party kicks off, everything is perfect for Cole. I mean, Kya makes sure everything is perfect. She has everyone in this house fucking whipped, I swear. Hargreaves is like her little lapdog, running around making sure everyone's drinks are full.

Since they're all freshmen, I'm pretty sure Kya's friends will be here soon. They don't exactly wait for the party to get rowdy before showing up. I head to the bar before they get there. I can serve liquor at our campus parties since I just turned 21 – the same day as our sick ass War Hogs victory. Too bad it came with a pretty big warning from Murphy to get my fucking shit together.

I know Murphy cares, but does he have to be such an asshole about it? After a few beers, I'm chatting with some chicks from the lacrosse team near the front door when I see her. This short brunette waves her hand in front of my face.

"Um, Jayce-y, did you like even hear what I said?"

"Oh my God, he's so drunk," she says when I don't reply.

"Yeah. I'll uh... I'll be right back."

Fuck. I take my eyes off Makeba for one second, and she slips into the crowd and disappears. I search the crowd for Kya's expansive puff of hair and sure enough, Makeba's standing right next to her with their other friend, who has different hair now. My throat tightens as I watch her quietly for a few moments. I don't know why I pause, but a part of me freezes and I watch her tip something back into her mouth and then laugh at Kya's joke. She twirls one of the long braids around her finger and I feel a tightening around my crotch. *Fuck.*

I'm like a goddamn teenager, getting horny at some chick across the room. I sip more of my beer and pull myself together to hunt her down across the room. She looks relaxed, much better than she looked in class. I hate that it makes me feel relief that she's okay. If she lets me, I'll take care of whoever did that to her.

I want to get Makeba drunk enough to tell me the truth about how she got those fucking bruises, and I want to get her drunk enough to blackmail when she's sober enough to fuck me. Total revenge... simple, right?

I push my way through the crowd, but by the time I get to Kya, her friends are gone. *Makeba.* She could disappear amongst the crowd here, and I would have no clue how to find her. Shit.

"Yo, where's Makeba?"

Kya snaps defensively. Geez, is this chick a security guard too?

"What the hell do you want with Makeba?"

"We're in class together," I explain to Kya.

"Right. So you want the homework notes?" Kya huffs sarcastically.

"Yeah."

I can't believe Kya's going to believe that dumb story…

"Do you really think I'm going to believe that dumb ass story, Jayce? Stay away from Makeba or I *swear*, I will take your nutsack and fillet it like a fucking largemouth bass."

"Sheesh ,I wasn't even lying."

I totally was, but I back off to continue my search in total secrecy before Kya legitimately kicks my ass or gives it her best effort. Luckily, I don't have to look far. Dustin texts me that the "dark girl" is in the hallway to the secret bathroom (no longer a secret thanks to Kya Ambrose's big mouth) we don't tell visitors about so we have somewhere clean to piss during parties.

I grab my weapon (a shot of tequila) and hurry to the hall, cutting Makeba off before anyone can see her and before she can escape. She seems surprised to see me, which is pretty fucking weird because I live here.

"Jayce!" she squeaks.

"Hey. I brought you alcohol."

"How did you even know I was here?"

"I followed your scent."

"Hilarious."

She tries to get around me, but I block her from escaping. Nope. I have her right where I want her, and I'm not letting Makeba Winston out of my sight tonight.

"Come on, drink up."

"I'm not dumb enough to take a strange drink from a student athlete. Kya says student athletes commit 91% of campus rape."

Kya always has a different fucking statistic for that one.

"That doesn't sound right."

"I agree with her. All y'all asses should probably be in jail. 100%."

She's funny.

"Fine. I'll take a sip first to prove it's not drugged. Then you can have the rest."

"I'll watch you, white boy."

"White boy? What's with that one?"

"Sorry, are you black and I didn't notice?"

I may not be black, but I like a lot of rap music. I shrug and sip the tequila. It's pretty fucking good.

"Come on, try it," I say, holding it close to her, but not so close she can smell it. I don't want her chickening out.

"I've never had tequila."

"Yeah? We can do shots together. I can be your first time."

"Jayce… we aren't friends. Why are you being a weirdo and bringing me shots in the hallway?"

My response isn't exactly a lie.

"I saw what happened to you earlier. You look like you could use a drink."

She buys my story. *Yes.*

"Damn straight. Especially since that asshole might come to this stupid party tonight."

"Which asshole?"

"Never mind, white boy. I'll use you as a shield until I figure out a way to tell my friends the truth without him popping out of the damn bushes."

"Huh?"

"Any more shots where that came from?" Makeba snaps. I stumble to answer her question and hoping that she likes my answer.

"I have a few bottles in my room."

Makeba narrows her gaze. "Nice try. Bring the bottles down here."

"Sure I can leave you alone?"

"I'll be fine, white boy. I'll wait here."

"In a dark hallway?"

"Yeah, I blend in. He'll never find me here."

"Sure you don't want me to kick his ass?"

"I'm from Queens, Jayce. I'll kick that white boy's ass on my own. Once I learn to fight."

"I'll get the liquor."

"Good boy."

I ignore that last weird comment and rush upstairs to get my liquor. Makeba is making this way too easy on me. She makes nothing easy on me, so whoever fucked her up must have her pretty scared. I'll take care of that once I get my revenge on her for not sleeping with me.

When I'm back with the liquor, Makeba sticks her phone in her pocket.

"Cool," she says. "I just told my friends half of the truth. So we're getting somewhere. Tequila?"

"Do we have to drink it in a dark hallway?" I ask her, handing her a bottle. I hope she pounds back the entire fucking thing...

"Just pour it up, white boy. I don't want to associate with you."

Again, I ignore the sting.

"Bottoms up, Makeba."

She gives me a weird look, but even then... she suspects nothing.

❦ 4 ❦

BRING HER UPSTAIRS

MAKEBA

There's something tight around my neck. It's thick, and it's squeezing me to death. I gasp for breath. Oxygen flows into my lungs easily. There's still something around my neck, but at least I can breathe. Thank God, I can still breathe. I grasp at my neck, trying to pull that thick thing away, but it won't move. I roll over and then the lights go on. My head feels weird. So weird...

If this is just a hangover, it's the worst hangover I've ever had. Tequila. Tequila... why did I let myself drink tequila? Holy shit... I gasp for breath and keep trying to pull that thick thing away from my neck. It doesn't work, and the light makes me nauseous. I want to throw up. I remember *nothing* and I especially don't remember how I got here.

The last thing I remember was Jayce's chest. He was shirt-less, and he had a little of chest hair. I don't know why I

35

remember that part. I stumbled forward, and then he just hoisted me over his shoulder and carried me to his bedroom. There was tequila and... oh God...

I scream. I scream and try to run away, but the tight thing around my neck yanks me back aggressively and I smack my head against a bed frame. My head throbs and my desire to throw up only gets stronger.

"HELP!" I scream, but my voice comes out exhausted and raspy, like I'm tired from cheering at a sports game. I scream again, but my voice barely comes out. *Shit..* I hear footsteps crashing down the hallway. Someone's coming to rescue me. Wherever the fuck I am. I'm trapped in a dark room and this thing around my neck is totally making my bruises worse. The footsteps stop at the door. I screech louder and then the door opens and lights come on.

Where the hell am I? I scream again for good measure. My first assumption is that somehow B.J. got me and trapped me in his bedroom where he was going to kill me and upload the video to the internet or something. But as my eyes adjust to the flood of light, I notice that the pristinely tidy room has clues everywhere. Skates. A hockey stick. Hockey pads neatly organized in a corner.

I'm in a hockey boy's bedroom.

Which one? I hear more footsteps, but with that thing around my neck, I can't turn around. I hear the door close behind me and my heart is beating so loud that it's practically in my throat. I'm tied up and leashed to a hockey boy's bed like a dog. This can't be good. I don't know how I got here, but I hope to God I didn't drunkenly sign one of those kinky consent forms our student counselor got us to print out to prevent situations just like this one.

"Hey, Makeba. Keep it down. You're fine," he says firmly.

His voice sounds so damned smooth for a New England boy. I hate that I like it. New Yorkers all sound like they're about to start a fight. Jayce sounds laid-back and classy – not too Boston, but not too uptight. Jayce's sexy voice means Jayce is coming to rescue me.

My unsexy voice screams his name. "JAYCE?!"

"Did you throw up?"

"Jayce, untie me! HELP!"

"No one can hear you out there," he says calmly. "I'm the only guy left on the second floor. The party's over. It's spring break."

"Spring break?"

"Everyone cleared out. I've been sleeping in Dustin's room. I promised Kya I'd let you sober up in here alone and get you to your train on time."

"Did you mention you TIED ME UP LIKE A DOG?!" I scream.

The only way I can move around is on all fours, so despite my personal pride, I crawl around to the other side of the bed where I can give Jayce a stern look and threaten him with all the strength I can muster to **let me fucking go.**

He doesn't budge.

"I didn't mention that. Obviously."

"Untie me! This is hurting my neck."

"You're right. I don't need it anymore. I already have what I need."

"What does that mean?"

Jayce shuffles over to me, considering me, but moving no closer to releasing me from his leather trap. His New Balance sneakers are basically at my eye level. He wrote his last name CLUTTERBUCK along the soles, with a tally in Sharpie.

"I have the blackmail I need."

He crouches down to my eye level, and I lunge forward like some kind of deranged pit bull. What was my plan? Biting him?

"Hey, that would have been perfect for my video. But I guess you saved your best performance for when you sobered up."

"What video?! And can you hurry and untie me?"

"Promise you won't run."

"Why would I run?"

"Good point," he says. "That would be dumb."

Oh my God, this white boy is way too easy to trick. He leans forward and I bend my neck so he can untie me. He actually does it. I don't care what stupid ass blackmail video he has or whatever dumb threat he makes. It's spring break. I'm getting out of here. If I don't get out of here now, there won't be any witnesses left on campus to overhear whatever twisted shit Jayce could do to me if I stay here.

If B.J. taught me anything, it's trust no (white) man.. I'm free and Jayce puts his hand on my neck gently.

"Sorry. I didn't think I'd hurt your bruises."

Fucking idiot. I lean forward again and I head butt him. Hard. Jayce groans and I have my chance. I lunge to my feet and don't notice that he also bound my ankles. I scream as I lurch forward and fall. Halfway through my fall, Jayce catches me.

"Hey!"

I squeal and brace myself against his chest. What the fuck? Is his chest made of literal iron? B.J. was my first ever boyfriend and the first guy I saw shirtless. He was okay, I guess, but Jayce feels like... a fucking man. I pull my hands away and try to move away again, but I yelp and fall onto his bed. Jayce puts his hands on his hips and gazes down at me.

"You lied," he snarls, all the gentleness vanquished from his voice.

Like he has any right to be mad.

"You kidnapped me! Of course, I'm going to make an escape attempt."

"Everyone's gone already, chica. It's almost noon," Jayce says. "You missed your train."

"NOON?! Jayce, I need to get to New York! I can't be here. I have a train to catch."

"I know. Change of plans, chica."

"No! Untie my legs, Jayce. Now!"

He's devastatingly calm and terribly amused. He's not even attempting to hide how fucking amusing he thinks this is. I want to strangle him.

"Don't think so," he says, running his tongue over his lip and then biting on it. I don't even want to know what sick, devious ideas are running through his peanut head.

"Why not!?" I shriek.

I sit up on his bed – which I'm still attached to by the ankle – and fold my arms on my laps waiting for this dumb ass white boy to come up with a suitable answer. This is Jayce we're talking about... I can get his ass.

"Because I have this..."

Jayce shoves his phone in my face and begins playing a video. Holy shit. I'm going to die. Jayce has something on me – and it's horrible.

I'm on all fours in the video, leashed to the bed.

"Bark like a dog, Makeba."

"No," I slur drunkenly, drawing out the vowel for several seconds.

"Bark like a dog. Come on. It'll be fun."

"ARF ARF ARF."

Then I fall over in peals of laughter like an idiot.

I want to fucking die. I want to pinch myself and have this video go away. Jayce chuckles in real life and then laughs in the video.

"Do it again," Jayce taunts.

"Are you filming?"

"No way. You can trust me. Just bark again…"

You think that's not so bad? It gets worse.

"I think you should pee like a dog, Makeba."

"I'm drunk. I need to go home."

"If you pee like a dog I'll take you home."

"What do you mean pee like a dog?" I whine. "Jayce…"

"Pee, Makeba. Just let it go. Let it all out."

"Let it all out," I repeat…

. . .

I raise my leg and pee.

"JAYCE, TURN THIS OFF," I shriek, interrupting the video.

Jayce presses pause.

"What's the matter? We didn't even get to the part where you take your top off."

"I took my top off!? That's assault."

"Uh, no it wasn't. I asked you to put it back on. You said you wanted your puppies to come get milk from—

"I did *not* say that," I interrupt. My voice is totally hoarse from screaming.

"Well, I coached you a bit."

"Jayce!"

"Once I edit this... it'll be perfect. I'll post it on every social media platform you can think of. I think we're going to go viral lil' puppy."

He smirks, and then the annoying bastard kisses me on the cheek. I wipe my cheek off and push him. He's insane. He's fucking crazy. I thought B.J. was the craziest white boy at Laguna Grove, but I've finally met the one and only.

"Why the fuck are you doing this to me?!"

"Because. I owe you," Jayce answers. "Payback."

His eyes gleam with self-satisfaction. What the hell is he so damn smug about?

"Huh? What the hell did I ever do to you? I mind my black ass business even when your white ass copies off my homework. Magnetism doesn't have a 'z' in it, by the way."

"You turned me down," He says. "I offered my gorgeous body to you so you could have amazing mind-blowing sex with me and you turned me down."

"Seriously?! You're going to humiliate me and attack me because I didn't want to have sex with you? Are you a fucking teenager?"

Taunting him is probably a mistake, but I'm officially freaked out and Jayce is right. I'm missing my bus back to New York, which means my strict ass Caribbean parents are going to wait for a girl at a bus stop who won't show up. I know they'll freak out. I can imagine my dad in his accent now lecturing me that he didn't leave Portmore to "come a farrin" and have his daughter turn into a fast woman. Doing anything off schedule makes you "fast" according to my dad.

One time I woke up at 8:30 a.m. and he was damn near ready to exorcize the white devil from me.

I can't imagine what he'd think if he saw anything from that video. Unlike Kya's dad, my father lives and dies by the belt. He proudly announces that it's the same belt his grandmother and his mother beat him with. That beast, which he named 'the tickler' is braided together with thick brown leather and has a broken metal buckle that stings when it lands on your skin... Oh hell fucking no. I'm too old to face the damn belt again because I got drunk and acted like a dog in a white boy's bedroom.

I won't get caught up like Kya. If Jayce asks about my parents, I'll tell him they're dead. But I need to get out of here, so I'm not the one who ends up dead instead. Jayce's scowl builds slowly.

"I didn't attack you. I lured you. And you drank the same amount of alcohol that I did. I was fine."

"I'm 5'10" and you're what, six feet tall?"

"6'4" actually," Jayce corrects me, which is super fucking annoying. But he is pretty tall. B.J. barely came up to my nose. I have nothing against short guys or anything, but Jayce's height definitely makes him easier on the eyes. Unfortunately, he's very difficult on the brain.

"Exactly. I can't drink as much as you can!"

He scowls and puts on some demonic, entitled expression.

"You asked for it. You wanted to forget whatever dick choked you out."

"You're not any better than the dick who choked me out," I snap back. "You tied me to your bed with a leather leash after getting me drunk. How do I know you didn't violate me?"

"Not true," Jayce responds calmly, like this is an intellectual debate. "I'm taller probably, hotter, better at hockey, and I definitely have a bigger dick."

"Is all you think about your stupid dick? I have a life to get back to, Jayce. LET ME GO."

"No."

"JAYCE! PLEASE!"

"I have a bigger dick than whatever guy fucked you up. That's important."

"It's important to literally no one," I yell again.

Why am I yelling? It has no effect on this dumbass. He just smirks more.

"Fine. I'll give you a little more freedom if you tell me why you won't sleep with me," he says.

Okay, I guess that's his way of telling me he didn't take advantage of me completely when he had me passed out drunk and utterly at his mercy. It's the bare minimum, but I need whatever clues I can find about what the hell happened last night.

"What the hell are you going to give me?" I snap at him.

"I'll give you a phone call."

"To the police?"

"No. To your parents," he says. "That's who you're so scared of disappointing in New York, isn't it? I know it's not a boyfriend."

"I don't have parents."

"That's a big fucking lie. I sit next to you in class, Makeba. I know you."

"I know nothing about you."

"Maybe you're not very *observatory*."

"What?"

I swear, I want to punch Jayce in the damn mouth.

"You heard what I said."

Jayce is a dumb ass. He might be a hot dumb ass, but he's still a dumb ass. And I learned my lesson with white boys. What would my dad say if he found out about B.J.? He'd call me fast. And he'd definitely call me fast if he learned I did anything with a worse type of white guy.

"Fine. I'll take the deal."

"Why won't you sleep with me?"

"This is so fucking stupid."

"You know what... I'll post the video," Jayce says.

I try to call his bluff, but he pulls out his phone and I blurt out the most embarrassing confession of my life. I don't even know why this is the answer I choose to give Jayce Clutterbuck. The words just spill out of my mouth of their own accord.

"I'm a virgin. I don't want to have meaningless sex with some racist ass jock. Okay? You might be someone else's type, but you're just… way out of my league. I'm not a joke or an experiment. So yeah."

Then it's quiet. So quiet. And I want to sink into the ground. I'm probably going to hell anyway for making that video. Might as well make it quick.

5

MY VIRGIN PET

JAYCE

Heat rushes past my ears. I know they're red. I have to adjust my trousers and ignore how heavy my tongue feels when I answer her. I need to deflect. Make a joke about it.

"You're a virgin? Wow, that means you haven't even had puppies yet."

Man, that video is hilarious. I laugh as I replay Makeba's embarrassing display in my head, but my laughing only seriously pisses her off. I play it safe. She doesn't notice how her confession forces me to react. I'm so hard that if I move ever so slightly, she's going to have enough evidence to make an unfortunate accusation against me. That's exactly the line I don't want to cross.

She scowls, which makes her high cheekbones look even sharper. She has a pretty face, no doubt. I don't know if it's my type, but I won't know until I taste her. That part will come soon. She's a virgin… fuck.

"I'm joking," I tell her, steadying my voice. "Chill out, chica."

She's just a little shakier than normal when she answers me. I'm curious about all the thoughts dancing around her pretty little head. Mine. If I do her, she'll be mine forever. It'll mean something alright. She won't need to worry about. I just didn't expect to get so lucky with her.

"Boy, I ain't your friend. Don't play with me."

I love when she says weird funny things like that. I need to keep her unsteady, so I can think. Piss her off a little more.

"You were a pretty funny dog."

The reminder of the video gets under her skin. I want her. I'll have to pull back a little if I want to make it happen. She's mine for days… Eventually, I'll break her.

"You're such a dick."

"See, now you're thinking about my dick. Weird how that keeps happening."

It's impossible for me to ignore my dick. I have never had to work this hard for him. It's painful, but I don't want to back down from the challenge. Makeba folds her arms and jostles the ankle binds that keep her attached to my bed. "I'm not thinking about your stupid dick."

Liar. She has to be a liar. I can't imagine what else she's thinking about while we're alone in my bedroom. This would be so much better if she stopped denying herself.

"Why not?" I whisper.

Seriously, that pisses me off so much. Makeba's a chick. A straight chick. Why doesn't anything I say or do impress her? She's so complicated. It's weird, but a little hot. Dustin was totally wrong. She is the hot one. And now, she's mine because I was smart enough to get some pretty sick dirt on her.

"Because... your dick does not interest me, Jayce."

That doesn't even make any sense. If Makeba won't come around to seeing things my way, I have other options to get what I want from her.

"You know, Makeba... I think the internet would love your video... I know a community of sick freaks who would love the address of a chick like you."

She doesn't even look scared. She just rolls her eyes.

"I could sue you. Untie my leg or I'll sue your white ass so hard."

"Oh yeah? How do you even sue someone?" I shoot back.

Ha! That was a shot in the dark, but it actually works. She totally doesn't know how to sue someone.

"Jayce! Just stop being an asshole for one second. Untie me, white boy!"

For a second? That sounds far too long. "Listen, you want something from me, right?"

Makeba's glare could kill me. I like that she's looking at me, which she never does unless she wants something.

"Yes. Several things," she says grumpily.

"Good. And I want something from you. So we can conduct a civilized trade negotiation. A white ass trade negotiation."

Her folded arms and her narrowed glare only mean she's looking at me more. I like her to look at me.

"You realize that makes it sound suspicious," Makeba complains.

"I'll teach you how to fight and I'll keep your video a secret, but... you have to stay here for the rest of spring break."

"Tied to your bed?!"

"I'll untie you, but if you try to run away, that's over."

"Okay. Fine."

"That's it? You won't argue? Protest for your freedom?"

Wow, Cole had a much harder time with Kya. This is going to be a piece of cake. I can't stop fantasizing about all the nasty things I can do to Makeba now that she's mine. She protests now, but soon... she'll beg. I just know it. There's only a little more resistance I need to break down.

"No. But only because I need you to agree to one thing. I need to call my parents. They're waiting for me in New York and if I don't show up, they'll call the cops."

"Seriously? Aren't you eighteen?"

"They're from Jamaica, Jayce. It doesn't matter if I'm 18. If I was 81, they would still be my parents. I have to listen to them."

I don't get her at all sometimes, but it seems like a harmless addition to my offer, so I don't think I have much of a choice but to agree. I hand her my phone and watch her every move.

"You realize I could delete the video," she says. "Right now."

"I have backups."

"Shit. I was hoping you wouldn't say that."

Makeba's pretty smart, but I totally planned this out. I'm ready for anything she could throw my way.

"Call your parents, chica. Before I change my mind."

Makeba scowls but then has an awkward phone call where she talks to someone with an accent and explains that she's staying on campus to do extra studying. When she hangs up, she sighs.

"You're a pretty good liar," I tell her.

"When you have strict parents, you learn how to become a good liar."

I grunt and sit next to her, which gives me some pretty sick ideas since she's still tied to my bed. I need to be patient with this one. I hate patience. It's the reason I hit first, think later. Tuck has a problem with that. Everyone has a problem with that.

I shrug and answer Makeba. "My step-dad doesn't give a shit what I do. I don't know about strict parents."

"What about your mom? She didn't whoop you or anything? Because that would explain a lot."

"She died the year after she married my step-dad. I was only three."

"Oh. Shit."

I need to change the subject.

"Yeah, whatever. We have a deal, right?"

"Yeah," Makeba says, shifting on the bed. "There's just one more thing."

"What?"

"I want to tell you what happened to me and then... I need to tell my friends. So I'll need my cell phone."

"Uh... your cellphone's in Ovie's cage. Sorry, chica."

"What? Wait... is that the terrifying snake Kya talks about that escapes all the time?!"

Our housemate and fellow player Dustin Rathbone has a bunch of exotic pets. Ovie, named after one of the greatest hockey players of all time, Alexander Ovechkin, is just one. That boa is pretty shifty and escapes all the time, mostly because Dustin's too high to remember to lock his cage.

"Uh huh. I'm taking care of him over spring break," I tell Makeba.

I know she'll freak out. Chicks always freak out about the snake, even if it's totally not a big deal or anything.

"Jayce!"

"You can go get it. He doesn't always bite. He killed a mouse on it last night though. So it's pretty fucked up in there."

Makeba's scowl brings a smile to my face. Fuck, she's so pretty when she's mad. Those lips fixed in that scowl are fucking delectable. She's so distracting.

"You could use my phone…" I suggest, "If you remember their phone numbers. I don't have any."

"Ugh! You know what? I'll tell them after spring break. Fine. It's not like they can do anything now."

I face her, taking in all the details I can about her. She's pretty, but it's like she wants to hide it so bad. I don't know why. Every time I look at her, she looks away from me all shy. Out of her league? Makeba is crazy as fuck, because she's the one out of my league. She looks like she dropped out of the sky. Chicks just don't look like that. Trust me.

"You can tell me what the fuck happened to you now."

"I can't."

"If I'm going to teach you how to kick some guy's ass, I need to make sure that the sorry motherfucker deserves it."

Her gaze flickers angrily to mine, like I've called her honor into question.

"Trust me, he deserves it."

Fuck, she is so secretive. I want to do whatever it takes to draw the secrets out of her, without even really knowing why. She's a chick – and a chick that hates me at that – I don't know why I'm so fucking interested.

"Then tell me what happened."

I hate she makes me beg for everything, but I can't seem to make myself stop begging.

"You just shouldn't be the first person I tell."

"Whatever, Makeba, don't tell me then."

"We made a deal!"

"Yeah, I know. I was trying to trick you into going back on your word so I could punish you."

Makeba rolls her eyes. "Seriously? Don't tell me your dumb plan next time."

I grin. I know I'm softening her up despite her glare. I watch her body relax and she turns ever so slightly toward me. She thinks she has all these walls up, but I can see straight fucking through them. I know she'll tell me if I ask. If I make her.

"Spill the beans, chica. Who choked you the fuck out?"

"Promise you won't tell Cole. I don't want Cole to kick his ass."

That's the last thing Makeba needs to worry about. Truth be told, I plan on kicking the dude's ass myself once I get my hands on him. But I nod, because I want the truth and unless I agree to whatever she asks, she won't tell me.

After a loud, dramatic sigh, the words come out. She can barely look at me as she explains that her ex-boyfriend, some sick English major punk, put his hands around her neck and threatened her.

"He exposed my best friend," she says. "And I've been too scared for my life to do anything. You don't understand, Jayce… I don't want to be weak."

B.J. Satterfield. I don't recognize the kid's name or anything about him. Makeba explains as much as she can, but she doesn't mention what blackmail Cole had on Kya that Mr. Satterfield discovered… She's pretty clever telling her story, so I can't figure it out.

Cole… my best friend, is an absolute legend for using blackmail to get his girl.

It's cool to see that great minds think alike.

Unlike Cole, I won't screw this blackmail thing up. I'll use my blackmail to get some hot sex and then I'll get out before anything can go wrong. This will be totally easy and totally worth it.

"You should have told your friends," I tell Makeba. "Sure you don't want that phone back?"

"Now you're an expert on my life?"

"No. But I have friends. I'd die for them. You never keep shit from your friends."

"Whatever, Jayce. Are you going to help me fight or what? I can save my friends from all of this by kicking B.J.'s ass myself once he gets back."

"Yup. I'll teach you how to fight. But it's gonna hurt."

"Whatever," she snaps. "Nothing can hurt more than this stupid ass hangover. Now untie me."

That hangover might be my fault. Not everyone can handle their tequila so well.

I untie her and once she's free, Makeba stands up and stretches. Her shirt hovers over her navel and wow. Her skin is so dark, it's almost purple and her stomach is flat and smooth without a single blemish or inflection in her skin. She almost catches me looking at her tummy until her shirt falls again.

"You are crazy," she tells me, wrapping one of her arms over her stomach. "There's no way in hell I'm staying in your room for an entire week."

"Why not? You agreed to it."

"You'll want to kick me out in about a day. I'm messy as hell."

"You can't be that bad."

"Look around, Jayce. I've already caused several mini-disasters. My friends are always on me about it."

Sure enough, as I slowly consider the state of my bedroom, I notice Makeba's right.

"Maybe I should keep you leashed to the bed, then. Or put you in a crate," I tease, glancing at a pile of shredded papers. I don't even know how she created a mess so fucking quickly. She pushes my chest hard, but not hard enough to hurt.

"Come on, white boy. Let's scrap. Teach me how to one… two…"

She throws the weakest punches I've ever seen against my shoulder. She has no idea that I can throw a hard enough punch to knock that B.J. character into the next dimension.

"Are you sure you don't want to get your phone?" I tell her. "Tell your friends the truth before I teach you how to smack down?"

Makeba raises an eyebrow, giving me an annoyed look like I'm too dumb for words or something.

"Boy, I ain't putting my hand in a snake cage for nothing. But I'll confess as soon as they get back. I promise."

"Then I can teach you how to fight. But I'm all stressed out from the mess in here."

Makeba wrinkles her nose and nods in agreement, moving her head around like she's searching for the source of the smell. "Yeah. It smells like… pee."

Shit. I totally forgot to clean that up after taking my hilarious video. It's halfway dry already in a corner of my bedroom.

"You did that. I should make you clean it up."

"Boy, watch it."

"I'm the one who has blackmail on you," I point out. "I can make you clean it."

"And? You have blackmail on me, so that means I have to be your damned pet now?"

"That's exactly what it means," I tell her.

For a smart cookie, Makeba sure is missing the point here. My genius plan to trap her in my bedroom and win her sweet, sweet forbidden frosh pussy is already under way. She doesn't have a fucking clue what's coming.

"Jayce… I'm staying here for a week already. That's punishment enough for both of us. I think we can agree."

"Fine. I'll clean up your gross mess, but then we're hanging out. In my bed."

"Since when did I agree to that?"

"What did you think you would do here for a week, Makeba? You already refused to clean up... I mean... come on."

"I thought you'd be like Cole... making me sweep your floor and fold your clothes."

"Unlike Cole, I can clean up after myself," I said. "What I can't do is fuck myself..."

"Really? You're incapable of masturbation?"

She gets me so damned angry.

"Makeba... seriously? What's so wrong with fucking me?"

"Everything! I want to have sex with someone who... is nice."

"Like B.J.?" I snap. I know it's a low fucking blow. She just told me the guy beat the shit out of her. Obviously, she made a wrong move. It's not her fault. Some guys are dicks.

"Fuck you, Jayce."

Yeah, I deserve that one.

"Come on, chica. I'll make it good for you. It doesn't have to mean anything."

"I want to learn how to fight. Not learn how to fuck."

"What if I taught you both?"

"Jayce…"

"Am I really that ugly?" I grin at her, because there's no way in hell Makeba can say I'm ugly with a straight face.

6

CONVINCE ME

MAKEBA

"Don't you want to lose it? I'm offering you the chance of a lifetime… sex with the hottest guy you will ever see naked."

"Have you ever considered the possibility that your entitlement and arrogance are a complete turn off?"

Jayce tilts his head to the side, a crop of his coppery-brown hair falling into his face. He pushes it out of the way and shakes his head. He's unbelievably simple sometimes. It should definitely get on my nerves way more than it does.

"No," he says, genuine confusion on his face. "I thought my arrogance would let you know I had a big dick."

"Jayce! This is harassment. And worse."

He perks up like a Golden Retriever about to go for a walkie-walk.

"Can I at least show you what you're missing?"

"No!"

"Okay... can I show you the top half of what you're missing?"

He gets off the bed, and before I can say anything, Jayce Clutterbuck takes his shirt off. Is he out of his goddamn mind? Am I out of mine? I can't look away.

"I never realized you had so many tattoos," I say stupidly. But it's only because I can't stop staring at the 6'4" pillar of muscle in front of me. He hasn't shaved his scruffy beard in three days and there are flecks of blond hair sprinkled throughout the thick brown. His hair is long because he's almost at the end of hockey season and the players don't cut their hair until the end of the season (according to Kya).

Tattoos are only the first thing I notice. He has black ink covering his shoulders. My daddy would hate if he saw me even looking at a man with tattoos like this. But that's not all. Jayce has a silver ring through his right nipple and a large tattoo across his chest that says La Vida Loca. He is crazy. Even his tattoo says it.

He has to be crazy to have a six-pack, too. Wait, it's an eight-pack. My bad. I suddenly realize that neither of us has said anything in a very long time. I clear my throat and pretend like Jayce's chiseled body hasn't distracted me at all. I have my head on straight and I'm way too mature to get lured in by some sophomore's ridiculous obliques or even his sexy nipple ring.

"I knew you thought I was hot. Liar."

Jayce gets on my last nerve.

"Are you five?"

"Out of ten? No. I'm definitely an 11.5. Look at this. Most guys don't even have this muscle."

"Jayce, maybe you should take a psychology class and learn about a concept called malignant narcissism."

Jayce shrugs and keeps tilting his body from side to side so his abs catch the light

"It's called self-esteem, babe. Hit enough guys in the ribs, you get pretty good self-esteem."

"Maybe I should try that."

I get up, ignoring Jayce's triumphant grin, and I hit him exactly in the ribs. My hands sort of graze his stomach a bit, but that was a total accident.

"OW! What the hell, Makeba!?"

Jayce should have seen that coming. He grunts and moves backward only a couple feet. But his face is red, so I must have got him pretty good.

"What? I thought you were teaching me how to fight?"

He groans and grabs his stomach.

"After a quick detour," he grumbles.

"I don't want a detour, Jayce. Now put a shirt on, or I'll hit you again."

"Oh, yeah?"

"Yeah."

I give him my biggest, meanest stare. Jayce Clutterbuck has another thing coming if he thinks he's going to distract me with an eight-pack when I'm only here to learn how to become the next Muhammad Ali. Jayce grins, which isn't the response I expect.

Then he drops his sweatpants and his boxers in one swift motion. They both land on the ground with a thud, weighed down by his wallet and his car keys, which thud and jingle on the way down. Oh my God. He did not just do that. I am not looking at...

"JAYCE CLUTTERBUCK, PUT YOUR PANTS BACK ON!"

Instead, he puts his hands on his hips and moves his hips from side to side.

"Come on, Makeba, what are you, scared?"

His dick. I'm looking at his dick. Oh, God. Oh, child. I don't want to look at his dick, but it just jumped out there like an elephant trunk and that shit is freaky big. I don't want to believe it's a dick because it's so enormous that it looks prosthetic. Scared. Yeah, I am beyond scared. There's no way in hell I had that dick in me when I was passed out. Now I know for sure.

Jayce might be deranged, but he's not a rapist.

"No, I'm not scared! I am disturbed."

"I thought you were going to punch me," Jayce taunts me. "Where's the punch?"

My cheeks are hot. They're so hot, I feel like my head is going to explode and fly across the room. I'm stuttering like a crazy person and I can't handle Jayce messing with me anymore.

"Jayce, there is an exposed penis in my face! I can't punch you…"

"That's what I thought," Jayce responds triumphantly. "My big white cock totally seduced you."

"Your big white cock did not seduce me."

As soon as the phrase comes out of my mouth, I see the stupid trap that Jayce Clutterbuck laid for me.

"So you agree that I have a big white cock? Which probably means that you're totally into it. Ha. Tricked you. I knew you thought I was sexy."

As difficult as it will be, the only choice I have is to try to reason with the dumb hockey jock.

"You didn't trick me, Jayce. I simply identified your dick. Yes, it's big. You can put it away now."

"Aren't you even tempted?"

A flash of anger crosses his face.

"What would I be tempted to do?"

"That's right. You're a virgin. You don't know anything about sex," he snaps, as if that's the worst insult in the world. Plenty of people are virgins at our age. It's not my fault Jayce has chosen the life of a man-whore.

"I know plenty about sex. Just because I'm a virgin doesn't mean I'm ignorant."

Jayce shrugs, completely unbothered, or perhaps confused again.

"Yeah, but you don't know how good it feels."

"Good enough to give people orgasms," I shoot back. I am probably totally failing to sound like an expert, which is making me more nervous as Jayce edges closer to me, completely disobeying my command to put more clothes on. His tattoos are closer and I can make out distinct designs on his sleeves. I pretend that I'm not just appreciating his biceps. It's totally about the great line art and shading. And those colors? Who would have thought black ink could have looked good on such thick, muscular biceps? Right.

"Have you ever had an orgasm, Makeba?"

Now he's way too close to me and Jayce has just asked me one of the most personal questions a guy can ask anyone.

I don't want to answer Jayce Clutterbuck, a guy who has more women in his bed than Hugh Hefner.

"Come on," he says. "I want to know. I bet you touched yourself at least once."

"No! I haven't done that. Girls don't... I don't... You know what, Jayce? Put your damn clothes on."

I don't want to look at him, but considering he's naked, it seems like the safest bet. If I take my eyes off him for a second, he might pounce. The last thing I want to do is fight another man when I already have to fight B.J.

Jayce is now red. Not all over. Just his dick, which is now pretty big. And hard. His face is red too. It just takes a second for me to notice his face.

"Suck it a little," he coaxes.

See, this was a mistake. Talking to Jayce Clutterbuck was a mistake.

"I'm not doing that!"

He gets all puffed up when he's offended or upset.

"Why not? It's a big white cock, and it's pretty happy to see you."

"Can you stop saying big white cock? It's gross."

Jayce laughs.

"Fine," he says. "I'll make you a deal."

"We are so twisted up in deals that I don't even know what's going on!" I scream at him.

Jayce scratches his head and I sense he has definitely lost track of our deals, too.

"Yeah. Good point. New deal… I eat your pussy."

"What do I get out of it?"

Jayce snickers. "I eat your pussy."

"So, your new deal is a gift?"

"Yup."

"This is the most suspicious trade deal in the history of trade deals."

Jayce shrugs. "I've never been with a black chick. I want to try. If you won't let me get my dick in, I can at least use my tongue."

"You are the biggest freak I've ever met," I snap at him. "What the hell is so different about black women and white women? We're all women. We just have some stupid slight differences. I don't get the big deal."

"I only know white girls."

"I know. That's why I don't want to sleep with your racist ass."

"I don't get it."

"I'm not surprised," I snap. "You don't seem to under-stand much of anything."

Jayce presses on, ignoring my insult. "So you'd sleep with me if I'd been with a black chick before?"

"I don't know."

Why didn't I just say "NO"?! What the hell is wrong with me? Now, I'm giving this big-headed idiot a reason to feel like he has a chance.

"But how can I get with a black chick if I don't have a first? Someone has to be the first. Congratulations, Makeba. I choose you."

He bows his head slightly, his long brown hair falling over his face before he scrambles to remove it. Jayce is out of his mind. I don't know exactly what's wrong with him, but something is definitely wrong with him.

"You're crazy."

"I want pussy."

"Are you just going to keep making passes at me until–

"Pussy."

"Jayce, you're dumbing it down even more."

"I want it."

He gets on his knees and drags himself over to the bed. I'm still fully clothed and still fully trying to ignore Jayce's nude body as it inches closer to mine.

"You don't get to have everything you want."

"I could take what I want," he says. "I already know that you can't fight back."

"That is disgusting, Jayce."

"I know," he whispers. "I'm kinda fucked up. But the thing is... you're the problem, Makeba. You keep saying 'no' to me and it's not what I want to hear."

"Too bad. I hear 'no' all the time," I hiss.

Jayce puts his hand on my thigh and just holds me there. He's firm and not overly aggressive. Even if he's acting like a creep, I don't feel scared that he'll hurt me. I feel like he's playing with me – a pretty twisted game, but it's just a game. My mouth suddenly feels dry, though. I don't know what to do or what to say to him. I've never been in a situation with a guy before. B.J. never held my thigh like that. He didn't want to touch me. Now, it makes sense. He was using me because I was convenient. He never liked me.

If a guy like B.J. thinks I'm lower than dirt, a hockey player treated like a God on this campus has to be playing a sick game.

"Why are you so freaked that I want you?" Jayce says. "I mess with you all the time. Duh, chica. It's about sex."

"We aren't toddlers," I snap. "You can't pull my hair on the playground and expect me to fall in love with you."

Jayce chuckles. "Love," he whispers. "Is that what you want from a guy before you do it?"

"I never said that!"

"Okay," he whispers, his hand slowly traveling across my thigh. "We might not love each other, but if you say yes… I promise it will be good for you. I won't be a dick."

"Why do I find that so hard to believe?"

"So you're thinking about it?"

"I'm not thinking about anything."

His hand moves further up my thigh and his thumb is dangerously close to my thigh crease. What I'm thinking is something I can't possibly put into words because it's so insanely wrong.

"You're definitely thinking about something. I can smell you."

"Jayce, ew."

"I'm serious. You smell all horny."

"Boy, bye. I don't smell horny. Get your hand off my thigh."

"Don't think so."

Jayce leans forward, gazing up at me with giant sorrel eyes and a look on his face like a puppy.

"Let me lick it."

"Jayce!"

"I want you."

Jayce reaches for the waistband of my leggings.

"Scoot your butt," he says.

"Jayce, are you hearing the word no? Are you capable of hearing?"

"Makeba... you are already humiliating me. Can you stop?"

"So you aren't capable of hearing?"

I scream again... "JAYCE!"

He rips my leggings off. This caveman literally rips my clothes off. Then he spreads my legs wide. Really wide. I shriek again and try to shut them, but Jayce's forearms keep me open.

"I knew you were horny. Makeba, your underwear is so wet. Don't worry, babe. I won't touch it. I don't want you to call me a rapist or something."

"You ripped my pants off and you're staring at my private parts!"

"False. I'm staring at all the hair on your bikini line. Damn, you don't shave..."

"Jayce!" I screech, desperate to close my legs on this invasive white boy's hands, but unable to force them shut as he runs his hands over me. "Mind your damn business."

Jayce runs his spread fingers over my bikini line and hot shame courses through me. Jayce, of course, has the most bizarre reaction to my discomfort.

"I like it," he says. "Hairy pussy is natural. It's all womanly. Now, can I please take your underwear off? I want to lick it."

It's like he thinks saying the word please makes up for the fact that he is ripping my clothing off against my will. Jayce edges forward, his nose plunging between my legs. I stick my hand out and stop his big ass head from diving right in.

7

DISGUSTING DUDE

JAYCE

"**M**akeba… why are you making this so difficult?" I grunt as she struggles to push my head away. I stick my tongue out, trying to lick her hand, but it doesn't work. She just shrieks and pushes harder. Her spitfire energy turns me the fuck on. She wants me to work hard, I know it. Challenge accepted, chica.

"Because…"

I stop pushing against her hand. If she wants more verbal foreplay, whatever. She sighs and nearly flops backward. She still doesn't look angry, just… weird. Maybe I just need to explain things to her. Chicks can get pretty confused.

"You're wet. That means you want me."

And Makeba thinks I'm the dumb one? I know how chicks work. Wet pussy means go ahead.

"Sex is more complicated than just being wet," she gasps. Her face crinkles whenever she looks at me, and I don't know why I get her so pissed off. I'm a pretty chill guy with some great ideas. I take a second and then I realize what's wrong.

This is deeper chick stuff. The stuff they want to talk about all the time. Feelings or whatever. That's easy too.

"Afraid of getting attached?" I answer with a smirk. Makes sense. I'm pretty hot and cool.

Makeba's response comes out flat and serious. "I am at absolutely zero risk of getting attached to you, Jayce."

Now she's pissing me off. Doesn't she want my tongue in her pussy? This is taking a long time and I'm already hard, anyway. I want to lick her pussy and then get her to fuck. I've never had to work this hard to get here before. I had to freaking kidnap her. Doesn't she appreciate how much effort that takes?

"Then what's the big deal?" I huff. "I want your pussy. You won't get attached. We do it."

She makes a frustrated grunt, which she usually does before calling me an idiot or something mean like that.

"Why do you even want this?" Makeba huffs.

Oh, that's a simple question.

"Pussy tastes good."

"You are so simple."

A compliment. Simple is good. That means go ahead.

"Thanks, babe."

I push my nose forward and press it right up against her panties. If she won't let me taste her, then the least she could do is let me sniff her. Once my nose hits the cotton, I'm high off her smell. I inhale deeper and push my nose between her lower lips, her panties dampening as they slide between her folds with my nose. Let me get all up in there and…

"Jayce! Jayce! What are you doing?!"

She's frantic, and it's kinda sexy. My pet's a little nervous, but that doesn't bug me. Chicks are nervous all the time because I'm hot. I like it.

"Fuck… you smell good," I whisper. My cheeks feel hot and I am so fucking glad I did this. Another amazing Jayce Clutterbuck idea works out great.

I kiss the top of her thigh because it's bare, and it's the first time my lips have touched her. Holy shit. She tastes amazing. It might be the lotion on her skin, but I really want to lick it. A lot. She gasps.

"Jayce…"

"I always get what I want," I whisper, running my tongue along her inner thigh and getting so fucking close. Once I hit the smell of her pussy again, I go crazy. I stick my tongue out and then…

She slaps me. Her hands sting. She can't throw a punch, but she can definitely through a good fucking slap in the face. What the hell did I do? The sting spreads to my teeth. Damn, she has a pretty tough hand. I finally move my head away, scowling as my cheek turns pink.

"What the hell was that for?"

She gets all sassy, next.

"You are not listening. But I'm tired of fighting with your ass. I'll let you eat me out, but only if you get my phone for me after. From the snake. Got it? And remember that I am in no way, shape or form attracted to you."

She is such a liar. But it's cool. At least I finally won and I get to taste some of that sweet ass puss.

"Yeah, whatever. Just let me have your pussy, chica."

"Can you think of anything else right now aside from 'pussy'?"

Makeba is full of simple questions today. There are so many places I want to put my dick. Her butt, for example.

"Yeah. Butt. Dick."

Makeba looks like she wants to kill me.

"You are such an idiot."

I nod, and Makeba almost cracks a smile. Almost. See, she just can't resist my charm. That's what makes this such a fucking treat, right? Winning.

"Okay. Can I eat your pussy yet?"

"You are like a puppy," she chides, and it sounds like a yes.

"Yeah," I answer, nodding. She's driving me crazy. Can this chick just open her legs and let me get all up in her wet underwear?

"You should be my pet," she sasses back.

"Makeba…"

"Yes," she sighs. "But I'm lying on my back and closing my eyes. I don't want to think about what you're doing down there."

Perfect. Makeba doesn't have a clue what she's agreeing to. I grab her underwear with my teeth and tug it over her hips, using my hands to help. Makeba raises her ass off the bed slightly and I grab her hips, pulling her against my face. My tongue juts out first, splitting her lower lips open and sliding between her juicy slit. Fuck…

"Jayce!" she gasps, but it comes out all strangled, like she's in pain.

"Uh huh."

"Oh my God…"

"Chill out," I murmur. "I'll take it easy on you."

I run my tongue down the inside of her lips, just getting a feel for her, or more like a taste for her. She moans a lot. Fuck. She is super sensitive. As I lick her clit, I stroke her soaked folds with my fingers and she moans louder. Making her cum will be so fucking easy. I keep teasing her with my tongue and eventually run my fingers over her entrance as I suck her clit.

Makeba loses control. Holy fuck, when she cums, she's even sexier than I thought she would be. Her hips push up against my face and I cup her ass cheeks, pulling her sweet pussy closer to my mouth and flattening my tongue as I run it along every part of her pussy and then down to her back door. She cries my name out again when my tongue touches her asshole. She goes wild again and runs her fingers through my hair. I think she's trying to push me away, but when I slip a finger inside her, she cries out loud and I know she needs more of my thick fingers and my tongue.

I make her cum twice before I take a break. I kiss the tops of her thighs, getting her juices everywhere as she shivers in my grasp. I have totally broken her... I know I'll get my cock in her soon. I just don't know how soon.

"Hey," I whisper. "Nice pussy."

She scrambles a few inches back, but she can't bring herself to glare at me. Her legs are still wide open and I can't take my eyes off her pussy...

"My phone," she gasps. "You promised."

Damn, she's cold hearted. But she makes me want to chase her down even more. I can't get enough. I'm not like Cole... I'm not confused about why I have Makeba down here. I'm going to get exactly what I want from her – sex. Her virginity. Everything...

I dash upstairs to get the phone from Dustin's room. He's coming back a day early from spring break so we can skate together. Cole will be in Boston training with the team there until the very last minute. Heading into Dustin Rathbone's dank cave always requires extra work. I have to take my shirt off just to stand the temperatures, so I head upstairs without bothering to put one on.

I use my set of keys to open the door and the humid tropical air hits my face. He has to keep this place just right for the reptiles and spiders. There are heat lamps and enclosures stacked on top of each other and tons of live feeder animals for the menagerie.

When he's gone, there's a glowing red light to keep the place looking properly fucked up.

I look in the cage for Ovie, and he's not there. Fuck. He got out again. Dustin warned me he only takes a few days to crack a new way of latching his enclosure, and just my luck, the fucking snake is gone. He could be anywhere… Cole's room, under the kitchen sink. He left some of his skin behind and a mouse tail. Fucking grim as shit.

I don't know how Dustin lives with these creepy fucking creatures.

"Ovie," I whisper as I grab Makeba's phone from behind a rock. "Where the hell are you?"

8

YOUR PUSSY TASTES GREAT

MAKEBA

Jayce flings my phone on the bed next to me. He's still shirtless, and I'm still trying not to stare at his tattoos. Or his biceps. Or the rest of him. It's not fair that he has the perfect body. It's not fair that his tongue can do all those crazy things. Thankfully, I was right. Even if he just made me cum, I don't feel any different about Jayce Clutterbuck.

He runs his tongues over his lips, immediately snapping me out of staring at the tattoo on his forearm. He shuts the door behind him and leans against it. The light filtering in through his window catches his abs. They actually glisten.

"Your pussy tastes great," he says. "It's different."

I squeeze my legs shut. Letting Jayce put his tongue between my legs was a mistake – intellectually. Physically,

I am still reeling from what this completely ignorant hockey player did with his long and flexible tongue between my legs. He's an athlete. He's dumb as rocks. He's not supposed to know how to find the clit, much less do all that stuff to it. Jayce didn't just find my clit. He used his tongue to make love to it.

Every inch of my thighs remains soaked and his presence makes my heart jackhammer in my chest. I have to remind myself that it's Jayce Clutterbuck standing in front of me and that he's a monster. We don't have a future together and he is definitely not boyfriend material. He's the furthest thing from boyfriend material, but I can't look away from his chiseled body.

There's something primal and untamed in me, and it's hijacking my rational thinking. I want more. Jayce will never let me live it down if I let him between my legs again, so I stiffen my body and sit up straight despite my instincts, struggling to maintain dignity around him, which seems so completely impossible. He grins down at me as if he knows something I don't and puts his hands on his hips.

He is so muscular.

"What are you staring at?" I snap at him. I don't want him to get the wrong idea about me. Just because he gave me an enjoyable experience with his tongue doesn't mean my feelings for him will suddenly change.

"Aren't you going to tell your friends the truth? Go ahead. I'm confiscating that afterwards."

"No, you aren't. You gave it to me."

I hurriedly unlock my phone and hope Jayce ignores my sass.

"Damn it, Makeba. Do I need to remind you I have a video of you pissing yourself on my phone? It's humiliating."

"You don't need to remind me, asshole."

I glance down at my phone, praying that my careless mouth doesn't get me into big trouble with the ignorant ass hockey player hovering over me. My friends are totally freaking out in the group chat and since I always answer texts, they already suspect something nefarious. I have to tell them the truth and I have to do it with naked ass Jayce Clutterbuck staring at me.

"Boy, can you go do something else?"

"Like what?" He pauses for a moment like he's genuinely thinking of an idea. "Eat your ass while you finish your text?"

Jayce has a glimmer of hope in my eye, like he's actually serious. I'm not going to let some man I barely know put his tongue against my butt hole... again. I know what Jayce was doing earlier. I glare at him. I gave him permission to lick one thing down there – not everything. He knew exactly what he was doing and now he's planning to do it again.

"No! No! Who the hell would say that? Get me some food, maybe. I'm fucking hungry."

Maybe if I send him scampering off on a little errand, he'll leave me alone.

"You are the world's most demanding prisoner," Jayce complains. My stomach is growling, and he's about to find out just how much more demanding I can get when there's nothing in my belly. Hunger + anger = the worst.

"Run along," I command imperiously, acting significantly more confident than I feel. If Jayce was going to get all aggressive on me, I would know.

To my surprise, Jayce actually does what I ask and exits the room in search of food. It's not a complete win because he locks the door and slides something under it on the other side once he leaves, so I couldn't get it open if I tried. I roll my eyes. Jayce may have the upper hand for now, but that won't last. Now that I know his true colors, I need to plot my escape and revenge.

Thankfully, I have a lot of experience from helping Kya with Cole. What Jayce has on me isn't half as bad except for the part where I pee. And basically the whole video. Okay, fine. He could ruin me. But I think I can get out of it. Whatever.

I rush to get dressed in his absence and then I text my friends.

B.J. leaked Kya's stories. I found out before break but didn't know how to tell you guys. I'm sorry I kept it from you. I was just in total shock and needed a day or two to process. I hope you can forgive me.

I shut my phone off when I send the message. I need to handle the Jayce situation a lot better before I get into a text message back and forth with my friends, explaining more. I just need to get the truth out and honestly? Once Cole knows someone messed with his girl, he's probably going to go crazy on that kid. At least they know the truth now, which takes one thing off my plate. Jayce returns in five minutes with a hot pizza.

"Where the hell did you get that?"

Jayce grins and slides into the room with that impish smirk on his face. It's not that cute of a smile, but it makes him look like a little boy, which softens up his hard, masculine features just the right amount. I can't help but smile back until I remember I'm supposed to be playing this tough.

"I stole it from the frosh on our team," Jayce announces proudly. "Just my luck. It was at the front door."

"Did you pay for it?"

Jayce has the moral fiber of a French fry.

"Do you know what stealing is, Makeba? Don't worry, it's pepperoni, so if you're vegan like Kya, you can still eat it."

He says this with a startling amount of confidence. Jayce is confident in pretty much everything he does, but it's always a shock when he's confidently wrong.

"Do you have any idea what veganism is?"

"Something about only eating dead animals," Jayce mutters. "It's totally fucked up."

I sigh. Sometimes it's best to let Jayce be the idiot he is. Plus, he can't be that bad. He got me pizza. Unless the box has spiders in it or something gross.

In case it's a prank, I command him aggressively. "Open the pizza box."

Jayce opens the pizza box, entirely oblivious to my suspicions, and the delicious smell of pepperoni pizza becomes impossible to ignore. Yummy. Jayce sits on the floor, and I'm ready to get into a grease fest when he asks. "Can you not eat on the bed?"

"Why not?"

"Kinda, gross, Makeba."

"Just wash the grease stains off."

"Floor. Now."

I roll my eyes but I listen to Jayce, mostly because of his sexy body and definitely not because of the words coming out of his mouth. With the fresh aroma of pizza in the air, I'm no longer a slave to Jayce's pheromones and I can think... and man, do I have a great idea. He's letting his guard down and that's the perfect time for me to strike. Jayce will never see this coming.

I follow him to the floor and sit cross-legged. He opens the pizza box and our eyes lock from across the greasy food.

"It's kind of like a date."

"Eating pizza on the floor of your bedroom is nothing like a date."

"Right. On a proper date, I would fuck you while I eat the pizza."

He nods proudly to himself, like this is the most brilliant idea in the world. Then I catch him staring at my boobs and take measures to cover my cleavage a little more.

"Jayce, I'm beginning to think you've never been on a date."

"Not really. I get tons of sex anyway," he responds casually. Tons of sex. Ugh.

He shrugs in such an annoying, entitled way that makes me notice another tattoo on his chest. I look away from him and take a slice of pizza since Jayce has done the same, and he's folding it in his mouth before sliding it in like a sub sandwich.

"That's not as impressive as you think it is," I retort, after watching him eat like an animal with disgust. "I wouldn't brag about being emotionally defective."

"Listen, chica. I am not a fucking detective."

"Defective, Jayce."

"Oh. Sorry. I lost some of my hearing a while back."

I knew that white boy couldn't hear.

"From one of your hockey fights?"

Jayce grunts because his mouth is full of pizza. Then he shakes his head.

"Step-dad."

"What do you mean?"

"He punched me in the head when I was nine. I got a concussion."

"Oh. Shit. I'm sorry."

"I'm the fucking idiot," he says. "Grew up promising I'd never be like him, but... I can't stop fighting."

"Why not?"

Jayce shrugs. "Everything I got going on, I put it on the ice. That shit comes out there too."

"Like, what else do you have going on?"

I can't imagine what complex thoughts could run through Jayce's head. He tunes out whenever he hears a word more than a syllable long.

"Pretty much just my step-dad."

"What about your mom?"

"She died."

"Oh."

Damn, that's sad. I never knew Jayce had all that going on. I feel a little guilty for being so harsh. I have both my parents and they're that married couple that kept the honeymoon phase going for decades. I know they want me to have a love like theirs, but what our elders don't understand is that we live in a totally different world from the one they did.

Men don't do commitment — they do pizza on the floor and sex in the dorms. There's no romance in any of that. My friends think that makes me cynical, but it's just practical. Not everyone can have perfect love the way my parents do. What they have is rare these days.

"He took care of me," Jayce says. "But he hit me. I didn't have anyone to stand up for me. I couldn't fight back. Until hockey."

Jayce's admission hangs in the air between us and stirs me to something close to sympathy. He may have had one too many pucks to the head, but he may have also had one too many fists too. Even an asshole like Jayce didn't deserve to be mistreated as a kid.

"I'm sorry."

I mean that. Jayce might be a bit of a dick, but no one deserves to grow up with abuse.

"Don't be," Jayce says, pivoting his gaze to mine and grinning. I don't like that mischievous look in his eye.

"What's that look for?"

"Sex," He says. "Sex goes great with pizza."

How can he talk about this stuff and then jump straight into sex? He seriously has a one-track mind.

"Jayce... we've already discussed this."

"Sex."

Great. Is he going to do that thing he does where he just repeats a word and hopes that it breaks me down? Because it won't work this time. Actually, I'm about to reverse Jayce's little plan upside down–and thanks to this pizza in my tummy, I actually have the nourishment to do it.

He'll never see what's coming.

"Sex?" I repeat.

Jayce nods–again, like a puppy. This can't be the story of how I lose my virginity… I always wanted it to be epic and romantic. I'll have to get used to the fact that I'm about to lose my virginity… for revenge.

9

SEX... AND PIZZA

JAYCE

If I keep saying the word "sex", eventually, she has to listen and give it to me. Crazy thing is, it works every time.

"Sex... and pizza," I say again.

I think she's finally about to agree. Makeba throws a balled up napkin at my head.

"Teach me how to throw a single punch first."

"Fine," I say. "Pizza break?"

"Yes," she says, and I wince as she wipes her greasy fingers off on my bed sheet. Makeba rises to her feet. She doesn't exactly have any clothes left because I went crazy trying to get to her pussy. After putting a finger in there, I want to follow a wise man's advice. My best friend Dustin Rathbone always says "get the whole dick in there" – and that's exactly what I want to do to Makeba tonight.

I already got her wet. I smelled and tasted her. I put my finger in her tight pussy and felt her from the inside as she screamed in pleasure. I want her.

Our eyes lock and I remember that my first task is showing her how to throw a punch. But I can't stop staring at her and for a while, she doesn't look away either. Maybe I should be worried about what types of thoughts are racing around her smart head. She's kinda brainy.

Nah, brainy or not, a chick is a chick. She has a pussy, and she wants to get it wet.

"Listen," I say. "Why don't you just let me kick that kid's ass for you?"

"I don't need a man to fight my battles."

It sounds like she has spent just a little too much time listening to Kya Ambrose's lectures. I don't see another way out except for agreeing with her. Makeba's pretty stubborn. I clear my throat and focus on teaching her what I can – enough to knock the lights out of some punk ass nerd.

"Okay. Fine. You want to make a fist like this," I show her, demonstrating proper technique so she doesn't break her fingers or wrists.

She tries and fucks it up totally. I reach over and bend her fist in the proper way.

"Like this, Makeba."

I close my palm over her fist and then I try to swallow, but it feels like an impossibly large knot is stuck in my throat. If I didn't know any better, I would say touching her is making me nervous. I don't get that way around chicks – especially not chicks who I already tasted.

"Like this?" she says, trying it on her own.

Her voice is so soft and her accent is a little raspy. I have to ignore how stiff I'm getting to answer her as she adjusts her fist a little closer to what I showed her. I move her thumb a little.

"Like this," I whisper. "There. You've got it."

Why do I want to be so gentle with her? The new fist shape excites her, and she makes another fist with her other hand.

"Okay, and I hit like this?"

She tries to hit my outstretched palm and I barely feel anything.

"You want to feel the force from your hips," I say. "Your lower body is a lot stronger than your upper body. Try it like this…"

We practice for a while until she can slam her fists into me pretty hard.

"Great," she says, out of breath and smiling after our lesson. "Am I ready to kick some ass yet?"

"Maybe we should learn how to kick first," I say to her. Fuck. When did it get so hot in here? I'm all sweaty and so is Makeba. Her skin looks really pretty and shiny with all the sweat. It's so distracting. She nods and a surge of regret floods me. I can't mess around with her anymore. I need to stop. I need to satisfy this inexplicable urge.

"I want to fuck you," I blurt out.

She sighs and drops her fists. I'm just relieved they aren't flying towards my face.

"You mentioned. Not exactly a romantic offer."

"Sorry. I'm an idiot."

"Maybe," she replies, "But it's okay…"

Then she kisses me. I think it's a trick or something, but she doesn't hit me in the face at all. She just keeps kissing me and then I get too hot to think about anything else but her pussy. Man, I want more of it. I grab her hips, which are slick with sweat, and pull her body against mine.

Kissing her breaks something in me. I can't hold back. I slide her lips apart and push my tongue into her mouth. Her body tenses for a moment, like she's nervous about kissing me so deeply. I don't relent. I push my tongue into her mouth again. You're mine. You're safe.

Her fingers dig through the stubble on my cheeks and she pulls my face close to hers, finally releasing her tension and pressing her tongue against mine as I kiss her.

I squeeze her hips against my body and then pull away from her to give her air and to see her. I need to know why the hell she did that and what she's thinking.

"Makeba…"

"You want to fuck me, don't you?" she whispers.

"That's what you want?"

"Yeah."

My heart throbs. This has to be a sick joke. I'm getting her into bed. It's going to happen for me. My cock surges to attention.

"Makeba…" I whisper. "Are you for real?"

"Yes," she whispers back. "What? Are you scared of sleeping with a black girl?"

She won't stop challenging me and I fucking love it.

I shake my head. I can't form words. I'm too hard and I'm trying everything in my power to stop myself from hoisting her against the wall and taking her there without another word and definitely without a condom. It's wrong, but it's how I want her. She's natural in every way and my dick wants her raw.

Makeba leans forward and her hand slowly cups around my cock through my sweatpants. She feels around for the size and weight of it, her hands traveling up the shaft over the fabric. Those fingers are so fucking gentle. Her hands near my cock are too perfect to ignore. My hips thrust forward urgently and I grunt.

"Damn," she whispers. "You're really hard."

"Yeah."

Her lips meet mine again and I feel a surge of suspicion, which Makeba dispels with a nervous smile. She isn't scheming. She's just nervous like I am. I guess it's because she's a virgin. She really wants me. A virgin.

"Try not to fall in love after I make you cum," I whisper.

She presses her fingers to my lips, and I take the hint. Shut it, Jayce, and let's fuck. Makeba moves her hands back over to my cock, curving her fingers around the bulge in my sweatpants and making me even stiffer.

"Do you want to see it?" I ask her. I just want her to stop playing with me and take my fucking clothes off. She opts for teasing me.

"I've already seen it."

"Up close."

Makeba's hand falls away and I sense I've said something to push her off or turn her away.

"I don't know what you want. I don't know what to say," she says, almost stammering.

I don't like that there's any distance between us. I pull her close to me again. I can almost hear how nervous she is. Fuck. I don't want to screw this up. For the first time in a long time, she's looking at me and she isn't looking away. I kiss her soft shoulder.

"Hey, it's cool. You're new to this. Let's just kiss for a while."

She has nice lips. Really nice lips. I could kiss them for a while and I want to kiss them again the second she pulls away.

"I don't want to make it awkward," she says. "Unless I already fucked that up."

It's kinda cute that she's all nervous. It's different. My cock still wants her. I don't care if she's nervous, or awkward, or anything. I just want her, in all her natural glory.

"I stood in front of you naked, swinging my dick around like a helicopter. I think I'm the one making it awkward."

She wriggles against me and I feel my heart racing as I wonder if I'm getting close or if I'm about to lose her.

"Okay."

I don't want that spit fire I dragged to my bedroom to disappear because she's shy. Whatever, Makeba. There's a first time for everything – and for everyone. I kiss her shoulder.

"I want you," I whisper. "It's your first time, and you're with a guy who wants you. Okay? Nothing bad is going to happen... I promise, chica. I'm a great fuck."

She gives me those large brown eyes and I don't know what the fuck will happen to me if I keep looking at them, so I kiss her and we both stop looking. We both stop doing anything except touching each other and pressing our lips together. I don't even realize how quickly we're both naked until Makeba grabs my cheeks, her body pressing forward against mine, and the warmth from her nude flesh seeps into mine. I need air.

"You are so cocky," she whispers. But she doesn't stop kissing me, which gets me hard and excited for her. Damn. She is so much hotter up close. And there are boobs. Boobs.

I pull away from her for a moment and her hands fall away from my face. I see that anxious worry again, and I want her calm. No freaking out, Makeba… trust me, I'm good at this.

"You are so hot," I whisper. "Seriously."

Then I reach up and grab her boob. She gasps.

"Jayce…"

God, her boobs are perfect. They're round. Soft. Not very large, but that doesn't bother me. It's more about the shape and how they feel – and the fact that they belong to the chick in my physics class who totally ignores me. I hold her by the waist with my other hand as I let my thumbs run over her nipples.

"Let it happen, Makeba."

"I don't really have a choice now, do I…"

I cut her off by kissing her neck and making her moan. I like how she sounds when I kiss her neck. I tease her more with my tongue and when she moans again, I move back to kissing her lips. Our kisses are fiercer now, and far more desperate for each other. We stumble together and kiss against my Alexander Ovechkin poster, then against my full-length mirror. She grabs my cheeks and my cock feels like it will burst if I wait another second to touch her.

I lead her back to the bed and we fall together, kissing and touching each other again. Makeba's legs wrap around me as I fall on top of her and I want to enter her so badly. She's soft in all the right places and her boobs...

"Boobs..." I whisper.

Makeba arches her back, allowing me access to her perfect nipples. They're like raisins, but they taste all sweaty and salty, like her skin. I want to lick them until she begs me to stop.

"Jayce..."

"I like boobs."

"Jayce!"

"What?" I whisper, kissing all over her breasts and running my tongue over her nipple again while she gasps and struggles to answer my question.

"That feels... it's making me... I don't know."

I slide my hand between her thighs and just press my fingers against her mound. Makeba shudders again, but pinned beneath my weight, she has nowhere to go. She can't do anything but yield to my hands, my lips... whatever I want to do with her. And the stuff I want to do with her will take us all night.

"You're wet," I murmur. "That's all."

"I feel more than wet," she says. "It's like... I'm warm..."

"Okay," I whisper. "You're sensitive. Let me taste you again and then we can finally do it."

"Do you have a condom?"

She's almost nervous as she asks, which I think is totally hilarious.

"Yeah. Duh."

I want to make her look at me when I enter her for the first time. That's the best part, and having Makeba wrapping her legs around me after all her comments about me being an idiot white boy... it just feels like pure victory.

She runs her fingers through my hair, her sexy boobs moving all hot and everything with each breath.

"Put it on," she says. "I'm ready."

Why does it feel so fucking good to hear her say that? I scramble for the stupid condom and put it on before I get on top of her again. This time, I have to part her thighs myself and I press my finger to her clit again, just teasing her awake.

"Hey," I whisper. "You sure about this?"

"Not exactly. You kidnapped me and it's a blackmail situation. But I guess it'll make a good story some day."

"Yeah, hot stuff," I whisper, and I say something that will totally piss her off for maximum revenge. "It'll be our love story."

Makeba wants to say something dripping with attitude, but I stop her by pressing the head of my cock against her virgin entrance. Her hips want to resist me at first, but I grab them and hold her in a comfortable position. She's mine. Every inch of her belongs to me. I pull her hips closer to me and slide my cock inside Makeba inch by inch. It's painfully slow, but perfect as I take her for the first time. Her walls resist my invasive member at first and then Makeba presses her palms against my chest, crying out from the novelty of an enormous cock between her thighs.

"Jayce…"

Fuck, it feels good to hear her call my name. I push deeper. I need to take her. I need to be her first.

Her hips rise to meet my push and my body pulses with heat from how incredibly tight she is. I bite down on my lower lip hard to keep from crying out. Holy fuck, she's tight. I ease my hips forward again and bury my dick between her legs.

Our bodies mash together and heave with the force of that first thrust. She's mine. I have her pinned to my bed and my cock stiffens between her legs as my body ignites with satisfaction. I slowly withdraw my hips and the shuddering moan from Makeba's lips pushes me over the edge into my pure animal desire for her.

Beneath me, her skin is such a perfectly dark brown shade in contrast to my pale skin that it's like making art with her body in my bed. She's different. She's not who everyone else wants me to be with. She's fierce, she's trouble, she's so goddamned attractive and so goddamned forbidden. I thrust into her again and never stop using my hands on her. When I feel a sensitive spot between her legs, I tease it and coax her very close to her first orgasm with a dick inside her.

"Cum for me," I whisper. "It's okay..."

I kiss her and push her over the edge with my fingers and then thrusting my dick deep between her legs. Makeba's first orgasm turns her into a writhing mess. Her inner thighs become sticky with her juices, and her entrance is gooey with her gushing juices. I kiss her and thrust deeper.

I want to cum. But I can't let myself do that without making Makeba cum a few more times. After her first orgasm, I slowly withdraw. Her soft features draw together in confusion.

"Don't worry. I'm not done."

"I wasn't worried..." she mumbles, but her voice is all sex-dazed and far away. I spread her legs and ogle her gushing wetness. Before I make love to her again, she needs my tongue. I love how great she smells and I just want to lick her pussy more than anything. I dive between her legs and Makeba grabs onto my long hair, moaning with each lick and exploding into another climax within a few seconds.

I keep going until her orgasms are throbbing, loud, and frequent. As she shudders, I kiss my way up her stomach and run my tongue over her breasts and neck before I kiss her and press the thick head of my dick against her entrance again.

"It's huge," she whispers. "It's so big."

See? All it takes is a few orgasms to loosen her up all the way.

"Yeah. I know."

Before she can give me lip about being arrogant again, I slide the head inside her. Her loud gasp encourages me to go even deeper this time. She wants to cum and I want to be inside her, making her cum for as long as she can go. I last a long time and Makeba cums a few more times before I feel the desire to finish. I move my hips slowly and then rock with her body, using those slow, deep strokes.

That's how I like to finish. nice and slow.

I kiss her slowly and when she pulls away, she's gaping up at me with those brown eyes. They're infinite. I ease my hips forward one last time and cum hard. One of her hands caresses my back as I finish and the other cups my ass as she pulls me deep. She digs her longish nails into my ass and I cum harder…

"Fuck," I whisper. "Five minutes and we can go again."

"Five minutes?!"

"Maybe three."

I roll off her, and Makeba immediately turns to face me.

"Go again? Is that even possible?"

I chuckle. She seriously underestimates how hot she is. "Yeah."

"Okay."

"We should have done this a long time ago," I say to her. And fuck, I mean it. She was so soft… so perfect. Nothing awkward about her or how we fit together. It's weird. I don't even want to kick her out of my bed or anything.

"We? You kidnapped me and blackmailed me here, remember?"

"I made you cum a bunch of times and taught you sex," I balk. Seriously? It's like Makeba appreciates nothing I do. I could eat her pussy like a hundred times and she'll still give me this look like I'm total scum.

"Wow, my hero."

"Finally. You admit it." She hates when I get all smug, which only makes me worse.

"That was sarcasm."

"I can make you cum."

"Jayce, that's not what I said."

I run my fingers along her lips and whisper, "Cum…"

"You're doing that thing where you just repeat stuff, Jayce. Snap out of it."

"Pussy," I whisper. "Let me lick it again while I wait. I promise it'll be good for you."

"You are so cocky."

"Yup. Big cock. Long tongue. That's all I need to keep you happy."

"Keep me happy… Jayce… you aren't keeping me at all. You're blackmailing me."

"Maybe I want to keep you," I grunt.

I put my hands between her thighs, peeling them apart despite her best efforts to squeeze them shut around my hands.

"Stop," she whispers.

"Why?"

"Because… you can't do that again."

"Why not?"

"It's not fair," she says.

Was someone keeping score?

"To who?"

She huffs at me next. "Why are you so annoying?"

"Pussy," I whisper. "Thinking about pussy."

Ha. She rolls her eyes and finally gives up fighting me again. I push her onto her back and spread her thighs open. I'm beyond ready to taste her some more. I can't wait.

Reluctantly, Makeba lets me eat her out again. She's all quiet when my tongue gets deep inside her and then she moans like a fucking angel when she finally climaxes. Her braids stick to her neck and her skin is slick with sweat. I kiss her inner thighs, her stomach, and I get between her legs again to make her cum some more.

Making her cum gets me hard again and we fuck until I can't fuck anymore. Every time she came, she got softer and sweeter to make love to. I enjoyed taking her slow. I can't stop thinking about how it just felt and how her body moved against mine.

I thought she would be awkward and all... like a virgin. I dunno. Boring. But I guess it's impossible for her to be boring with her sharp tongue, those bright eyes and that soft fucking skin. It's dark out and even with pizza breaks, we're both covered in sweat. Makeba doesn't even crawl out of bed when it's time for us to sleep.

"Come close," I whisper. "I'll hold you."

"I don't need you to give me the full virginity experience, Jayce. We're not even friends."

"Yeah, but... my lips still smell like your pussy, so this is just like basic respect."

She mutters something under her breath and then calls me a white boy again, which doesn't even bother me (even if it's kinda racist). I fall asleep with Makeba tucked underneath my bicep. I don't remember sliding into sleep, but it must have whacked into me like a freight train. The last thing I remember is how she smells. Her fingers trace the outline of my tattoos as I cuddle her close and her smaller body next to mine makes it so easy to fall asleep.

Only thing is, I make a total fucking mistake trusting Makeba Winston.

In the morning, everything between us changes.

10

SO LONG AND THANKS FOR ALL THE DICK

MAKEBA

The leather leash he used to tie me up fit easily around his neck last night. Using various neck ties from his dresser, I secured Jayce's arms and legs. He won't get free. He can't. I think he'll wake up when I've done it–even after I push him off the bed.

I guess I was pretty good at tricking his ass.

I took his nighttime sleep aid–several doses worth to be sure–and crushed it under my nails before crushing it all over his half of the pizza when we took one of our sex breaks.

It was too easy.

A part of me feels like shit for using Jayce to lose my virginity and then getting back at him like this. But too bad... he's mine now. And it's my turn to have a varsity house pet. Even if I know Jayce can't get free, I can't exactly fall into a peaceful slumber with him tied up and with our roles reversed. I need a plan. I need to know what to do with him.

The only problem is the deadbolt on his door. I don't know what freak designed this house with a deadbolt–something evil hockey players definitely don't need–but I don't know where Jayce has the key. If I want to get out of here and get some breakfast, I'll need to get the key from him and I'll need to do it fast, which means waking him up and facing his certain rage now I turned the tables.

There's no better way to get things done than to just rip the band-aid off, right? I grab the water bottle off Jayce's desk and pour it on his head. Well, I throw the water. Aggressively.

"WAKE UP, DUMBASS."

Jayce blinks stupidly as water falls into his eyes and blinds him, only making him blink more. He's slow to react. Man, I must have got him good with those sleeping pills. I take my phone out and get a picture of him like this–tied up to the bed naked. How's that for blackmail, Clutterbuck?

He looks up at me like I've betrayed him, like I owe him anything at all...

"Makeba?"

I want to think that those large coppery-brown eyes are gorgeous looking up at me with that look of sheer desperation, but I am too caught up with my smug satisfaction.

Dumb ass Jayce Clutterbuck could never and I mean never get my ass caught up for long. Ha!

"Oh, how the tables have turned," I say in my most dramatic villain voice possible. Raven would have been proud of me.

I don't know what I'm saying or doing. It just sounds like something dramatic to say at a time like this, when I finally have the upper hand over annoying ass big dick, Jayce. Who does he think he is to torture me with pizza, orgasms, and tying me to the bed?!

"Makeba… What the hell?" he coughs, sputtering and spitting out water. Oops. Maybe the water was a little too much. But then again… he got me drunk off tequila and took a humiliating video of me with copies everywhere. He deserves a taste of his own freaking medicine.

Jayce shakes his hair, shaggy brown hair falling out of his face and then groggily glances around before testing his binds and learning the unfortunate truth about his circumstances.

"That's right, Jayce. I knocked you out with sleeping pills and tied you up. You're my pet now. My dog…"

My smug smile makes his thick dark eyebrows pinch together, and he tests his binds again. Jayce is pretty strong, so I'm a little worried that they'll give, but I keep my face steady as I watch him failing to break free. He's gigantic. I can't believe I pulled this off.

"Damn it, Makeba, can you knock it off? Untie me."

His pleading gives me life. This foolish ass white boy really thought he could outsmart me, didn't he? He thought I was a dumb frosh and now he's the one who needs to beg me. Ha.

Jayce writhes on the ground again and I slightly regret not putting a shirt on him. I mean, he's easy on the eyes and with his muscles all tense and stressed, he looks very fit. But he'll probably be freezing, lying on the floor shirtless for the next five days. Too bad. He should have thought of that before kidnapping me, getting me drunk and tricking me into acting like a dog. I am never drinking tequila again.

"No way. I only woke your sorry ass up so I could get your keys and get myself some food. I'm outta here, white boy."

Jayce glares at me, but doesn't immediately reveal the location of the keys. He doesn't have to worry. I'm an expert at finding stuff in a messy room. It's one of my hidden talents.

"This place is a mess," Jayce shoots back, grunting and fighting his binds again. "I hope you plan on cleaning up before your great escape."

"I don't."

Jayce flashes me an intense glare, like there's a part of him that's planning to end my life. This white boy is tripping.

"Makeba... I'm not giving you my keys and I'm not letting

you out of here. We're going to die here together, if that's what it takes."

"Don't be an idiot, Jayce. You'll get hungry long before then."

"Hungry? Who's hungry?"

Both of our dumb stomachs growl together, betraying both of our weaknesses. But I'm much smaller than Jayce. I don't need as much fuel as the 6'4" hockey player. I have to tell myself that he'll crack before I do. I pull the chair away from his desk and sit a few feet away from him, clothed in his oversized Laguna Grove sweatpants and a clean white t-shirt from some hockey sleep-away camp.

"I can wait," I say calmly, even if my stomach then growls louder.

"So can I," Jayce says. "You know, this is fucked up, Makeba."

I roll my eyes. Jayce has lost his mind. So it's fucked up when I do it to him, but when he does it, it's totally fine?

"But it wasn't fucked up when you did the same thing to me? Got it."

"I did that as a joke and to get you to fuck me."

"Blackmail isn't suddenly okay because you did it to get sex."

He has the morals of a tarantula.

"Why not? It worked."

"Jayce. Have morals. Please."

"No way, chica."

"Okay, if you won't have morals, at least tell me where you put the keys. I've been searching around this place for the past ten minutes."

"At least you've been busy," Jayce grumbles, flopping over dramatically and flashing his annoying sorrel eyes at me. "You can't keep me tied up here like this. I'll starve to death."

"I'm a generous master, Clutterbuck. I'm going to feed you two to three times a day. If you're good, I'll even take you for a walk."

His ears perk up. Sigh. I am definitely not untying Jayce. I have a survival instinct, you know. That was just a clever lie to trick him into giving up the location of the keys. It doesn't work.

"I'm not telling you where the fuckin' keys are."

I get up and walk over to him.

"That's fine. I'll just play DMX songs on repeat until you give up the location."

"I like DMX."

Of course, this annoying ass white boy loves DMX.

"Whatever, Jayce. Point is, you're going to give up the location… soon. Take your time. Feel the burn of hunger.

The rest of the hockey players are finally all gone on vacation. I heard them leaving at 6 in the morning."

"You're cold hearted," he spits at me. "Did I ever tell you that?"

"Sorry, I couldn't hear that over the sweet sound of my victory. I'm calling my friends."

"Don't I get a phone call?" he asks, grunting and wriggling against the binds. Damn, this man is powerful. Thankfully, my knot skills are pretty good.

"No. I'm not giving you a chance to get any of your sick buddies up here. You're stuck here for spring break, Jayce. That's just the way the cookie crumbles. Five days as my varsity house pet. I can't wait."

I take my phone and start searching for Kya's name in my contacts list. She'll have to add Raven to the group call once she picks up. The second the phone rings, Jayce howls like a greyhound. I glare at him, but he only makes his howling louder. Before I can shut him up, Kya picks up with an urgent tone.

"Oh my God, Makeba! You're alive."

"Of course I'm alive. I'm fine."

"Is that a dog in the background?"

AWOOOOOOOOOOO! AWO! AWO! AAWOOoo-OOOOOOOOoo.

Jayce is serving big crackhead energy acting like that. I

throw one of his hockey gloves at him and he yelps like a real hit dog.

"Something like that..."

I want to give Kya a chance to freak out about the last thing I told her before I announce that I'm holding Jayce Clutterbuck–one of the most terrifying hockey players on campus–captive in his own bedroom.

"We got your news about B.J. I am so sorry for what you went through. Are you sure you're okay?" Kya gushes. "We need to kill him.,"

Kya worries about stuff a lot and I know she would do anything for her friends if we were in trouble.

"I'm fine. I promise. I'm mostly healed up and everything."

Kya doesn't sound convinced. I can't blame her, but I don't want to push B.J.'s buttons. I want a sneak attack.

"What he did was fucking vile," Kya spits with resentment. "He was your boyfriend. I'm going to have to work up the courage to talk to my dad and see if we can sue him. And he hit you? We need to report him to the school, Makeba. This is domestic violence. If a man thinks he can go around just hitting a fellow college student, a woman pursuing her education as we are free to do, then he has another thing coming."

This sets Kya off for a while, but she's not entirely wrong. Cole's voice in the background breaks up her lecture for a second.

"Who you talking to, babe? And does she have a dog?"

Jayce hasn't stopped howling since he recovered from the hockey glove to the face. I shoot him a glare and consider giving him a good kick in the side, but that would definitely count as animal abuse. Jayce gives me a cocky smirk as I glare at him. Whatever, Jayce. You still aren't the winner here.

"I'm talking to Makeba and she doesn't have a dog... wait, do you?"

AWO! AWOoooOOOOOOOOOOoooo!

"It's a long story..." I clear my throat and glare at Jayce again, who only stops to pant and gasp for air. "Can you get Raven on the phone, too? I need to talk to both of you."

"Of course! We need to take down stupid B.J. the second we get back on campus."

Yeah, by the time they get back to campus, my little house pet will probably froth at the mouth and prepare to kill me. I need to give my boring black girl crew an update ASAP because shit just got a little less boring for the crew with Jayce on a leash.

It takes a few seconds to get Raven connected, but once she's there, she's on it.

"Okay, whose ass are we kicking? Makeba, are you alive?! I have been blowing up Mr. B.J.'s goddamn phone and if he thinks he's going to get away with this, he'll be sorry."

"Hey, Raven. I'm good. And yeah. I'm actually going to kick his ass myself."

"You are?" Kya said. "Are you sure? Makeba, you said he hurt you."

"Well… I got myself into a situation, then I got myself out of a situation and basically, I can fight now."

"What situation?" Kya asks.

Raven continues, "Listen, I don't care. You aren't handling him alone. What kind of person does what he did to you? I wish you told me sooner…"

"Wait, what situation?" Kya repeats.

Shit. There's no getting anything past Kya Ambrose. Her experience taking down her dad's mistresses with her mom has basically turned her into a world class detective. I take a deep breath and glance over at Jayce, who has advanced to very annoying wolf howls and dramatic yelps for attention.

"Jayce Clutterbuck sort of kidnapped and blackmailed me."

"He did what? Oh, hell no. COLE!" Kya screams at Cole off the phone. "Cole, get over here. One of your feral ass big hockey butt white boys has become a problem."

"He's not a problem," I interrupt. "And please, don't get Cole involved. He has team loyalty, remember?"

Cole's voice sounds like it's coming from the other room when he says, "Babe, what?"

With a well placed "never mind", Kya gets off free and Raven speaks ups.

"Some hockey guy is blackmailing you. How is that not a problem?"

I hold my phone closer to Jayce, whose howling hasn't abated a single second since I got on the phone. After treating my girl crew to a few seconds of deranged hockey boy wolf howls, I sigh and put it up to my ear.

"Hear that? It's Jayce. I freed myself and used my talents to tie his ass up, and he's basically my pet now."

"He's your pet?!" Kya says. "Makeba, explain."

My friends can't even imagine what kind of spring break I've been having. Hey, it wasn't all bad. I lost my virginity and lost count of how many orgasms I had. Poor Jayce. Little did he know that his humiliation was waiting for him on the other side of my virginity.

I walk over to Jayce's bed and sit just out of arm's reach of him as I explain the story to Raven and Kya. They both coax the story along with "oh no he didn't"s and "get his ass" peppered in at the right places. When I finish, Jayce is glowering at me, absolutely loathing my epic recounting of my brilliant revenge plot. He just hates that I used him for sex and not the other way around. This cocky ass hockey player didn't have a clue who he was dealing with.

Thank you Jamaican ancestors for my skills at escaping bondage.

"So wait... you lost your virginity as part of a revenge plot?" Raven asks once I tell them everything. "That sounds just like this book I was reading. But then the guy comes back like ten times more powerful. So be careful."

Raven is always reading something oddly helpful in her romance novels. But I don't know. I don't see Jayce getting out of this before I figure out what to do with him. I could make an embarrassing video, but I want to come up with something better, even if it takes all of spring break. For now, I'll just keep him fed and plot with my girls. I glance over nervously at the dumb, sexy hockey player, who has finally stopped howling and has curled up against the foot of his bed. He's half asleep, like a golden retriever after a long walk. I roll my eyes and turn my attention back to my conversation with my friends.

"Don't worry. I just need to know where he put his keys and I'm free."

Raven and Kya give me advice on where to look and I step over Jayce and around him as I search his bedroom. He gets really nervous when I look at his hockey bag and I reach my hands in, moving around his jersey and his spare gloves before...

"I found them!"

Sucker needs to work on his poker face.

Kya celebrates. "Score!"

"This is epic," Raven responds with a giggle.

I cover the microphone so I can give Jayce one last epic goodbye.

"I'll bring you food once I've eaten. Sayonara, white boy. Thanks for the big white dick."

Jayce lunges forward like a worm, but I dodge his body launching toward mine and escape to freedom. I still need to get out of the hockey house with none of the guys staying on campus for break noticing my escape, but that should be easy. I throw up the hood on Jayce's hoodie and bend my head, hurrying through the halls all the way to the front door, where I finally escape to freedom.

I won. This stupid hockey boy thought he could capture me, kidnap me, and control me – then worse, manipulate me into some insanely hot mind-blowing and incredibly confusing first time sex. But I won... and now I need to figure out what to do with my big old varsity house pet.

BIG SEXY CAN DEFINITELY HELP

JAYCE

If Makeba thinks she's going to get away with this, she's fucking crazy. I've been patient. Five days, sleeping on the floor without a shirt, utterly relying on her for food, water and entertainment.

It's been a fucking nightmare. She read online that solitary confinement is inhumane, and she's taken it upon herself to ensure I get "plenty of socialization". **I hate it.**

She comes over and sits there and doesn't even try to have sex with me. We just talk. It's fucking weird. I mean… The sex was great, right? I know she came. I know it. I'm not one of those clueless fucking guys. We connected. And now, Makeba's treating me like a fucking dog.

She even calls me her dumb golden retriever, emphasis on the dumb. Whatever, just because I thought those dog treats were real beef jerky doesn't make me dumb. She doesn't know what it's like to be tied to the bed all freaking day and not even get your dick sucked.

Every day I stare at her snacking in the chair across from me, lost in a million dirty thoughts, and she doesn't even look twice at me. She doesn't even like me.

Makeba even laughs at me when I get all excited to see her. I haven't eaten in fucking twelve hours. Of course, I'm happy to see her. It doesn't help that she's wearing all these dumb spring time outfits–like that short yellow dress. She hit me on the nose when I asked to see what was underneath it. What's wrong with her? Why isn't she totally horny and in love with me?

We had sex. It was like… the coolest sex I ever had with a chick. Now, she makes me bark on command and every-thing, like our night together, didn't even mean anything. It's totally fucked up. Her idea of revenge is pretty twisted, and she doesn't even have feelings for me. She's just different from other chicks and it's dumb, but it's so hard to stop thinking about her.

At least with all the time I have alone, I have time to think. I'm not so good at thinking, especially not after a rough day on the ice, but I think hard enough that I remember something Makeba doesn't know. Rathbone's coming back early so we can skate together. If he times it right, he'll get here before Makeba and I can get free. I'll head out to skate and then Rathbone and I can put our stupid fucking heads together and come up with a plan to out-revenge one smart fucking chick. I can't wait to get her back in my bed and force her to confess why our great night in bed didn't make her fall for me. She's probably crazy, huh? That would explain a lot.

The night before Dustin comes, Makeba's late with dinner. But I have an ally. Ovie...

It's been days since I've seen that motherfucker, but he's finally hungry for another mouse and without Dustin (or me, the guy taking care of him) catching him and returning him to his cage, he's going on the hunt. Unfortunately, he comes slithering under the crack in my door, which is way too fucking big now that I think about it. Once he gets his head through, it might take him a while, but Ovie can get his whole body under a door.

I hate to admit it, but I've been alone long enough that Ovie feels like my best fucking friend as he sticks his head under the door. Fuck yeah. He's coming to save me. I don't know how, but he's been one of the bros for so long, he'll help me think of something.

"Ovie! Come on buddy... come on..."

Ovie slowly slithers over and then he pushes his way across the floor, lying next to me with his head at my feet and his body all stretched out. Ovie's so goofy, man.

"Hey, Ovie, any idea how to untie a knot?" I whisper. He's quiet. Whatever, he's just a snake. And speaking of snakes... Where is that chick with my dinner? I keep waiting another fifteen minutes. By then, Ovie has his body on top of mine, like he's trying to give me a big hug. He's moving really slow, and it tickles a bit. Big guy must really want a mouse. Too bad I'm tied up and can't feed him.

Makeba pushes the door open finally and screeches like a banshee.

"JAYCE!"

"What?" I reply, coughing a little. Ovie's hug is getting pretty tight.

"There's a SNAKE!"

"Yeah…" I answer, coughing again. "It's Ovie… he's named after–

"Alexander Ovechkin, the greatest hockey player of all time. I heard you the first seven times you told me about that damned creature. How the hell did it get out!?"

"I dunno. He's pretty cool, though."

"That doesn't change the fact that it's going to EAT YOU!" Makeba shrieks. She's frozen in the doorway and looking at Ovie like he has two heads. Geez, it's just a giant boa constrictor. It's a pet.

I swear, I have to wonder who the dumb one is some-times. Snakes don't eat people in real life, Makeba. Duh. Ovie eats mice.

"Makeba," I grunt. "Ovie eats mice."

"He's literally squeezing the life out of you!"

"It is getting kinda hard to breathe…"

"How do I get it off?!"

"I don't know. I'm pretty hungry. Can you get me some dinner?"

"Can you fucking prioritize?" Makeba shrieks, throwing a plastic fork at my head.

"Buy new ties? Yeah, I'll have to considering what you did to mine…"

I thrash against the stupid neckties tying me together. She literally used all of them.

"JAYCE! There is a snake trying to squeeze you to death. FOCUS!"

Ovie's hug is getting pretty tight.

"He's just hungry. You'll have to get one of the live mice from Dustin's room."

"LIVE MICE?!" Makeba shrieks. Her nostrils flare with rage and there's fire in her eyes. I can tell she's considering leaving me there and letting Ovie hug me to death.

"Yeah. Just hold it by the tail and he'll get it."

She's looking at me like I just told her to eat vomit off the floor.

"Have you lost your fucking mind?!"

It's getting pretty hard to talk, so I just shrug and try to say something which comes out more like a cough.

"OH MY GOD!" Makeba screeches. "I'm going to go to JAIL! Jayce, where are Dustin's keys?!"

She shuffles around my room, flinging books, papers, pens, and hockey equipment fucking everywhere in her search. I struggle to choke out a response.

"Un...lock...ed."

Makeba leaves, and I know she's returning when I hear her screaming from down the hall.

"AIIIIIIIEEEEEEE! Ohmigod. Ohmigod. Ohmigod. Ohmigod. Ohmigod."

She pushes the door open, holding out a live mouse by the tail and shrieking loudly. The mouse isn't having a good time. I don't know why Dustin insists on live mice instead of frozen ones. I guess he's just a freak like that.

"I don't even know why I'm saving your life right now!" Makeba shrieks.

Ovie can smell mouse. He knows mouse. He eases his grip and stops, giving me one of his big friendly hugs while Makeba shrieks again. The mouse is putting up one hell of a fight.

"It's fucking fighting back! The mouse is fighting back!" She shrieks, waving the poor terrified mouse around as she tries not to get bit. The boa smells the mouse's fear. I cough and writhe forward a little. Damn, it's hard to breathe.

At least Ovie's already loosening his grip. Ovie's flicking tongue probably sniffs out that mouse and he's choosing that easy, exciting prey. Makeba shrieks again and then drops the mouse, who bolts. Ovie slithers away from me and finally... I can breathe.

"That snake almost killed you!"

"That's your fault for tying me up here."

"I thought it was in a cage, Jayce. Why are your freak reptiles — AIIEEE!"

The mouse darts back across the floor, making the mistake of crossing too closely in front of Ovie, who lunges and wraps his mouth around the creature. Makeba screams again.

"He's EATING THE MOUSE! Ohmigod, Jayce, STOP IT!"

"How!? I'm fucking tied up!"

"AIIEEEE! This is nasty! It's so nasty!"

She keeps screaming even louder than before.

"Calm down, Makeba!"

"Calm down!? You want me to calm down... here's your food, Jayce. Catch!"

She throws something at my head in a bag.

"What the hell is that?"

"Dry Cheerios."

"That's my dinner!? I'm starving."

"Then you'll really enjoy it. I can't be in here with this snake, Jayce. I'm out of here."

"You tied my hands, remember?"

How the fuck did she get all the power here?

"Use your mouth to open the bag, then."

Has this chick lost her mind?

"My mouth? Makeba, chica… you're forgetting prisoner's rights."

"You don't have rights, Jayce. My friends are coming tomorrow and we'll decide what to do with you then."

"Your friends?! Makeba…"

"Sayonara, white boy."

And then she's gone… I swear, Makeba is the craziest chick I know. But when she leaves, I can't help but crack a smile. She has the upper hand for the moment, but she doesn't realize that Dustin Rathbone will be here before her friends and when he finds Ovie missing, I have the first door he'll knock on. In the meantime, all I have to do is squirm my body across the floor to the baggie of Cheerios Makeba left for me. I swear, she treats me like I'm really her pet. It's massively fucked up and when Dustin Rathbone gets here, I know he'll help me get her back for this with some sweet ass revenge.

Didn't our insanely hot sex together mean anything to her? Something is majorly wrong with that chica if she can't even connect to the hottest guy ever who just took her virginity. God, she was tight.

I only get a few of the Cheerios with my tongue before I accidentally kick the bag across the room. Fuck. Ovie is totally chill now that he has his mouse. I am so jealous. I would give anything for a mouse right now. I just need to get my macros in and these fucking Cheerios Makeba left me aren't doing it for me. There's definitely protein in mice...

Several hours later, just when I think I'm about to die of hunger, I hear Dustin Rathbone's giant clunky footsteps hauling his gigantic ass down the haul.

"OOOOOOVIEEEEEE. Are you in Jayce's room!?"

"DUSTIN! DUSTIN, HELP!"

The colossal idiot doesn't hear me until he gets to the door.

"Yo, Jayce... what's going on?"

Eventually, I get the stupid motherfucker to understand what he has to do. He runs down to the truck to get some tools. A screwdriver. A crowbar. Normal Dustin shit. Before you know it, he has my door off the hinges — and it's totally fucked up.

"That's going to cost a shit ton of money in school fees," Dustin says, throwing the door into the hall. "What the fuck happened, brah?"

I grunt and squirm, struggling to face him, which barely fucking works.

"Dude, your plan totally worked. For all of five fucking minutes and then that fucking frosh tricked me and tied me to the bed."

Dustin steps into my room and chuckles. He cut his shaggy head of hockey flow over break, so he looks different and less grungy. He's still a piece of shit – the worst of all of us.

"Can I take a picture? Your junk is basically out."

He reaches for his phone and laughs when I look at him like I'm going to kill him. I haven't exactly ruled it out.

"No, you can't take a fucking picture. Untie me."

"Ovie! He looks great, Jayce. Good job keeping him well fed."

I don't bother telling Dustin that I nearly became Ovie's next meal. Dustin releases me from the stupid binds and lets Ovie climb over his shoulders. My wrists are raw and I am fucking thirsty. Not to mention starving. I sit up and look around my room. How the hell did she get it so fucking messy in here? I search on my floor for a white t-shirt and tell Dustin about the best sex I ever had and the tragedy that followed. Ovie slides over Dustin's hands and shoulders and Dustin glows, smiling as Ovie slithers around him gently. Those two idiots love each other.

Makeba could learn a thing or two from Ovie…

"That chick is the most cold-hearted chick I ever met. I thought virgins were supposed to be nice."

Dustin laughs.

"Bro, she fucked you up good. You lost weight, man."

"I'm fucking starving. And yeah, she fucked me up. Dude, I slept with her. Why doesn't she have feelings for me?"

I don't want to tell him all the ways it was weird with the emotions and stuff. Dustin isn't really an emotional guy.

"No way, so my plan worked?"

"No, it didn't fucking work. I've been on my bedroom floor for the past five days. No sunlight. No skating. It was worse than apartheid, Dustin."

"Do you know what apartheid is, Jayce?"

"No. But it was really fucking bad. Just like this."

Dustin pauses for a moment, totally lost in thought.

"Yeah, I don't know either," Dustin says. "Let's get you cleaned up, brah. You smell like ass. We'll hit the rink in twenty."

He's right. I smell like shit. Dustin could stand to give me a little fucking sympathy.

"Got it."

I take less than twenty minutes to get ready. I am so fucking eager to get out of my bedroom and plot revenge on my nemesis. She's so beautiful and she drives me fucking wild. I guess I didn't see it because of all my prejudice and stuff, but once I had her close, it was like... woah. I am a total idiot.

Dustin skates onto the ice first and he is so much faster than me. I haven't worked out in five days and a diet of Cheerios, pretzels and Hot Cheetos has me totally weakened. I begged her for vegetables. I fucking begged. She showed absolutely zero mercy. This chick is brutal, and I need to be just as brutal in return. We shoot for a while, zeroing in on the net with no goalie and practicing chipping it in.

We have a couple games right after everyone gets back to campus and we need to be at peak.

"Brah, why didn't you ask me for weed?" Dustin says, when I complain to him.

"I wanted a discount."

"Oh, yeah. Fuck that. No discounts for you."

"Asshole."

Dustin grins and passes to me. I shoot on the empty net and Dustin passes me another puck. We skate for a while and plot. It'll be a matter of time before Makeba realizes that I've escaped. By then, she'll no longer have the upper hand and the rest of Pesthouse will filter back on to campus after the holiday. I'll get sweet ass victory over Makeba and she'll realize she made a total mistake not falling in love with me.

"Why do you even care about this chick so bad?"

I fucking hate Dustin. I swear.

"Who says I care about her?"

"Uh, it's pretty obvious, bro."

"Obvious? Shut the fuck up, Dustin. You know what's obvious–

"Chill out, man. I'll help you get her. We just need to kidnap her again and prank her big time."

"Like how?"

"I'll pretend I'm going to... you know... bang her. And then she'll confess her true feelings."

"This sounds like you're just going to bang her."

"Dude, what you're talking about is rape. It's not okay. That's why you pretend you're going to do it and when she's all freaked out, you stop."

"And that's not just as bad?"

"No, dude. It's totally legal. Especially if she forgives you after."

"Can you come up with a better idea?"

"Maybe Ovie can help," Dustin says.

He's getting closer. Ovie's only one of Dustin's terrifying pets. There are better ways to scare the crap out of Makeba. I toss an idea out there.

"What about Big Sexy?"

I don't know how Dustin will react. He can get pretty protective of the guys and gals in his collection, but he just smirks.

"Oh yeah," Dustin answers with a nod. "Big Sexy can definitely help…"

THE WRONG GUY

MAKEBA

I realize I messed up when I approach Pesthouse and see Dustin's truck out front. After he kidnapped Kya in that thing, Raven and I created a spreadsheet of the hockey boy vehicles so we could avoid further kidnapping situations.

Shit. I dash back to campus with my baggie of Cheerios because I know the jig is up. If Dustin's in the house, that means Jayce is free and if Jayce is free... I need to call my friends because he will 100% come after me. This is an emergency. I already know that this trifling ass hockey player has anger issues, and he's worse when he's hungry. Honestly, he might not even be alive since I left him with that snake. Hopefully, the mouse was enough to keep Ovie occupied for a while. Crap.

I can't believe I never considered that these stupid hockey

players could intervene for each other. I need backup ASAP.

I get Raven on the phone first and she insists on getting her parents to drive her back to campus early, even if I tell her I just need advice and I don't need a full-blown intervention. After the B.J. situation, I totally freaked my friends out and they don't want to leave me alone. Raven calls Kya, who is reluctant to leave Cole's side at first, but agrees when I remind her that Jayce still has blackmail on me and if he releases it, my entire life will fall apart. I could get myself expelled and worse.

I can't imagine explaining to my Jamaican parents that I got kicked out of a prestigious private university because I was drunk and acting like a dog on the floor of a white boy's bedroom.

I'm too scared to leave my room until Raven knocks according to our agreed upon code in the group chat. Damn, she got here quick. I don't know how she convinced her parents this was an emergency, but here she is.

Knock-knock-knock. Knock. Knock.

"Raven?" I whisper, just in case it's a Jayce Clutterbuck trick.

I would recognize that voice anywhere. Thankfully, I'm safe.

"It's me."

"Is an evil hockey player holding you at knifepoint?" I ask. In this situation, it seems wise to double check.

"Nope."

Thank God.

I thrust the door open and Raven saunters in with bags of yummy smelling Thai food. My stomach grumbles in eager anticipation. I've been so freaked out I forgot to eat. I never forget to eat.

"I picked up takeout on the way. You said you barricaded yourself in. I know you need your snacks."

My friends are seriously the best. I'm starving. I can't imagine how Jayce feels either on his diet of Cheerios. Not like I care — it's just that starving his ass out will probably piss him off enough to do something unthinkable.

My stomach twists into a nervous knot, but then succumbs to the delicious curry smell from Raven's plastic bag. I can worry about Jayce later.

My desire for food overwhelms my worry that Jayce will come back for me.

"Thank you… I'm starving."

"I was out with my friend Sydney, and I was just talking about you when you called. I got here as fast as I could."

Raven wraps me in a big hug, and I hug her back. I feel safer already having someone here. When she pulls away, Raven gets all serious. I worry I did something wrong, but her words bring me some relief.

"I reported B.J. to the dean," she says. "I'm sorry I didn't ask your permission, but… I don't want him to get away with what he did. She might email you tomorrow to talk."

We officially get back to classes tomorrow, which means avoiding Jayce will become a tough project. We have physics together and I'm sure he's not above stalking me and hunting me down. I'll have to be alert. Vigilant. Unfortunately, Jayce isn't the only deranged white guy I need to worry about. Raven went on ahead and reported B.J. Who knows how he'll respond to that. She did the right thing, at least. That was better than what I did.

I know I should have reported B.J. earlier. The more time that passes, the dumber my choice feels. My embarrassment for waiting so long already just paralyzes me further. I don't want the deans to get mad at me for not reporting him right away, or to accuse me of lying. B.J. doesn't exactly give the impression that he's the type of guy who would strangle someone. He has a slight frame, a boyish haircut and he can turn on the charm when he wants to. It's just that he rarely wants to. And he definitely didn't want to turn on the charm with me.

"Thanks," I start. "But… I don't want to get him in trouble and have him come after me. I might try to talk the deans down."

I recognize a flash of anger on Raven's face — rare for her, since she's a total cinnamon roll.

"He deserves to get in trouble," Raven says. "Kya's still a couple hours out. Let's talk B.J. and then we can talk about Jayce Clutterbuck and how the fuck you got him tied up."

It's not just that I tied him up. We actually had sex. I won't keep any of the details from my friends — at least not about the events that happened between us. But I don't know how to explain the emotions to them. I'm not exactly some super experienced femme fatale or anything. I don't know if sex is supposed to have... feelings. I definitely can't have any of those feelings for Jayce, so for the moment at least, I push whatever weirdness I feel far out of my head.

I don't know where to start when explaining the Jayce situation to Raven. How the hell do I explain I lost my virginity to him and locked him up within twenty-four hours and then for the past five days, I've been taunting him and feeding him Cheerios? I don't even know how to explain to her that our time together wasn't totally horrible, either.

Not like that matters. He's going to kill me when he finally gets his hands on me. Maybe she's right that tackling B.J. is the better idea.

I explain as much as I can and I also explain that I learned how to fight.

"I think I can beat B.J.'s ass and teach him a lesson."

"Wouldn't it be much easier to let the dean handle it tomorrow?"

"Raven, he's just going to lie his ass off. It'll be my word against his. And in the meantime, he'll know I talked. He threatened to kill me and trust me, I believed him."

"I'm sorry," Raven offers. "I wish you had told us."

The more I can hear how much this kills her, the guiltier I feel for not speaking up. I feel like I need to explain myself. I'm a strong woman… but it feels like this dumb event made me weak. Raven puts her hand on my back and it works to comfort me. I confess the truth to her, even if it makes me feel stupid to admit it.

"I was just too frozen to speak up," I whisper, the words choking in my throat.

From the time I was a little girl, my parents told me that I couldn't afford to be weak. They drummed it into me from my childhood that black women are strong no matter what. I tried for years to expunge every bit of weakness from my system that I could.

Then I let some idiot blindside me with hands around my neck and death threats. I didn't even love B.J. I still let him hurt me. When I close my eyes, I remember that powerless feeling like it's still happening. My body tenses again and I try not to let myself cry. I'm good at holding my tears back when I need to. But that doesn't make the hurt go away. That doesn't stop me from freaking out about how far I let B.J. go before I could even escape. That scares the crap out of me. How could I let some guy do that to me and just… freeze?

Raven's still trying to comfort me, which is helping a little.

"It's always worth it to speak up," Raven says. "Even if you're scared, I'm here for you."

We talk about B.J. some more and then Raven asks me to detail everything that happened with Jayce. Talking about Jayce is harder than talking about B.J. At least my situation with B.J. is simple. He attacked me. He exposed Kya's secret. We don't know what he'll do next. He's a problem we need to solve, but Jayce is… something different.

I don't think I'm drawn to him, but when I close my eyes, I can't stop thinking about what happened between us. He really does always get what he wants, doesn't he? But what the hell does a guy like Jayce really want with me? I want to think it's just sex, but he can literally have sex with anyone he wants. Why me? Why not Raven? Why not the cool black girls who hang out with the basketball guys or the black girls from the sororities who at least like partying, beer and whatever other jock stuff Jayce likes?

I'm the wrong girl for his world, and he knows it. Kya's wealthy and her dad plays professional sports. She might not see it, but she fits into Cole's world more than she realizes.

"I need to know what Jayce did to you," Raven says. "If he hurt you–

I quickly cut her off. He might have humiliated me and pissed me off, but if I think about it, Jayce never hurt me. He was gentler than I expected.

"He didn't. He tied me up and blackmailed me, but… he didn't hurt me. Then I got free."

"How?"

This is it. The moment of my big confession. The tips of my ears feel warm as my tongue gets all tangled. I don't know how to say it, so I just say it.

"I had sex with him."

Raven shrieks. It's loud enough to wake the dead and attract Jayce from ten miles away. I know it's a paranoid thought, but when you piss off a hockey player twice your size, you get a little paranoid about him popping out of the bushes and exacting revenge on you.

"Was it good?!"

"That's your first question?"

"Love blossoms in unexpected places," Raven teases. I can already see that hopeless romantic gleam in her eye. I swear, she would tell me a guy was the love of my life if he asked me for quarters at the laundromat. She sees the potential for romance everywhere.

"We just had sex, and I used it to trick him. Knocked him out. Tied him up. Easy as pie."

She doesn't need to know that I was sweating, huffing and grunting like a sow in heat as I pushed Jayce's gigantic unconscious ass off the bed and she definitely doesn't need to know that I made a noise that sounded just like a bark as I moved his ankles to tie them together. Yeah. Easy peasy. That's what it was.

"Sex..." Raven whispers, focusing on exactly the wrong part of the story. "With Jayce... You know, I thought he was racist?"

His damn dick didn't feel racist. I think it's probably a good idea to keep that intrusive thought to myself.

"I don't know. It was just sex."

"With Jayce?! I can't believe he would... you know... want to sleep with you."

Okay, there's throwing shade and then there's getting a read, and Raven sounds like she's about to read my ass. I raise an eyebrow.

"What are you trying to say?"

"It's not that," Raven insists. "I thought you said he hated you and scared the crap out of you!?"

"He did! He's the one who asked."

"And you said yes? You consented?"

Considering what we just talked about with D.J., I can understand why she's all freaked out and asking about consent. Did I consent? It's hard to remember, and it's definitely not the typical hook up scenario they present us in those freshman seminars. At first, I couldn't bear to look at Jayce's muscles or his naked body or his dick. He touched me and then there was this... change? I don't know how to describe it.

"Yeah, I guess."

"Do you have a copy of your consent forms?"

"Girl, do you still have those?" I mutter. I thought we weren't taking those seriously.

"I'm serious!"

"No. But I'm fine. It didn't traumatize me or anything. He was… I mean, I have nothing to compare it to."

"Neither do I," Raven says, wide-eyed, but clearly unable to help me. "Still a virgin. Still lame."

"You're not lame. And I'm not different because we had sex."

"At least you know what sex feels like. I'm still a dumb virgin running out of jojoba oil."

"Your time will come. How long is it supposed to take that spell to work?"

"I don't know. The instructions were vague," Raven says. "My friend Sydney says I need to stop fantasizing about Mr. Right and just find a decent black king to hold me down."

"Decent advice… do we have any options for you in our year?"

Raven shakes her head. "I swear, they hide the eligible black men."

"And what about your internet white boys?"

"I'm just messing around," Raven says. "You don't really know who the person is behind the screen, anyway. My Mr. Right is going to fall out of the sky."

She's only half-joking, but I appreciate the distraction. I don't want to think about Jayce anymore. Raven's right— we both thought he was racist, but he didn't feel racist. When he pulled me against him and cupped my hips in his firm grasp, I didn't feel invisible. I just don't know how to describe what I felt. Thinking about his kisses only makes my damned confusion worse. It's Jayce. I shouldn't feel anything. But damn, sex hormones hit different.

We talk about Raven's love life a little more until Kya returns to campus. Her dad just bought her a new car to apologize for wrecking her boyfriend's face. I don't know if she's going to forgive her dad, but Kya has definitely adjusted to her new silver Mercedes. When she arrives at my dorm room, she looks incredible – as usual – and she has tons of gifts for us from Cole's new gig. Hockey jerseys, lanyards, t-shirts and all types of merch. I'm not really a hockey fan, but I can't say no to free stuff.

Once she unloads her gifts, Kya gets right down to business. Raven isn't the only one of my friends who has reported B.J. to the dean. Kya confesses she drafted her email as soon as she got my text and she had Cole read it several times before sending it along.

"You told Cole!?"

Great. Cole is probably going to put his fist through B.J.'s face and I'll be the one to pay the price. Kya notices the worry on my face and offers necessary reassurance.

"I made him promise not to attack B.J. If anyone else gets involved, the school might decide he's a victim. Cole gets that."

"I don't want B.J. to kick my ass in the meantime."

"There's going to be an investigation," Kya assures me. "Don't worry. We'll get through this, queen."

"Duh," Raven says. "We won't leave you alone to handle this, Makeba. Trust us."

My friends stay true to their word and they surround me like guard dogs for the next three days. Jayce skips our Monday physics lecture for some hockey training event with recruiters and coaches, so I don't have to worry about running into him. Kya gives me the heads up so I don't have to freak out or skip class myself.

I worry less inside the school buildings, anyway. Our school is safe. Not even Jayce Clutterbuck is dumb enough to attack a female student in public. Still... I know I need to keep watching my back.

Jayce has anger issues and if he turns his rage on me, I'm screwed.

After three days of constantly looking over my shoulder and worrying which of the crazy white boys I've upset is going to attack me, I finally have a meeting with the dean. My friends volunteer to accompany me and they promise me that Dean Petrosky will do everything in her power to help me. I actually believe them... until I step into the office and Dean Petrosky begins with a bigger let down than I could have ever expected.

"I really wish you had reported this sooner, Miss Winston. With no physical evidence, it's your word against his, and Mr. Satterfield has denied your claims vehemently and threatened legal action for defamation."

Kya's arms have been folded the entire time. Raven's are on her hips. We look more like the angry black girl crew than the boring black girl crew.

"Dean Petrosky, this man has threatened the life of a female student," Kya intones. "Physical evidence or not, Makeba's in danger."

"I certainly wish to take you seriously and we will note this report on Mr. Satterfield's record in the event of future incidents."

"You're going to sit around and wait for him to attack another girl?" Raven blurts out. "How does that make any sense?"

Raven exchanges romance novel recommendations with most of the female staff she encounters at Laguna Grove and I'm fairly certain she knows Dean Petrosky – and what type of crazy sex books she reads – but even her solid connection won't budge our freshman dean into action.

"My hands are tied. We have to follow school policy to the letter here. If you're concerned, we can move your schedule and classes to allow you to avoid–

"So Makeba gets punished? Her life gets ruined?" Kya interrupts. "How the hell is that fair? This man attacked my best friend and I want blood."

Dean Petrosky clears her throat and raises an eyebrow, sympathetic but immovable to our complaints.

"I promise, if any further incidents occur, you will report them immediately and we will take immediate action. Do I make myself understood? And Makeba, we can work with you so that your class schedule and activity schedule don't clash with Mr. Satterfield's for the rest of the semester."

"I don't want to drop any of my classes," I explain. I'm taking physics to get my science credit out of the way, and I don't want to start the semester over. My other classes are actually interesting and I can't imagine leaving any behind just because B.J. Satterfield is a damn freak.

"We'll move your sections around. We'll arrange tutoring. We want to work with you, Makeba."

"This is bullshit. I'm waiting outside," Kya seethes, storming out of the room. Raven gives Dean Petrosky a sympathetic look.

"She's passionate. I'll go talk to her," Raven says apologetically, running after Kya, who hasn't stopped angrily monologuing since crossing the threshold of the dean's office. I sit across from Dean Petrosky and try not to tear up as I stare at the dying succulent on her desk next to a framed picture of our Dean and her golden retriever. I have no choice, do I? I need to move my schedule around.

At least that will make it harder for Jayce to stalk me, too. I suppose since I was there I could have reported him too, except I don't want the Dean to know that I held him captive several days longer than he held me.

I switch my classes around and then meet my friends for a passionate lunch where we unpack all the B.S. and hold each other up over soggy dining hall salads.

"This is such bullshit," Kya says.

Raven defends her fellow romance novel fan.

"Dean Petrosky is trying. It's not her fault our school policy sucks."

"We should protest," Kya says. "We should just burn our bras."

Raven and I exchange hidden glances. Sometimes, Kya's protest ideas don't exactly make sense. We love her anyway, but her passion needs a little tempering.

"I don't want the entire school to know some gamer geek choked me out," I grumble.

"Fine," Raven says. "Then we have to orchestrate a beat down."

"A beat down?" I say. "I only know a few moves. And honestly, maybe a beat down is a dumb idea."

Raven continues, "Yeah, but all together... we can beat his ass. I'm just saying."

I expect Kya to disagree, but she's right there with Raven.

"She's right. Three on one evens things out. I can borrow one of Cole's hockey sticks and just... right in the ribcage."

"That's a little violent," I mumble.

"That's what a beat down is," Raven says. "Violence. I used to be his friend. I know his schedule. We can find him after class, follow him to his room, and just jump his ass. When are you done today?"

"2:30 p.m.," Kya answers.

"I'm done at 3 o'clock," Raven says.

"I'm done at 2:30 too."

"Perfect. B.J.'s last class ends at 3:15 p.m.," Raven says. "We used to vape together on Wednesdays. We'll find him in his room and then we'll get his ass."

"Sounds like a plan," Kya says. "And what about hockey on Friday? Are you two coming?"

"Duh," Raven answers. "We wouldn't leave you alone with the wolves."

"Thanks, queen."

After lunch, we attend classes. My new philosophy section is packed to the gills with weirdos. The biggest weirdo in my new philosophy class is Dustin Rathbone, another ass on the hockey team.

I only know him as the freaky hockey player with the snake, but I think he's been taking too many lessons from those nasty scaly reptiles. He won't stop staring at me. And I mean staring like he's going to eat me. Halfway through class, his staring gets under my skin. He's a predator and I feel like I'm his prey. The uneasy feeling makes me want to step out to the restroom, but I'm lucky this time. Our professor calls on "Mr. Rathbone" and that finally breaks his eye contact.

Dustin's weird ass behavior would freak me out but Kya is coming to get me after class and she's struck fear into the hearts of a few hockey boys right now, so I know Dustin won't try anything if she shows up on time. Towards the end of class, I wait for him to leave first before I head out the door to meet Kya. She texts me when she arrives and I just hear the vibration and know it's her. Seven more vibrations follow. So yeah, it's definitely Kya.

Dustin's standing in the hallway across from my classroom, talking to a junior girl I don't recognize. He turns his head, obviously staring at me as I talk to Kya. Then he winks at me when I catch him and walks away. White boy, what? I look away from him and try not to meet his gaze again. My shoulders drop in relief once he's around the corner. Great. I know I can't move philosophy sections again, but Dustin gives me the creeps.

I don't know why Raven calls him 'the hot one'.

We all know he's evil and that he has a menagerie of freak nasty pets that the administration technically doesn't permit on campus. His boa constrictor practically has a hit list. The damned thing almost ate Jayce…

Kya's ready to fight when she meets up with me. Possibly too ready.

"Why are you wearing a karate uniform?"

"It's for the aesthetic," she says. "Beauty and the beat-down."

"Isn't it a little overkill? When did you buy this?"

"I took karate in high school to level up my female empowerment. I sucked."

"That's comforting, since we're going to beat a guy's ass," I mumble.

"Don't worry, I also brought this. Cole broke his spare stick."

"A hair dryer with a diffuser on the end?" Is this a beat-down or a blow-out?

"It's a weapon," Kya says gleefully, stuffing it back into her giant Longchamp purse. "Come on, let's go get Raven."

I glance over my shoulder as we walk down the hall towards the staircase so we can head out of here and into the English building. That's when I see Jayce coming around the corner surrounded by a crew of hockey guys and finally get confirmation that Ovie didn't eat him alive. (Surely it would have been in the news by then too). He looks exhausted, and he's wearing a gray hoodie with his hockey jersey over it. Gray sweatpants. His dumb sneakers. And he's staring. Big time.

His gaze is worse than Dustin's because I can see the vengeance on his face even from the other end of the hall. He's watching me. Hunting me. I want to deny it, but I know him well enough to know he won't let this go. He's stubborn.

And even with Kya right next to me, I don't feel safe. If I let my guard down, Jayce will have his stupid revenge. I link arms with her and look away, pretending I don't see him. Kya doesn't notice him, but I don't think I could walk into a room with Jayce Clutterbuck and avoid noticing him. He stands out with that head of golden brown hockey hair and that aggravating smirk on his face – not to mention his impressive height. My father would say he was "as tall as a mango tree".

Jayce stands out because even if I hate his guts and he hates mine… he was my first time. It feels like such a long time ago already. It's weird. I didn't think too much about it at first, but now, the longer it's been, the more I crave him. It's like finishing my giant bag of pretzels and knowing that I can't go to the store for another three days. I just want more so badly. Jayce is harder to quit than my snacks. It's just a harder itch for me to scratch. I have to put him out of my head anyway and stop being so crazy. He looks at me like he wants to slaughter me. That's not a turn-on, it's a red flag. Even if his gaze forces my thighs to squeeze together against my will.

Kya and I lean on the wall outside of Raven's English class, waiting for the lecture to finish. I won't lie – her class sounds kooky. Raven loves taking classes with the most insane course names. I think this class is about poetry because there's a student dramatically reading what sounds like a deranged text message exchange with the fervor of Martin Luther King Jr. and an affected stutter like King George VI.

After a few painful lines, Kya gives me a look.

"What is wrong with some people at this school?" she whispers.

"Girl, white people crazy sometimes."

"Black people crazy sometimes," Kya mutters. A fair counterpoint.

"Facts."

Then the poem concludes with a primal shriek/roar and I wonder if Kya and I need to rethink our fair conclusion. We don't have too much longer before Raven emerges and we're saved from yet another one of the creative endeavors of our fellow students.

"Beat down time?"

Damn, she doesn't waste time. I guess I can't waste any time either. I don't have anymore time. This is it. I need to confront B.J.

Raven checks his online status obsessively as we walk over. She finally makes a delighted noise.

"He's online. So he's definitely in his room."

"Perfect. How are we going to get him to open the door?" Kya asks.

"Easy. I'll tell him I'm there to smoke weed. He's been asking me to forgive him and hear his side of the story since I blew up at him."

"His side of the story?" I answer, trying not to quake with rage. I'm remembering why exactly I need to execute this beat down so badly.

"Don't worry," Raven answers, smirking. "We'll get his side of the story."

She slams her fist into her palm and I feel so much better having backup. Dean Petrosky was right. I should have just reported this earlier. Then I wouldn't have to go through all this vigilante justice. The freshman boy's dorm stinks of socks once the front door swings open. It's in a nice brick building, old school and preppy like the rest of Laguna Grove. Unfortunately, the ripe smell kills the vibe once you get inside and you remember that whatever nice ass house was here before got wiped out to house hundreds of stinky eighteen-and-nineteen-year-old boys accustomed to having maids do their laundry.

We hustle down the hallway, praying no one catches us. Any boys back from their classes early are probably holed up in their rooms playing video games or getting ready to head down to the fields for practice. I know the way to B.J.'s room, but I let Raven take the lead since she's our lure—and since she doesn't give me a proper choice. Once she gets to the door, she raps on it without hesitation.

"Wake up, loser. I'm here to smoke some weed and chill."

I hear B.J.'s voice squeaking from the other side.

"Raven?"

"Finally here to listen to your side of the story."

"Finally..." B.J. mutters from the other side of the door.

If this boy doesn't...

B.J. swings the door open and we spring into action. Kya and Raven shove the door open long enough so I can get inside. I push B.J., taking him by complete surprise, and then Raven shuts the door, shoving a chair under the handle. We don't exactly want him getting away. By some stroke of luck, my shove pushes B.J. over his gaming chair and he stumbles backward, losing some critical momentum, especially since we already have the element of surprise. All I have to remember is what Jayce taught me...

I swing at his face once B.J. stands up and I scream in a mix of terror and excitement when I land a punch. Listen, I never said I was a thug. I'm just a chick trying to stand up to herself. B.J. yells because I guess I got his nose. And he just keeps yelling with his hands against his face.

"Should I hit him again?"

"No," Kya says, getting around me and whacking him in the stomach with her hair dryer. He groans and doubles over, sitting on the gaming chair before Raven pushes it back across the room. B.J. groans as the chair slams into the wall and his hands finally come away from his face. Blood. There's blood everywhere, and he's still screaming.

"YOU BROKE MY FUCKING NOSE."

"Good!" Raven yells. "You asshole. If you ever, and I mean ever, try shit with any of us, we'll do so much fucking worse."

"What kind of asshole hits a woman?" Kya snaps at him. "She was defenseless. You are seriously disgusting."

"Yeah," I say, kind of annoyed that my friends took all the damn drags I'd been saving up. "And you were a bad boyfriend. I had sex, by the way. With a guy ten times hotter than you. You always bitch about the people at this school, B.J., but you aren't any better. You're just another stuck up rich kid who thinks he's a victim whenever someone says 'no' to him. Stay away from us. I mean it. Sayonara, white boy."

"Sayonara?" Kya whispers. "Where are you getting this from?"

"I don't know. Roll with it," I mutter.

"We're taking this," Raven says, grabbing a box of chocolates off B.J.'s desk. "Come after us, and I'm going to put you in the ground myself."

Damn. I might not be a thug, but Raven seems to have a little thug in her. Then again, she might just be quoting a romance novel. I can never tell with her.

B.J.'s just whimpering and looking away from us.

"Let's go," I whisper. I think we got our message across. I'm still curious why Raven grabbed his box of chocolates. We take our things and stalk out of the boys' dorm, feeling ourselves beyond belief. My fist hurts but I did it. I actually threw a goddamned punch. I have this weird urge to tell Jayce about it but… it's not like he would care. His only interest in me is probably distributing his blackmail tape and ruining my life. I don't know why I'm assuming he hasn't done it already – or that's not what he's planning. Now that I've dealt with the B.J. situation, I can't exactly ignore the fact that Jayce still has dirt on me and he hasn't unleashed it… yet.

Whatever. I guess now that I can throw a punch, if word gets around, my dumb blackmail tape won't matter. No one wants to bully a chick who can fight. And I just beat up a guy. Hell yeah. Nothing can puncture this good mood. The best part is the stolen snacks. I'm downright gleeful about getting some chocolate in me.

"Why did you take B.J.'s box of chocolates?" I ask Raven once we get outside.

"Girl, that ain't chocolate. That white boy's parents send him so much money… he buys like an ounce twice a week. There's enough weed in here to last us the next two years."

Okay, not chocolate, but I won't complain about inconveniencing B.J. by hooking ourselves up with his entire stash of weed. Thinking about weed makes me giggle and also reminds me of the time Jayce called it reefer to me. He has a weird sense of humor.

"You took his weed?"

"And what the good God damn hell is he going to do about it?" Raven answers with a grin. "We won. We broke his fucking nose."

"Damn right we did," Kya says. "I even got blood on my outfit. Good thing I didn't wear anything expensive."

"Girl, the karate costume..." Raven says. "You're doing the most."

I'm in too much of a good mood to let this turn into anything close to a fight.

"Who cares, ladies?" I remind them. "We fucking won."

Ha. It feels amazing. I turned B.J. into a whimpering mess. I got free of Jayce on my own. I'm even liking my new class schedule. Now, we even have weed. It's at least party currency, even if I don't really smoke. I'm on top of the world and nothing can take me down. *Nothing*.

❧ 13 ❧

THE SUNFISH GAME

JAYCE

Cole should be here. He isn't. They want him playing with his future team in practice this weekend, so our first game back from spring break and we're missing the one guy who keeps this team together. He's the glue. The responsible one. The dude we all look up to. I miss that colossal idiot. I know I'll screw up today without him. I can feel it. I've been seething all throughout our practice skate because I can see her in the stands and I can't wait. I can't wait a whole three hours before I touch her. Before I take her back to my house and get sweet revenge.

I know Dustin wants me to focus, but it's hard when she's there, smiling with Cole's girlfriend and that chick who always has her nose in a book (even at hockey games). What the hell is making Makeba so fucking happy? We haven't had sex in… I dunno… I'm guessing, but… I think it was somewhere around 16 days, 9 hours and 26 minutes. She's laughing. I can't believe she's fucking laughing, and she's not even looking over here. She's not even looking at me.

Well… she won't be laughing for much longer. She won't be laughing after Dustin and I–shit.

I miss a practice shot on an empty net, and Dustin elbows me hard.

"Get it together."

"I'm fine," I growl at him.

I'm not fine. I have a semi and I can't stop thinking about getting my hands on Makeba. I want her again. I want her now. It's the worst timing ever, but I wish she wasn't here tonight. I don't need any distractions and I especially don't need Dustin's arrogant fucking reminders.

"Tuck's going to kill you if you're off your game tonight. We need this. You need this."

How fucked up is my life if I have to get my wisdom from Dustin?

"I know. It's just…"

"Stop thinking about later," Dustin urges. "We'll be fine. Just let old Dusty Rat take the lead."

"That's not a good nickname, Dustin."

"Worked throughout high school. Now get your shit together or I will let Ovie squeeze you to death."

He finally admits that the damn snake isn't 'harmless' at all.

"You told me those were just friendly hugs."

"I lied. Now shoot. And actually get one in for once."

Fuck. Dustin's right. I can't afford to screw up, even if Makeba is doing everything in her power to piss me off by showing up to my game after ignoring me completely. Does she really think she can just do that? We had sex. She should be feeling things in her stomach and getting distracted at practice or whatever. Not like that's happening to me. I can handle this.

"Fuck off, Dustin…"

Shit. He's right. I need to get my act together. We get off the ice and Tuck looks like he wants to shove his shoe up my ass.

"I don't need to tell you anything," he snarls when I make eye contact. Message received. It would just be much easier if she weren't here. If she weren't distracting me. She's wearing another scarf around her neck and I have to wonder if that motherfucker put his hands on her again. I need to find that asshole and turn him into mincemeat.

Tuck doesn't start me on the ice, which pisses me off. He's still mad about my last few penalties and he doesn't want us starting off the first period with a man down. The first five minutes of the game feel slow. The guys are skating well enough, but the Susquehanna Sunfish whiz past in their obnoxious fucking orange uniforms and get smooth control of the puck.

After five painfully slow minutes of game time, I'm desperate to get on the ice. If my step-dad were here, he would remind me I'm such a fucking disappointment and that's why my ass is warming the bench right now.

A disappointment. Invisible. That's what I'll be if I don't turn this shit around. I'll just prove him right. God, I hate I think of him at all, but the thought of proving him right only makes shit worse for me.

After last year, I told him to stop coming to my games. It's the only time he pretends to care, but I'm done pretending. I don't need him around just to fuck with my head.

Tuck's considering the play, and I know he's deciding whether it's worth the risk to put me in next. Fuck. I have to stop letting distractions get to me. I just need to put the work in and I'll get everything I want. Once I stop fucking up, that's what happens. But I need to stop fucking up first. I need a chance.

"Coach..."

"Not now," Tuck snaps.

Dustin gets the puck, passes it to the kid from Boston and the kid swipes it into the goal. We score.

First goal of the game between the Susquehanna Sunfish and Laguna Grove Vipers goes to Laguna Grove #16 Dale Miller.

The crowd goes wild, but my cheeks are hot. I should be out there helping the team and putting in the work I'm capable of, not sitting on the bench like some type of uninitiated frosh. I know I did this to myself, but I'm ready. Makeba won't be able to look away if I pull off stellar playing out there. I know chicks.

She wants a guy she can root for. She wants a winner. A hard worker. She wants a guy who can protect her, but keep his ass out of prison–or in my case, the penalty box. She wants to feel safe, but not scared. She's a good girl. She needs a better guy than the shithead I've been.

"Coach..." My voice is desperate. I don't bother hiding that. Tuck has played this game. He knows how it can get under your skin and become everything.

Tuck glowers at me like I deserve this bullshit. I'm good enough to be out there on the ice with Dustin and the rest of them.

Tuck indicates that he'll put me in soon with a warning that I had better fucking listen to. "You stay out of the box..."

I respond halfway between a nod and a grunt, which had better be good enough for Tuck Murphy. I replace DiMaggio on the right wing defense. It's a tough position, especially against Susquehanna. They have nothing to do out there other than drink and play hockey, and they're tough. I recognize two players from travel hockey in high school. Big Mac O'Reilly, Skinny Shit Sheldon Torrence. Talented kids. Well, they were when they were half my fucking height. I thank my early growth spurt for my hockey skill, but in college, it doesn't give you much of an edge when the other dickheads finally catch up.

Big Mac plays offense for Susquehanna and he swerves the puck around our center, Adam, and pushes the black disc down to my neck of the ice. I dart over to block the other forward and Mark Kane takes Big Mac. That dude has definitely improved his skating skills since I knew him. He passes to their #34, and the guy swerves around Kane. He's doing great until he gets to me. I flick the puck out of our ice and they don't have time to score. Fucking, safe. Tuck sees it. Makeba sees it. I feel the surge of adrenaline strengthen and then… it happens. Anger.

Big Mac mutters some shit under his breath to me. What did that motherfucker say? I chase him down the ice after the puck, covering my area with a wide stance and my stick held out as my eye fixes on the puck. I want to put Big Mac's head through the glass, but I can't let that distract me.

My breath comes out hot as my skates drag me across the ice. Don't think, Jayce. Just play. And don't get too fucking angry. Benji Coyle's playing Cole's position today and he takes a shot on the goal that our hat trick champion wouldn't have missed. It's not Benji's fault. He's getting better, but he's no Cole Seabrook. The crowd groans, but Dustin offers the kid words of encouragement. Good. It won't help any of us to lose hope when we still have a point ahead.

After the missed shot on goal, we lose control of the puck to the other Susquehanna forward who hurtles past Dustin and swerves around the Canadian kid replacing Adam in the center position. Fuck… I chase after the puck to get to it before the little shit makes it to Barkov, but he switches up on me and passes across the ice to Big Mac who rocks the shit out of Kane and easily slips the puck into the goal past Barkov.

Next goal of the game goes to Macaulay O'Reilly of the Susquehanna Sunfish…

"Laguna Grove pussies…" Mac grunts after the goal. What the hell did that motherfucker say? This time, I can't ignore the burn. My body reacts long before I know what I'm doing. This is pure instinct. I'm an animal when I dig my skates into the ice to stop in front of Macaulay. Bullshit ass name for a big fucking asswipe.

I drop my stick and take my gloves off, sliding over to Mac so I can break every fucking rule Tuck Murphy set out of for me and punch him in the face, but Kane gets there first. My chest tightens as he lands the first punch. Envy. Desire. Rage. All of it courses through me, but then I'm fucking relieved that I didn't get to Mac first.

Kane's a better fighter. He plays fair, I don't. I'm a scumbag once I get a guy in my hands and I don't know how to stop. With his gloves off, Kane pushes Mac and then throws a mean left hook in his face. Kane's a southpaw which Mac doesn't see coming at all. Kane drags him on the ice, throwing hit after hit, and our school goes wild. We aren't supposed to fight like they do in the league and Kane definitely gets in a couple dirty punches in before the refs pull him off.

I'm just relieved that I'm not the one in the box.

"Watch your fucking back," Mac spits to all of us as they drag them both into their respective penalty boxes. The crowd boos the decision to throw Kane in the box, but he really couldn't have expected anything different throwing a hit like that. At least it's not my ass on the line. I glance over at Makeba and I swear she's looking at me, but then she looks down at her phone. Maybe not.

We hold the game in a tie until the end of the first period. Susquehanna's ranked dead last in the league. The guys are big and some of them are skilled, but like I said, there's nothing down there to do but drink and play hockey – most of the guys prefer drinking. Hockey's just a side gig. Our college has many big league hopefuls and we send plenty of guys to the minors too. That's probably where I'll land if I don't get my shit together.

Tuck trusts me enough to start me in the second period, but it doesn't matter because the game stays tied the entire brutal twenty minutes of ice time. I'm soaked and fucking red by the end. Dustin's the only guy on the team who isn't tired. It might be because our offense has been fucking slacking all period. No goals, and plenty of fighting Sunfish on the ice. I have to hard check that idiot O'Reilly several times because the fuck head wants revenge for what Kane did to him. My ribs and chest hurt.

I probably have several bruises and the worst ones won't even hurt until tomorrow.

I don't know if I have it in me to start the third period. Tuck knows how I get when I'm tired. Aggressive. I get aggressive. And I've pissed Mac off enough that I know he's going to push me to swing on him. Everyone knows about my temper and controlling it seems like a fucking bad idea the worse my ribs hurt. I can't relax. And whenever I start to relax, I think about her. Not just her face or whatever, but the sounds she made when we were in bed together. Oh, God… that was perfect. She was perfect.

I feel Tuck's hand on my back telling me I've run out of rest time in the third period and since the game is still tied, it'll take every ounce of energy I've got in me to keep it that way. At least Tuck trusts me, even if I haven't smoked a single joint yet and I haven't exactly obeyed his instructions. I guess I found a new way to work out some aggression…

I have a rough start on the ice. The Sunfish have the fucking puck again and Hargreaves looks like he's about to pass out from exhaustion. We can't have that… we hardly have any time. Five minutes. Don't look at the clock, Jayce. The puck sweeps across the ice and I block the pass, shooting back up to Rathbone who misses a shot on goal. Fuck. It was a decent shot, but the Susquehanna goalie is the size of a fucking rhino and takes up most of the net. No excuses, we need to get a goal in. After the Sunfish steal the puck again, Kane pushes it back up to their ice and Dustin takes another shot. He misses again.

We run out of luck. Big Mac skates around Hargreaves, who doesn't even seem to notice it and when he runs into Benji, he flicks the puck through his legs, tossing it across the ice to #10 on their team. The big hairy motherfucker feels me coming up behind him and before I can make it to the puck, he tosses it back to Mac, who shoots and scores.

2-1 in favor of the Susquehanna Sunfish. I feel a knot in my throat that I can't afford. We need to keep playing. We have to fight for this. In the last three minutes, Mac cuts in front of me again on my way up the ice and I push him. He shoves back, but there's something about the way he hits me that pisses me off. I elbow him and then take a swing – a very illegal swing that's going to get me in the penalty box. I don't even fucking care.

I hit his face again and ignore the blood. My cheeks are red and my mind goes black until I hear the refs yelling and feel an arm around my stomach. The crowd's cheering for me, but I'm sinking. I screwed up. Fuck. I let my rage get the better of me and in the blind flurry of fists, I majorly screwed up.

Jayce Clutterbuck in the penalty box for fighting. 2 minutes.

The crowd boos, but they're only taking my side because I'm on their team. I can feel Tuck glaring at me from across the ice and I don't bother looking up because we have less than two minutes left and if they score in those two fucking minutes, I cost us this game because I couldn't control myself. My heart races for the next minute and a half. Susquehanna scores again. It's not Mac this time. I got him too damn good for him to get back on the ice. You're welcome, Murphy. Still, it didn't matter.

We lose the game. *We lose the game to a team called the fucking Sunfish.*

You can hear a spider walk across the wall. It's so damn quiet as the crowd filters out of the rink. How the fuck can we party after this? This big deal game was a sure win, and we didn't even make it to overtime. Tuck does worse than ream me out once I'm off the ice. He's quiet. We're all quiet as we take our pads off and shower together. There's nothing for us to say until we get on the ice together again. By then, I should have my rage situation worked out. That's if Dustin still wants to see my face after I let the team down.

After I dress, Dustin comes up behind me and flicks his towel against my leg.

"Hey, asshole. Ready for action?"

"We still doing that?"

Dustin snickers and I steel myself for whatever smart ass comment I know he'll make.

"It's clear you need to get laid," he says.

See? There it is.

"Yeah."

"Don't beat yourself up. Or anyone else, for that matter..."

"Mac's a prick," I remind him. "And he deserved that. This wasn't me acting out."

But it was. That blacked out rage scares the crap out of me.

Dustin surprises me. "Agreed. Anyone in your position would have beaten his ass way sooner."

"You're just saying that to make me feel better."

"Yeah. You're a fucking idiot."

"Great. Tuck's going to chop my balls off and feed it to that new dog of his."

"I thought that was a cat," Dustin says. He's great with reptiles but hardly knows the difference between a poodle and a pit bull.

"No. Anijah wanted a Pomeranian," I grumble. Tuck spoils that chick. If I had a girl, I'd spoil her like that. But I wouldn't let her anywhere near my crazy ass teammates.

"Crazy. Man… that chick is crazy," Dustin replies, either referring to Anijah or someone he's texting. Hard to tell with Rathbone.

"Whatever."

Dustin throws his arm over my shoulder. "Hurry. I'm getting hungry for hot chicks."

"I'm not letting you sleep with her," I remind him. "No sloppy seconds either."

"What if she wants me?" Dustin teases.

He knows how that gets under my skin. I don't dignify him with a response.

"At least I get to watch you bang it out, right?"

"No."

Dustin shrugs. "Unless you change your mind."

"I won't."

"Suit yourself. Let's go get our girl, brah."

"My girl," I grumble. "My girl."

Dustin laughs, but I don't like sharing. It's not my thing. Once I want a woman, I want her for myself. I almost want to hit Dustin in the face just for suggesting otherwise. But it's just Dustin... he talks a big game, but beneath that terrifying douche bag exterior, I'm sure there's a human being. Probably.

We get into the truck with our gear–just the basic stuff you need for kidnapping. An empty sack of coffee from Dustin's last trip to Costa Rica, duct tape stolen from a frosh, lots of rope Dustin had lying around, and a truck bed that can definitely hold a kicking and screaming frosh.

"Any idea where she is?" Dustin asks.

"No clue."

"We'll have to hunt then," Dustin grins, a glimmer in his eye. "I think I might have a way of finding out."

"How?"

"You know that chick she hangs out with?"

"Raven."

"Yeah," Dustin says. "I use this secret profile to follow her online."

"Why?"

"Mind your fucking business, dude."

Dustin's rarely this defensive, so I let it go. He keeps his personal life tightly under wraps. I know he sleeps with women, but I also know they all hate him after. I don't know why.

"Okay…"

"I'll message her," he says. "Light work."

"Won't that blow your cover or whatever?"

"No. I'm catfishing her. I have a totally secret identity."

"Why?"

"Can you stop asking all these fucking questions?" Dustin grumbles.

Now I have to confront him.

"Damn, Dustin. Defensive, much?"

If he's defensive, I'm on the attack. I know I'm still riled up from the game. Dustin's helping me. I should leave him alone. Luckily, everything I say rolls off him.

"I'm not fucking defensive. Now come on."

Dustin messages Raven from his creepy anonymous profile. I glance over his shoulder, but he tilts his phone away.

"She actually talks back to you?"

"Yup. She thinks I'm a townie named Brett McClure. Pretty sick, huh?"

I know Dustin means sick in the good way, but it's definitely just sick. It doesn't take him too much longer to pry the information out of her.

"Fuck. They're going to some dumb frosh afterparty. We'll have to wait outside and get her there."

I can't help but want a drink just thinking about parking outside some dumb party for hours. It's probably on the worst side of campus, too.

"Where is it?"

"Marquess Hall."

I groan. Exactly as I predicted.

"That's on the other side of campus."

"No worries, brah. All we have to do is lie in wait," Dustin says, sounding cheerful, and sounding like he's done this before.

Dustin has a fucking weird idea of how to spend a Friday night. I'm too tired to argue. We fought hard in that game. Too hard. Susquehanna shouldn't have been such a big fight. They're the fucking Sunfish for Christ's sake. Dustin's unbothered. Once we pull up to our spot behind the trees in front of Marquess Hall, he pulls a joint out of his pocket.

"Are you fucking serious?"

"You don't expect me to do this sober."

"I kind of do…?"

"Why?"

"Because I taught her how to fight, idiot. Anything could go wrong. She could have practiced. She tied me up. This chick is crazy."

"Chill out, brah. We'll be cool."

"I'll be cool. You're going to be stoned out of your mind."

"Yup."

Dustin lights up and doesn't bother cracking a window until I ask him if he minds. Then he tells me not to crack the window, but I can't fucking breathe with all that smoke in here.

"Want some?" he offers after a few puffs.

"No, thanks."

"Are you sure? Might take the edge off."

"I'm not on edge."

"You're more nervous now than when you were fucking up during the game."

"Can you shut the fuck up?"

"Don't think so."

"Fine. I'll have some."

I take the joint from him when Dustin drops the other shoe.

"That's going to cost you," Dustin coughs.

"Are you fucking serious?"

"I coat these joints in resin. I'm not losing a dime. $10 for half of this."

"You're already almost half done!"

"Cough up the cash, Clutterbuck."

"Fine."

Dustin is such a piece of shit. I give him $8 and a few coins from my pocket. He makes me write him an I.O.U for the remaining change on the back of a receipt floating around his truck. Who the fuck buys $400 worth of condoms, lube, a tarp, and a shovel?

Finally, he hands over the joint. I take a huge hit. Everyone says I need to smoke more and chill out, but I hate the taste of smoke. This one is smooth – really smooth. Fuck.

I cough and press my fist to my chest. That is one strong ass joint.

"What the fuck is in that?"

"Enjoy it. You'll see green…"

"Dustin…"

We're going to be too fucked up out of our minds for this to work if we're not careful.

"Chill out, brah. Let the good vibes hit you."

He takes another hit and passes it to me. I already feel fucking catatonic. How the fuck can I take another hit? I don't know how, but I do and man, we feel good.

"Let's play some DMX," Dustin says. "Yeah. DMX."

We get through about half an album before Dustin sits up and squints like he's seeing something in the distance. It's dark out, but Marquess Hall is well lit with the requisite blue lights to keep the college chicks safe.

"Raven. That's her," Dustin murmurs.

"We're not looking for Raven."

"I know that, brah. But Makeba's with her. Duh."

"Shit," I whisper. I finally see her and my chest tightens. I know she saw my fight. I probably scared the crap out of her. Why won't she realize that I'm not some creepy fucking guy like her ex?

I nudge Dustin. "How are we going to separate them?"

Maybe it's the hard fucking game we just played, but I never expected her to have company, which seems stupid now that I see her and Raven with linked arms.

"Leave it to me," Dustin says confidently.

Dustin pulls out his phone and begins texting furiously as "Brett McClure". I swear, Dustin is such a fucking weirdo. He only gets away with this shit because he casts spells on women. That has to be how he does it. After a few minutes of tapping, Raven and Makeba hug and part ways.

"What the fuck did you say to her?"

"That I was her secret admirer and waiting for her outside the library."

"Dude… that's fucked up."

"What? It worked."

"Secret admirer?"

"Chicks like that stuff."

"Oh yeah?"

"Yeah."

"Sure you don't want to bang her?"

It's Dustin. He probably just wants to bang her. But he denies me all smooth, like he doesn't give a shit about the chick he spends all day texting.

"Not at all, brah. Look, Makeba's coming this way and she's alone. Let's grab her."

We hop out of the truck. I'm still off balance from Dustin's primo weed, but at least it helps me relax. I don't feel my heart getting all quick and fucked up, even if we're talking about Makeba. She pulls her jacket tighter around her shoulders as we split apart and hide in the trees close to where she'll have to pass to get back to the freshman dorms. Raven heads in the other direction towards the library, making Makeba isolated and easy prey – Dustin's words.

We're hiding in the trees when she walks by and Dustin totally doesn't do jack shit according to plan. He pulls the old school hockey mask over his face and jumps out of the bushes.

"Surprise, frosh!"

Makeba screams, naturally, and then he grabs her.

"Get your ass out here!" he yells as I'm running over. I swear this motherfucker has lost his mind. We could have done a sneak attack like we planned, but Dustin Rathbone's high ass almost blows our cover. Makeba fights like a fucking rattlesnake until we get her tied up and in the truck bed with a bunch of blankets and comforters so she doesn't freak out.

One problem. She's freaking the fuck out.

"We didn't put enough duct tape on her," Dustin grumbles. "Come on, let's blast some 50 Cent until we get to the house. She's making too much noise."

"We put plenty of duct tape on her. I'm not trying to kill her."

"You aren't?"

"I swear to God…"

"I'm just playing man. Let's take our captive back to the house and have a little fun."

"Yeah. Just a little fun…"

14

UNLEASH THE ROACHES

MAKEBA

I know Jayce is the asshole responsible for this, which is why the red light filtering past my blindfold surprises me. It's not just the red light–it's my body. I'm naked except for my underwear, which isn't exactly my best pair. It's hard to find stuff on my floor, so I'm wearing my most worn out black lace bralette and a pair of lace underwear–with a rip on the butt. Don't judge. If it fits around my hips, it still works. I wrestle against my binds, but the thick painful ropes don't have any give. It's hot in here, and humid, but I don't know where I am... at first.

The blindfold falls away from my head and I shriek when I see my captor. Not Jayce. Dustin Rathbone. I know I'm in his bedroom because of the menagerie of cages and terrariums covering every surface and, in some cases, stacked on top of each other. Not to mention the smell. Reptiles shit like every other pet. I gag as I come to.

If I really think about it, the red light and the humidity should have been a dead giveaway. I've never seen someone transform their normal college bedroom to look like such a damn dungeon.

"Hello, Keeber."

"It's Makeba."

"I knew that. It's called a nickname. Now… you're probably wondering why I've brought you here to my special chamber."

Dustin makes me uneasy. His staring in philosophy class suddenly makes sense. I don't know how long he's been planning this or whether he's planning it alone, but I don't care about any of that. I know I need to get out of here. And report his ass to the dean!

"That's the last thing I care about. Untie me."

Then I get my confirmation that stupid Dustin Rathbone isn't acting alone. I'm tied up, so I can't turn around and see him standing behind me. I'm surprised I didn't feel his creepy eyes on the back of my neck.

"We won't be doing that, Makeba," Jayce answers.

His voice sends a chill through me, but seeing them together conjures up a much less tolerable sensation.

Next to each other, they're both physically imposing, violent, and tense, like predators about to pounce. I sense their instincts because I have instincts of my own–prey instincts that heighten when I'm nearly naked in a room with two large, imposing males. Considering my state of dress, my thoughts rush to a dark place. My throat tightens. Jayce knows that I'm not experienced. He wants to punish me by sharing me. Degrading me.

I need to get out of here. Fast. First, these crazy ass white boys tied me up and then they cut my clothing off and fastened my hands together and my ankles to Dustin's college bed. The only way I can move is by squirming like an inchworm, and the only choice I have about where to go is to throw myself off the bed, which wouldn't even put me any closer to escape. Reason. That's my only way out of this new Jayce situation. I shouldn't have told Raven I was fine. I let my guard down and that was exactly when Jayce struck.

"Jayce, I get it. You're mad," I tell him. Empathy. That's what crazy ass white boys need, right? Because of the childhood trauma? He doesn't budge.

I continue reasoning with him. "This is way too far. You know it. I think you want to let me go. This is assault. It's a real kidnapping. You put a bag over my head!"

"Sick move, brah," Dustin nods. Jayce grins.

"Chica, the fun has just begun."

"You don't get it."

"No," Jayce snarls. "I understand perfectly. You thought

you could get away with using me for sex. Now, that's exactly what we're going to do to you."

"What?" I gasp.

Jayce smirks. "We're going to rape you, chica."

I don't know if he's serious, but he looks serious and… he has a boner. I can't ignore the tent in his pants. It grows as I gasp for air. Hyperventilating. Shit. I prepared to fight B.J., but I couldn't have possibly prepared for this. Jayce is so much worse than I thought. This is beyond a prank. He's going to rape me.

Fear hits me like a freight train. My throat tightens, but I manage a strangled scream.

"HELP! HELP!"

"We've got music playing downstairs," Dustin says, moving away from me and towards one of his gross ass cages. "No one can hear you scream. We planned for everything. Revenge is a dish best served… with cockroaches."

Cockroaches?

He hoists up his travel cage with three of the most disgusting creatures I've ever seen. Jayce informed me before that they were Madagascar hissing cockroaches and I don't care what nationality they are or how they communicate, because these damn roaches are the biggest and nastiest things I've ever seen in my life. I try to scream the word help, but the scream just comes out in a loud tangled shriek of epic proportions. Dustin laughs.

"Dude, she's losing it," Dustin whispers.

Rape. He said he was going to rape me and that sent a surge of fear through me, but nothing beats the unparalleled terror I feel about large roaches. They're everywhere in Jamaica and once, my dad brought one back in his suitcase by accident. I woke up to it suckling on my palm one morning after he came back from a trip, and I was never the same.

I scream louder. I beg them to stop. I'm screaming like it's going to be my last day on earth. I'll probably have a heart attack. Dustin rattles the cage and my lungs expand to accommodate the loudest scream I've ever unleashed in my life.

"We haven't even got to the worst part..." Jayce says smugly. "Unleash the roaches..."

I fucking hate him. I'm never going to forgive Jayce for this. I swear.

I scream and thrash and do everything I can to escape as Dustin slowly opens the cage and then tips it over my bare stomach. I feel the nasty little legs like hundreds of bristled toothbrushes rustling over my skin as the roaches get a feel for my stomach and then split off in different directions. I scream and scream and scream, but Jayce and Dustin just laugh at me. It occurs to me that if I keep my mouth open, one of these damn things might just walk up in there. So I close my mouth and keep trying to scream and thrash to get the damn bugs off me. Tears stream down my face as I fight hard against the binds, but I'm powerless. I'm worse than his pet now–I'm pet food. I can feel the roaches tasting me and my body convulses harder as I weep. I can't hold the tears back this time.

After a few minutes of my screaming and crying, the roaches crawl back to my stomach and Dustin scoops them up lovingly and puts them back in the cage. Tears stream down my face and because I'm tied up the surge of fear and adrenaline turn into rage and trembling. I can't speak because I'm so choked up. Despite the pure terror flooding my veins, I find the words.

"Fuck both of you."

"Is that what you're into?" Dustin sneers. "Don't worry, I can get my cock nice and hard for your black cunt."

A surge of emotion crosses Jayce's face as he barks a response. "Shut the fuck up, Dustin. Stick to the plan."

"Right. The plan."

He sets the roaches' carrier cage back on top of another nasty terrarium and reaches for another. This time, I can clearly see what Dustin Rathbone picked up and my terror kicks into overdrive.

"AHHHHHHHHHHHHHHHHHHHHHHHHH!"

I shriek so loud, my rib cages rattle and I feel like I used every drop of oxygen in my lungs for this blood-curdling howl.

"Chill out, chica," Jayce says. "We haven't even let them out of the cage."

"Jayce, NO! I've had enough! Set me free and let me OUT OF HERE!"

Jayce snickers. I can't believe there was ever a moment where I thought his laugh was sexy or I thought he was anything other than a cruel, stupid asshole. I can't believe I allowed myself to even think he cared about me just because he held me tightly while he fucked me. He's a monster, and it was all just a fucking mind game to him. I see that now.

I can't back down. I need them to let me out of here before they torture me more. I struggle to steady my shaking body, but the adrenaline is searching for a way out. My voice wants to tremble, but I don't let it.

"Should we stop?" Dustin asks, looking sincere.

"YES!"

His face changes like a demon's. The sincerity falls away as if Dustin had only studiously mimicked the sincerity. Cruelty remains in its place–and disdain. The terror returns to my face and Dustin's amusement returns. He's a fucking sadist.

"Nah," he snickers. "I don't think we will."

"Open the box, Dusty," Jayce presses. He's still glowering at me. Punishing me. He hates that I won't bend to him and now, I never will. I won't let Jayce in ever again. I just won't.

"Sure thing, brah."

Dustin whispers, "Pastrnak… make her yours…"

He tips the cage over and the tarantula raises two of its hairy legs. I inhale slowly and sharply. I know they can bite, and I know the bite will hurt like hell if I screw up. Pastrnak. That's probably another dumb fucking hockey player. The spider stands perfectly still on my stomach, which only makes it more terrifying to me. That nasty ass spider is on my stomach and all I can do is quake in fear. Its fat abdomen drags across my stomach as it slowly scuttles towards my boobs. Dustin chuckles.

"Pastrnak loves tits. Always has…"

"GET THAT THING OFF ME!" I shriek.

"No way," Jayce says. "You deserve this, Makeba."

His eyes linger on me, fury tinging his dark gaze. The audacity of this one. I return his outrage.

"I deserve this? For what? For not letting you kidnap and blackmail me?"

Jayce clenches his jaw. I've never seen him this angry. Now I know what the guys at the other end of his fist normally feel. The chill runs down my spine and I suddenly notice the apex of my thighs. My body tenses as Jayce leans forward.

"No," he growls. "God, why don't you even realize what you're doing to me?"

Okay, I knew Jayce was a crazy ass white boy when I met him, but now that he has an ally in the world's most deranged hockey player to have ever existed. I have done nothing to him.

"Quiet, Makeba," Dustin snaps. "You're freaking him out."

I make the error of looking down at my belly, and I shriek. Jayce's distracting voice desensitized me to the brush of arachnid legs against my bare stomach. But now, I can't avoid how far this has gone. The freaking tarantula rears up on its hind legs, its pedipalps gyrating like a slow wine in a dancehall. It's like someone has their foot on my lungs. I can't breathe.

It's going to jump, or bite, or something. That damned spider is so big that it looks like it's going to open my mouth with its gigantic fangs and climb inside. I can't take it anymore. I don't want to scare the spider, but my fear response overwhelms my senses. Gooseflesh floods every inch of my bare skin and my horrified shriek rattles the floor.

I shriek and shriek while Dustin and Jayce laugh and mock me.

"What's a matter, Keeber?" Dustin teases. "Scared?"

"LET ME OUT OF HERE!"

Dustin chuckles and then sneers at me, "But you haven't even met Big Sexy. That's a bit rude, Keeber."

Dustin lifts the cage up to my eye level and Big Sexy scuttles to the glass.

I scream again. Big Sexy is just like Pastrnak, rattling around its damned cage with a fat abdomen protruding grotesquely and eight horrifying hairy ass legs. The name suits Big Sexy because it's the biggest effing spider I've seen in my life.

"No! Jayce! Dustin! This is too far! Stop it!" I screech.

I've settled for begging and silently praying for mercy–but mercy is the last thing on the hockey boys' minds. Dustin ignores my screams, his creepy, anime villain voice falling to a devilish whisper.

"Funny thing about Big Sexy is he's been getting bigger," Dustin says. "I think he might start eating sluts next… grow even more. I think he'll like how you taste."

"JAYCE! You can't let him put that damn spider on me! You can't!"

Dustin lovingly strokes the clear side of the cage, whispering something nasty to Big Sexy.

"Why not? You rejected me," Jayce protests. "When are you going to learn, Makeba? I get what I want. Always."

"What do you want? Jayce, what the hell are you talking about?" I scream.

He ignores me.

"How the fuck did I reject you?!" I shriek as he folds his arms, closing himself off to me again. He's lost in his outrage again. No sympathy, nothing but a cruel stare and a command issued coldly at my expense.

"Dustin? Get Big Sexy in here."

"Where? Can we put him on her tits?"

Only a freak like Dustin would name his damned taran-tula Big Sexy. Jayce snickers, but there's a flash of anger before he does it.

"Get Big Sexy AWAY from me!" I shriek.

"But him on her pussy," Jayce says. "We'll see where he goes from there."

"Jayce, NO!" I screech. "Dustin… please… you don't have to go down with him."

I must be desperate if I think Dustin Rathbone will sympathize with me. I've heard enough stories about him from Kya to guess that he won't help me. He delivers exactly what I expect–cold-hearted brutality.

"No fucking way, princess," Dustin whispers. "I'm going to enjoy this."

But Jayce isn't so brutal. He can't be. We slept together and I know what he's like naked. I know that somewhere beneath the vicious asshole who lets his anger get the better of him, there's a guy who would have the decency to show me mercy.

"JAYCE, PLEASE! What do I have to say to make you stop? Please. Just tell me."

I think that I'm breaking through the ice between us at first. His eyes lock with mine and for a moment, I see the man behind the beast. I run my tongue over my lips, preparing what to say next, but the pause is just enough for him to break eye contact with me. Just like that, the moment's over and I wonder if I'm imagining anything between us at all.

He just wants me because I don't want him. That's it. There's nothing real behind those dark eyes.

Jayce glances at the collection of cages and his evil eyes glaze over with desire as he stares at some fat ass lizard.

"Dude, can I get the skink?" Jayce asks.

I'm invisible to him again. Just someone for him to torture. But I still need to get out of this. There's no way I'm letting any animal called a skink near my body. I've suffered enough. I'm just lucky Dustin's taking his time with Big Sexy.

"Yeah. Bergie loves licking toes," Dustin murmurs as he fusses with the lid on Big Sexy's cage. I lose track of Big Sexy when I hear about the toe licking.

"WHAT?! He enjoys licking toes? Oh, hell nah. JAYCE! Have MERCY!"

Jayce has to hear my desperation now.

"Mercy?" Jayce snickers. "You don't deserve mercy."

"Why the hell not?" Makeba shrieks.

"Because... you know what... never mind. I'm getting Bergie to lick your toes."

"JAYCE, NO!"

Dustin tips Big Sexy's cage over and I heave as the large abdomen smacks the top of my mound through my underwear. I freeze. I can't even scream anymore. I'm so scared. Big Sexy just sits there, but the uncomfortable weight on top of my underwear makes me want to combust on the spot. Tears silently stream down my face. Jayce. I made a mistake messing with him. I thought because I could handle stupid ass B.J. that Jayce Clutterbuck would be light work. But I can't handle this. My teeth chatter as I try to plead with him for mercy again. I should have never let Raven out of my sight...

Jayce shows no mercy. He runs his hands up my legs. Big Sexy feels the vibration from Jayce's contact with my skin and runs off my underwear toward the center of my stomach. My throat constricts so tightly, choking off my access to oxygen.

Dustin murmurs, "Interesting. Big Sexy has grown like 15% since his feeding. He must be hungry, Keeber. I can put him in your underwear. Give him something to eat."

He laughs when I just shudder and spill more tears in response. My body wants to run, but I'm immobilized, first by their binds and now by adrenaline as Big Sexy rears its legs again, pedipalps waving madly.

Jayce pulls out a lizard and holds it like a potato, bringing it over to my toes where I can't see him. I shudder with anticipation of something cold and horrible. Big Sexy shakes its legs, unleashing some hairs onto my stomach. Then, I feel the slightest wet sensation on my big toe. A tongue. It's a freaking lizard tongue on my toe. No.

Jayce snickers. "He's tasting her. Pretty funny."

"Should I film it?" Dustin asks.

"No," Jayce responds.

Why? He wants evidence of all my other humiliations. Why won't he let Dustin film this one? Maybe there's a part of him that still wants to protect me. I regain control of myself. Big Sexy rears back down off his hindlegs, which does wonders for regaining my ability to form sentences. The itching on my stomach gives me even more motivation to get out of these binds. Whatever that spider did to me makes me feel like I have radioactive fleas on my stomach.

"Get that reptile off my feet," I snarl. "Now. And stop this shit or I swear, I'll go to the dean as soon as you're done."

"He's not just a reptile," Dustin snaps. "Bergie is a blue-tongued skink named after the talented hockey player Patrice Bergeron... Bergie..."

"Did I ask you? Do I look like I give a crap?!"

I shriek again and Jayce shifts Bergie a little so he can get to the toes on my dry foot. My sopping wet foot sends a chill up my spine the second I expose it to the humid air in Dustin's bedroom. The skink's tongue juts all the way out, wrapping around my toe and sliding up and down. I gag, and it's just enough to loosen the tight knot in my throat and allow me to scream again.

"EW! EW!" I keep shrieking the word over and over, but it doesn't stop their torture.

There's no sympathy in either of them. I have to submit to this until it's over and Jayce expects me to learn my lesson. I can't win. I don't think he has anger issues at all. Jayce just can't stand not winning. He has to be the best. He has to be on top. That's why he's so fucking angry all the time. It has nothing to do with his damn past.

Jayce moves Bergie from toe to toe until my feet are wet. I have to push myself out of my head to survive the ordeal without passing out in terror. I don't know what they'll do to me if I pass out – if Dustin will make good on his threat to put Big Sexy in my underwear, for example.

After a torturous amount of time, Dustin scoops Big Sexy off my stomach, but not before the spider drops more of its nasty itchy hairs on my burning belly. I suddenly feel like I'll do anything just for them to set me free. I thought I could win against Dustin and Jayce. Well, I didn't know about Dustin. I thought I could win against Jayce. I was wrong.

"Please…" I whimper. He's broken me. I finally feel like Jayce Clutterbuck has broken me. "Please, Jayce. If you aren't a cold-hearted asshole, you'll see that I mean it. I need you to stop."

"How dare you call me cold-hearted," Jayce sneers earnestly. "I made love to you and you acted like it was nothing. You tied me up like a dog and fed me dry Cheerios. I lost 5 lbs of muscle."

Dustin laughs.

"Sounds like you two have a lot to talk about."

"Fuck off, Dustin," Jayce snarls. He doesn't take his eyes off me and I hate that I don't want him to. I want him to see me. I want to do anything to make him stop.

"I'll give you space," Dustin says, thumping Jayce on the back and taking responsibility for his blue-tongued monstrosity.

The skink reluctantly lets go of my pinky toe, giving it one last furtive lick as Dustin tugs it away. He puts the squirming lizard on his shoulder as he struts out of his bedroom, leaving me alone with Jayce. My captor's eyes burn with rage. But my heartrate slowly stabilizes. It's almost over. It's almost over.

Mercy. He finally showing me mercy, but I'm not in the mood to celebrate that.

"Have you lost your mind?!" I hiss.

"What do you want me to say?" he murmurs, stroking his stubble and then raking his fingers through that long mess of brown hair.

"Nothing!" I snap. "My stomach itches because of those hairy fucking spiders. I'm half naked, my toes are covered in lizard spit and you TIED ME UP!"

"I want you to beg for mercy," Jayce says.

He isn't listening. My heart thuds as I imagine them keeping me here for days and subjecting me to some of the untouched cages. Dustin barely has room for his personal possessions. There are so many animals in here.

"Are you out of your mind, Jayce? I'm not begging you for mercy. This is too far."

He just commands again. "Beg."

"No," I snarl.

I don't know why I'm still fighting him. I know I can't win, but I don't want Jayce to think bending me will be easy.

"I said beg."

"And I said no."

Jayce's voice drops. "Dustin's not here. He can't stop me from manhandling his creatures. I'll get the emperor scorpion out next. And Alexander, named after Alexander Ovechkin, the greatest hockey player of all time, isn't friendly."

"He has two pets named after the same guy?"

"Focus, Makeba. I'm going to torture you until you beg... so you'd better do what I ask. Now."

"Do you not realize how crazy this is?" I hiss. "I'm a freaking freshman. You don't care about me. So what, I'm not in love with you. That doesn't affect you. Don't you have hockey games to worry about... especially since you lost the last game?"

"That's it. Alexander... You're coming out."

The scorpion thrashes around the bottom of its enclosure

like it's having a seizure. That's it. I have to put my pride on the line.

"JAYCE, NO!"

"Then beg…"

"Jayce…"

One last moment of resistance. I'm giving it all I've got. His voice is steel.

"Beg," Jayce snarls. "Beg, Makeba."

I don't want to crack, but I've handled more than enough of Dustin's menagerie. I have to take the one way out that Jayce is offering. I just need to beg. I need to grovel.

"Please… don't do this. I'm begging you," I whisper. Fuck, the words hurt. I almost wish I'd taken the scorpion when I see the smile spread across Jayce's face. He fucking loves winning.

"Beg more," Jayce sneers. "Or I'll put Alexander on your belly and fuck you until he stings."

I know he's just trying to shock me, but there's a part of me that doesn't know what Jayce is capable of anymore. He's not the guy I thought he was. Not even a little.

"You wouldn't," I say as forcefully as I can muster.

"Beg," he hisses.

"Fine!" The words are so painful. But I can't stop myself from saying them. I just want relief. "I'm begging you to let me go. I'm pleading with you to just let me go."

"Do you really mean that?"

"Of course I fucking mean it. I'm begging you to untie me. Begging. Exactly the way you want."

A smirk teases across Jayce's face.

"Good girl," he murmurs, coming close to me and running his hand over my cheek. Then, he kisses my cheek and my throat constricts again. He pulls away and smiles more genuinely. I've never hated him more. I'm too shell-shocked to come up with a revenge plan, but I know I'll need a good one.

Jayce pauses and I get the distinct sense that there's a catch. It's Jayce Clutterbuck. Of course there's a catch.

"You'll do it?" I ask him. "Right now."

"Sure, cupcake," he whispers, running his hand over my breast and resting his thumb on my nipple. I dry swallow and my legs tighten together. I don't want him to take this even further. "But I want something in exchange."

Now I know for sure this white boy has lost his whole ass mind.

"What do you want?"

Sex. I know he wants sex again. He's made it clear how much it bothers him I turned him down. He just wants another conquest – another chance to experiment. I expect his answer.

"You'll find out after I untie you. Agree now," he says.

See? It's definitely sex.

"To what?" I ask him again. I'm not agreeing to sex. No way.

"Makeba… you're really not in a position to negotiate," Jayce murmurs, staring at my nipple as he teases it to a pebble with his thumb and forefinger.

I squirm beneath his roaming fingers.

"Are you serious?"

"Agree to what I want, Makeba. Just agree."

15

I ALWAYS GET WHAT I WANT

JAYCE

Makeba's gorgeous body trembles as she agrees and finally accepts what we both already know – she can't win. Untying her is pretty risky right now, because she's probably pissed off. But soon, I'll make it up to her. I can't stop watching her as I get her free. Her little nipples stand up straight, and I want so badly to rip her bra off and run my tongue over them. Patience.

First, I needed to get her attention, and finally I have it. Sure, she's a little shaken up, but we'll work on that. Finally, she's paying attention to me. That's what matters.

Once I undo her binds, she sits on Dustin's bed, still shaking off an excess of adrenaline and rubbing her wrists, which are just as raw as her ankles. There's an allergic reaction happening on her chest and my throat tightens. Fuck.

This was her punishment. She deserves this.

When she finally meets my gaze, she doesn't smile, but glares. I guess I don't know what I expected.

"So, what did I just agree to?"

"How bad do your wrists hurt?"

"You don't fucking care."

"Makeba..."

"Look," she snaps, holding them up to me. "They're rubbed raw."

"I'm... Look, Makeba. You agreed to my request. That means–

"Hurry and tell me what your freak ass wants."

Here goes nothing. I know she's thinking about punching me in the face. If she tries, I won't stop her. Still, I need to make my confession.

"I want us to go on a date."

"Have you lost your mind?!" she hisses.

"You agreed, so you have to go," I grumble. "No take backs, chica."

My heart pounds a million miles a minute. She doesn't fucking know how nervous I am. She doesn't know how weird it is to deal with a chick who says the word 'no' all the time.

"And if I don't go?" Makeba protests. "You'll kidnap me and torture me with some nasty reptiles?"

Dustin's voice comes from the other side of the door. "Actually, spiders and cockroaches aren't reptiles, Keeber."

Fuck off, Dustin.

I snap at him, "Can you get the fuck out of here, Rathbone?"

"Yeah, dude. No problem."

I wait to hear the colossal idiot's footsteps lumbering away down the hallway. When he's gone, I turn to Makeba. I enjoy looking at her, especially now when she's half naked and sexy and she's already said yes to me. I just need to remind her of what happens when she says no...

"I'm taking you out," I command her. "You agreed, so you're coming. Sunday, 11 a.m."

"Why the hell do you even want to go on a date with me?" Makeba snaps.

I bristle at her tone. She's giving me that look like I'm nothing again and I hate it. I hate feeling invisible to her.

"Isn't it obvious?"

She looks at me like I'm an idiot. Why else would a guy plot with his best friend to kidnap a girl and torture her with a bunch of animals? Why can't she figure it out yet?"

"No, dumbass. It's not obvious."

I can't help but crack a smile. For all her frustrations, she's so… patient with me. I'm the total opposite. Rage first, think later. Here goes nothing… again.

"I like you. Duh."

Makeba laughs. I swear… she laughs at me. My ears burn with embarrassment. After all this, I'm still a joke to her? When she realizes I'm not laughing in return, she sobers up quick.

"Holy shit, you're serious."

Makeba itches her stomach more furiously. The bumps grow and more tarantula hairs sprinkle onto Dustin's floor. Those suckers must hurt her fiercely.

"Yeah. I'm serious."

Makeba snickers again. Yeah. Maybe I shouldn't have listened to Dustin.

"Jayce… listen. I'll go on your stupid date, but after that, we're done. No more torture, no more revenge."

I don't agree to that. I'm not ready to agree to that. The thought of being done with Makeba Winston feels worse than a verbal beat down from Tuck Murphy. I can't let that happen. She gets off the bed and I rise with her. She's tall for a chick, but she's still tiny compared to me. I don't want to let her go just yet. She's still itching her stomach and now her arms. I run my tongue over my lips as I watch the perfect curve of her ass through her underwear as she searches for something on the floor of Dustin's room.

What the hell is she looking for? Fuck. She bends over to lift one of Dustin's dirty t-shirts and her breasts almost fall out of her bra. I'm instantly sporting a semi.

"Don't tell me you idiots fed my clothes to some disgusting iguana," Makeba interrupts my fantasy of taking her right here in my best friend's bed.

"No," I grumble. "But your clothes are unfortunately out of service at the moment."

I can't remember what we did to her clothes, but the thought of Makeba covering up right now fills me with dread. I want to watch her prance around with that glistening skin and those gorgeous tits. She's blissfully unaware of the effect she has on me.

"What am I supposed to wear? Jayce. Focus. I need to get the fuck out of here now that you have what you want."

Her gaze flashes nervously to mine. She has nothing to worry about. Unless she gives me a good reason, I won't need to tie her up and torture her again. I hope.

"I'll get you something from my room," I offer.

"Oh, hell nah. I'm not letting you leave me in here at Dustin's mercy. He's deranged."

"Yeah. Okay."

"What is wrong with you, Jayce?" she says. "You tortured

me because you wanted to date me? Do you think that's normal and attractive to women?"

I stick my hands in my pockets.

"I don't know how to deal with women who say 'no'."

"Well, if you want to have someone, you'd better get used to the word 'no'."

"Like you're the relationship expert?"

"I might not be a relationship expert, but I know torturing someone with spiders doesn't exactly show your feelings."

"You made me angry."

She rolls her eyes.

"No, Jayce. You got angry on your own. Now get me a shirt. Hurry."

Damn, I guess I rattled her pretty good. Oops. Maybe the skink on her toes was too far. Maybe it was kidnapping her. There's no real way to tell. Plus, I think my plan worked out great because now... we have a date. A real date. Yes.

By then, Makeba will see that I'm not the stupid asshole she thinks I am. I'll prove it to her. Sure, I tortured her a little, but I wouldn't have done it if I thought it wouldn't work.

She moves towards the door, which means moving closer to me, although I can see her scouting the best angle to dodge around me. Not so fast, chica. I defend our net from guys twice Makeba's size. I sidestep and keep my gaze on her. I don't want to lose sight of those hips or those tits soon.

"You can't go into the hallway like that."

"You should have thought of that before stealing my clothes."

I know she's just saying this to piss me off. I hate that it works.

"I don't want my friends seeing your ass or tits."

"Dustin saw everything, and you didn't care."

My throat tightens. She doesn't know how much it hurt me that he had to see her like that. But I needed his help. That was necessary. Plus, I know Dustin won't make a move on her. I can't speak for the guys on the team who eagerly wait for sloppy seconds from the older guys on the team.

"He knows you belong to me."

I watch for her response. I want to know how she feels, but Makeba betrays nothing. Damn, she's good. But I won't budge. I'm in the habit of getting what I want and she's what I want right now.

"Belong to you?" Makeba intones. Sassy, as usual. I should have expected that. If talking won't work, I have other ways of getting what I want.

I press my finger to her lips before she can say anything else. Her lips are so fucking soft. Touching them makes me want to kiss her. But I can't do that – not while she's still shaking in terror. I want to wrap my arms around her, but I steel myself.

"You need clothes."

Makeba replies in a huff. "Then you'll need to give me the shirt off your back and I'll follow you to your room and get sweatpants."

"Will my shirt cover your ass?"

"So you would have a problem with your teammates checking out my ass?"

"Yes," I grunt. I don't want anyone checking her out. I meant what I said. She belongs to me. I'm tired of pretending that's not what I want.

"Take the shirt," I grumble, hoping I can distract her from chiding me by taking it off.

I take my shirt off and hand it to her. My chest tightens as she slips into it. The enormous shirt fits her like a dress, and relief floods me when it covers every bit of her. Unfortunately, she still hasn't stopped itching her stomach. Fuck. I need to fix that.

Now that I'm calm and now that I have her, there's a bit of something weird happening to me. Remorse. I wish I hadn't hurt her. I clear my throat and give her another once over. There's something special about seeing a woman in your clothes. Actually, it can be fucking annoying if they're just doing it to brag to their friends or something about sleeping with a dude in Pesthouse. With

Makeba, it's different. I feel like protecting her. I want to protect her. At least I do now that she finally agreed to go on a date with me.

"You have a mental problem," she grumbles as she adjusts the shirt over her ass, which fits her like a dress. The white tee looks so good against her skin. I can't keep staring at her without my cheeks going all red, so I look down and away from her.

"Probably."

"And you don't like me. You are just freaked out that we had sex and I didn't immediately fall in love with you."

"That's not true."

Makeba snickers. "You're not that hard to read."

"That's not what everyone else says."

Makeba rolls her eyes. "Whatever, Jayce. It was seriously just sex."

I hate that she can say that so easily. Wasn't she a fucking virgin? I thought virgins were easy, but Makeba's the most difficult woman I ever met. She twists the truth out of me even when I want to hide it from myself My reluctance melts and I say 6 little words I've never said to a woman.

"It wasn't just sex for me."

Our eyes meet for an excruciating moment. I can tell she doesn't want to look at me, but I don't know why. She glances away and shakes her head, like she's trying to banish something. Probably me. I've lip-read her call me a 'white devil' under her breath several times in physics class.

"Stop it."

"Why? We had a good time, Makeba."

"You blackmailed and kidnapped me! And then you kidnapped me… again. Are you seeing how that may be a problem?"

"What the hell does a guy do to show a chick he likes her, then?"

"Figure it out by Sunday at 11 a.m."

Fuck. She is so impossible to impress. I swear, I don't know what to do to get her attention — to win her damn respect. Maybe by Sunday she'll be in a more forgiving mood. Earning her forgiveness and impressing the crap out of her on Sunday is my best chance at keeping her reluctant attention. Chicks at Laguna Grove all like the same crap — fancy restaurants and date spots they can brag about on social media.

Makeba's different from the other chicks I've been with. I have to do better for her.

"Come on, asshole," she grumbles after a few moments of me staring blankly at her. "Let's get some clothes. I need a fresh shirt too. This one smells like your armpits."

My armpits smell just fine, thank you very much. It's just a few days of sweat. Makeba scratches her arms and thighs. She's only spreading the tarantula hairs around.

Nothing but a good shower will stop the itching. Yup, now Makeba needs rivers of warm water flowing over her curvy flesh and making the hairs stand up on her gorgeous dark skin. Fuck. Now I'm thinking about her in the shower and my semi turns into a full-blown boner.

I hide my arousal in my sweatpants as I walk ahead of her and push the bedroom door open. After Dustin's humid and extremely hot bedroom, the hallway feels like Siberia. I put my arm around Makeba's shoulders, drawing her body close to mine. That does nothing to solve my boner problem and touching her only gets me stiffer. Control yourself, man.

"You cold?" I whisper.

She doesn't push me off, so I pull her body even closer to mine. She smells like my sweaty armpits thanks to that shirt. My cock jumps because she smells like me and that activates every possessive instinct that I feel.

I'm glad we're alone.

"No, I'm not cold," she says, "You?"

"Nah."

"You're shirtless."

"There's ice in my veins, chica."

Makeba rolls her eyes, but she can't help moving her body closer to mine. She's reluctant to step into my bedroom with me. Her body tightens as we approach the doorway and my hand slides to her lower back. Makeba hovers at the door and then glances suspiciously over her shoulder.

"You won't stick me in a cage and start feeding me dog treats if I walk in there, are you?"

She scratches the top of her bare thighs and then her arm again.

"Nope," I whisper. "But you can hang."

"You just released me from captivity. Why would I hang with you?"

"I don't see your friends around," I point out. "And I'll eat your pussy."

She doesn't want to show me that my offer appeals to her, but I can tell from the slight curve of her lips and the gentle raise in her eyebrows that she vividly remembers the last time she had my tongue between her pretty dark brown legs. Her toes dig into the hardwood floor.

"Jayce…"

I know that warning tone. It's the tone that means she's going to make me beg and she won't have a lick of remorse about it. Luckily for her, I have an answer to every one of her protests.

"We're going on a date Sunday. Nothing wrong with me eating your pussy tonight."

"Boy, it's not that. I'm covered in itchy ass tarantula hair or whatever the fuck." Her itching gets more furious. "Sex is the last thing on my mind."

"Who said anything about sex?"

I smirk, and she rolls her eyes. Progress. She's thinking about sex, which means I have a chance.

"Oral sex has the word sex in it."

"Oral sex? Makeba. Chica. This isn't biology class. Eating pussy. Giving head. Cleaning the plate. That's what you call it."

"Cleaning the plate? Jayce, ew."

I wriggle my eyebrows and run my tongue over my lips. It's easy to lose myself thinking about her pussy. Different. But delicious.

"Whatever. I'm covered in nasty bug juice," Makeba grumbles. "I'm not doing that with you."

She can't keep turning me down forever and she can't keep up that coy embarrassment about sex. I've heard her moan and honestly? I want to hear those moans again and again.

"We could get clean. Together."

"I doubt you could ever get your twisted ass mind clean," she grumbles. It's hot when she argues. Really hot.

"I'll clean your pussy in the shower," I tell her. "And your ass."

"Jayce..."

"With my tongue."

"Jayce!"

"Now you complain about my dirty talk? It's almost like you hate orgasms."

"I literally always complain," she hisses in frustration. "And I don't hate orgasms. I never said that."

"Well I never listen. Duh."

"Jayce, no… We're not eating each other's anything or cleaning each other's platters or whatever. I'm getting out of these itchy clothes in my bedroom."

I step in front of the door so she'll have to throw a pretty decent punch to leave.

"I have an ensuite bathroom. Better than gross frosh showers. I used to shit in the shower as a freshman. You never know what's in there…"

She pushes against my chest, which obviously does nothing to move me.

"That's disgusting!"

I shrug. She doesn't know if I'm telling the truth or taking credit for Dustin's hilarious dookies.

"This shower is squeaky clean," I whisper, touching her cheek. She doesn't swat my hand away. Yes. I'm close to breaking her.

I know she's thinking about it because she can't stop itching her stomach. Tarantula hairs are a real bitch. I woke up in Dustin's with Big Sexy eating a cockroach on my face once after a big party and I didn't react well. Trust me, I know the pure pain of tarantula hairs.

"I'm only considering saying yes because that damned nasty spider dropped its fibers on me and I think I'm going to scratch myself to death."

Fuck yes.

"Then get naked, chica."

"You're not coming anywhere near me, Jayce. Get me a towel and sit on the bed."

I puff my chest out and scowl.

"I'm not your dog. I don't need to listen to you."

Makeba's unmoved by my aggressive display. She scowls, even while itching her stomach.

"Towel. Now."

Just because I want to eat her pussy, she thinks she can tell me what to do. Makeba is one crazy frosh, but I get her the towel because it's the best chance I have at seeing her naked.

Makeba snatches the towel without even saying thank you and she steps into my bathroom, locking the door behind her. No ass cheeks. No tits. I won't get to see anything. I'm livid. Does she really think she can get away with this? I try the handle again and it doesn't work. Then I put my eye next to the peephole and this crazy frosh stuffed toilet paper in the gap so I can't even see her butt. Makeba is impossible.

My cock is unbelievably stiff, imagining what she's doing in my steamy hot shower. I wonder how the water runs down her back and if she's soaping up her juicy breasts and rock hard nipples. They're so dark and I like them that way.

I want her. Every dark urge in my body makes me want to break the door down and take her in the shower. How the fuck am I supposed to resist her? I pace a little and try the door. Makeba sings one of those popular chick anthems. Her voice is pretty good. I need to get her naked in my bed. Now.

I can't think with my cock this hard. I idly grab myself through my sweatpants. Fuck. He's big. And he wants Makeba. I don't just want to stick my head between her legs and enjoy the scent of her thighs or the taste of her thigh crease. My hand slides down my pants and I wrap my fingers around my bare cock.

I can finish before she stops showering. Thinking about my tongue between her thighs almost gets me there. Imagining her in the shower drives me wild. My head spins as I picture pushing her up against the wall and spreading white soap suds over her incredibly dark skin. I pump my cock hard as I imagine spreading her lower lips and spearing her on my cock.

I love watching my big white dick disappear into her body. My cock responds to the fantasy of entering her again, this time watching her gorgeous dark-skin bounce against me as I fuck her from behind. Her ass... It's so soft. I imagine sliding my hands over her perfect ass and spanking her a little as I get lost in the moment. My cock stays rigid, unwilling to give in to my pumping fists. I can stay lost in this fantasy of fucking Makeba's brains out forever.

I have to finish before she gets out of the shower. I picture her breasts again, the way the soft dark brown globes peer out of her shirts, the way her nipples respond so eagerly to my ministrations... Fuck. Here it comes. I finish into an old t-shirt, my chest heaving with bliss. Thank fuck I finished in time. I hear her turn the water off and I toss the old t-shirt into my hamper and walk over to the bathroom door, leaning against the frame. One look at my eight-pack and she'll melt. I press my ear to the door to hear what's going on in there.

Makeba struts out of the shower, her gorgeous legs still dripping and her braids wrapped up in a tight knot on top of her head. She's so fucking hot. Not to mention she has no clue what I'm planning for her.

"What the hell are you planning?" Makeba snaps. "With your creepy white ass standing in the doorway?"

I scowl. Shit.

"I'm not white. I mean... I'm not creepy."

Fuck. She always gets me so tongue-tied and she doesn't even know she's doing it. That's the fucked up part. A part of her has to have at least guessed, right?

"Then what the hell were you doing since you're not creepy?"

"Tequila?"

I reveal the hidden tequila shot. If it worked before–

"Do you really think that's going to work on me again?"

"Uh… no. That's for me."

I take the shot of tequila because I'll probably need it to keep my brain working and come up with some good fucking ideas for a change. I don't know what's wrong with me. The tequila burns on the way down, but not as much as Makeba's glaring.

"Clothes, Jayce."

"Uh… no way, chica. If you want fresh clothes… I want fresh pussy."

Makeba's scowl turns into a furious glare.

"I already agreed to go on a date with you. We don't need to be doing anything–

You know what… sometimes a guy just has to go for it. I kiss her, but not so long that she gets scared. Just long enough that she knows I don't want to keep arguing about our feelings for each other. I just want us here. Right in this perfect fucking moment. She smells like my soap. She's mine.

When I pull away from our kiss, she won't break eye contact with me. She just says my name, and it's almost enough because at least it means she's paying attention to me.

"Jayce…"

My thumb teases her lips. I like them. They're plump and delicious, and such a pretty color. She tries to speak again, and I press my finger to her lips forcefully. No. I can't let her finish. I can't let her push me away.

"I fucking want you."

My forcefulness surprises me. I want her more than she could know. It's hard to keep my hands off her. It takes all my restraint to fight my impulses. If I don't restrain myself, I'll hurt her, and she's the first person I've ever met that I feel guilty for hurting.

"Why?"

"I don't need a reason to want you."

"You tortured me minutes ago. I'm still shaking in terror over that damned skink."

I put my hands on her shoulders. She's right, she's still shaking. I rub her shoulders a little and kiss her forehead until she stops.

"I'm a complicated guy," I respond once she's still. Safe.

"Maybe you're too complicated."

"I think you like complicated."

Makeba protests, as usual. She's still in her towel, but she's slowly getting dressed, one item at a time. It's hard to take my eyes off her, but she has no problem searching around my room for clothing. She won't look at me yet.

"You don't know what I like."

Does she really believe that? I've had so much time to study her. I think we know each other pretty well. We know each other's weaknesses. That's what makes it so easy for us to keep these walls up between us. But I'm ready for the walls to come down.

We're both tense and silent for a moment. I know exactly what she likes.

"You dated a guy who treated you like dirt," I whisper. "You like complicated. But there's good complicated and there's bad complicated."

A gentle smile teases across Makeba's face. She has a bra on and her underwear, but she's still using the towel to cover up. She grabs one of my clean t-shirts and uses it to dry her hair without asking. My chest does a funny flip as I imagine pressing that shirt to my nose later and smelling her freshly washed scent on it.

"You're bad complicated, Jayce," she says while studiously analyzing my face.

"Maybe," I whisper. "But I don't want to hurt you, Makeba. If you were mine–

"I'm not yours."

I won't let her blow me off.

"If you were mine, I wouldn't hide behind a computer screen to bully your friends, and I wouldn't push you around. I protect the people I love, even if they're fucking idiots like Dustin and Cole. I would protect you. I would claim you and I wouldn't care what anyone said."

"That's romantic," she says, but her tone is neutral. Fuck. Why can't I ever get through to her?

My dumb brain just blurts out the next best thing I can think of to prove how I feel. "I think you're hot, too. That helps."

"Charming," Makeba says.

Great, I'm losing her again. Why do I always say the wrong thing? Why is it so impossible for us to break the walls down between us? Is it because of our skin color the way she thinks? Or is it something else? Some real reason we can't be together. Whatever it is, I'll punch through it, break it down, do whatever I need to so Makeba can be mine. I don't want to let her go.

"It's not just your looks. Duh," I tell her. "Come on, this was always here between us. Why do you think I sat next to you in physics?"

Makeba raises a skeptical eyebrow and I know she's going to remember something awful I did that I totally forgot. Shit. I feel like a jackass when she replies.

"You asked my high school GPA before you sat down and openly asked to copy my notes."

Sure, maybe it was a weak excuse, but I thought she saw right through me.

I try to act casual, but I don't feel casual. Remembering the first time I saw Makeba makes me feel weird.

"I approached you because you're sexy, okay? And you're different. I wanted to get to know you."

"Jayce… half of you 'getting to know' me comprised little racist ass comments."

She's still making this so difficult. Challenge accepted Makeba.

"Doesn't it matter that I didn't think that stuff was racist at the time?"

Makeba folds her arms. No. Don't push me away.

"No," she says. "It still hurts. And you still hurt. You want me because you can't have me. If we really got together, you wouldn't be able to handle a black woman. You would want someone safe instead. This is just about the chase for you."

Makeba has me all fucking wrong.

I turn her words on her. "You don't know what I like."

But my cheeks burn with embarrassment at some things she's heard me say all the times I tried to piss her off for my entertainment. Sorry, chica, blondes do it better. My throat tightens. Why am I such a fucking idiot? My guy talk doesn't seem so innocent now. I keep wondering why Makeba won't see me, but maybe the problem is I'm not seeing her. I don't notice how I'm hurting her by being such a fucking dick.

"Isn't it true?" she pushes back. "I hear how you and Dustin and all your little friends talk. You want blondes and brunettes and white girls that fit into your little clique and make you feel like an alpha on this campus. I barely fit in with people of my race. I tried the white guy thing. It's just not going to work."

She gets me so pissed off sometimes... She leaves me no choice but to do this.

"I'm sorry."

"What?" Makeba sputters.

"You heard me."

Now she looks like a bewildered doe. Ha. One point for Jayce.

"I did but... did Jayce Clutterbuck just apologize?"

I can do it again for good measure if it will help.

"Yes. I'm sorry."

I mean it. I really am sorry. And I really want her. I feel like an idiot about it, and I probably always will. Her response confuses the shit out of me.

"I'm shook, honestly."

I don't exactly know what that means, but I can guess.

"It's hard to see these comments as more than harmless jokes. Guy talk."

"That's a privilege, Jayce."

"I get that. I think."

"I don't want to get stuck explaining shit like this to you."

"Why not?" I push back. "I want to learn. You call me racist all the time and I take it. If I was such an asshole, I would have tied you up and stopped listening a long time ago."

Makeba raises a skeptical eyebrow.

"You realize that you very much tied me up, right?"

"Yeah. Realizing that now," I mutter awkwardly. Shit. I should have come up with a better example.

"Jayce. I'll go on the date, but I expect nothing and I don't want you to expect anything. I already dated a white guy."

"So now you know what all white guys are like? Isn't that racist?"

She rolls her eyes, but she has to admit that I have a point.

"B.J. choked me out," she says. "You spend most of your time in trouble for punching people in the face. Maybe you are the same."

"I'm not your ex, Makeba," I say. I don't know why I feel so angry saying that. I don't want to be her ex, obviously. It's like I'm just angry that she has one at all. She should have been mine. She should have always been mine. And that little fucker dared put a hand on her.

"I know," she whispers. "But you could be like him. Any guy could be just like him. That's the scary part."

Now she fires me up. That pathetic excuse for a guy deserves far worse than what happened to him. Men who hit women and harm the innocent deserve nothing but a shit pie and a kick in the nuts. That shitty little asshole doesn't speak for me and he doesn't speak for all guys. Believe it or not, you can choose not to be a violent fuck to the woman you're supposed to love.

"Your ex was a little shit who put his hands on a defenseless woman. I'm not that guy, chica. I'll prove it to you."

"You don't have to prove anything to me."

She's so strong. She doesn't want a man working his way in and standing up for her. It's like she thinks I'll take away her strength if I get too close. If she lets me handle shit for her. I know her ex and I have a plan for him. A plan she won't approve of, obviously.

Makeba's afraid to be the type of woman who can't handle shit on her own. She's fierce and independent. She's ashamed that she ever let something like this happen to her. I love her fucking fire and I want her to burn me up so damn badly.

Fuck. I'm such an asshole. I want her to care about me so fucking bad, and it's just because I've totally fallen. I just want her to let me in and I have no fucking clue how I got here and when I cared so badly about Makeba Winston.

"I have everything to prove to you," I say. "You're the first black girl I've ever been with and... the first person I'm taking on a proper date."

And the first person I would kill for…

"Shut up," she responds. Makeba's always so resistant. I know it will take a lot to prove to her I'm different. But I'm up for a challenge and anything beats sitting there, seething, and giving in to my rage.

"I mean it."

"That doesn't make this special," she says. "You're only doing it to get something you want."

"Makeba…"

"I know, I know. You want me to believe you mean this? Fine."

"I'm sorry about the bugs. And the snake."

"And the lizard?"

"Yeah. And the lizard."

"And what about the spiders?"

"I covered those under bugs."

We stare at each other for a few seconds and Makeba laughs.

"That was fucked up, honestly."

I crack a smile, but I'm nervous that it's a trap.

"Yeah."

"I don't know if I can forgive you."

She's serious about that because the smile drops from her face.

"Makeba..."

"Prove that you mean it with this date thing and that you care about me for something more than just sex. Maybe then I'll give you a chance. Maybe. I already got my shit rocked by some white boy, I'm not letting it happen again."

"You are so hard to get," I grumble. She already knows I secretly like it, so my protest only earns a smirk.

"Maybe that's good for you," she shoots back quickly.

"Yeah. I guess so."

My gaze falls to her perfect boobs again.

"Stop staring at my chest."

"Sorry."

Naked. I want her naked. Makeba interrupts my fantasy.

"Hoodie, Jayce. Pass me a hoodie. Something that doesn't smell like pure ass."

I stand at attention and at her service for the night.

"Got it."

❧ 16 ❧
TWO WEIRD ASS PUZZLE PIECES

MAKEBA

I leave Jayce's place late. We don't have sex and I leave him with just a kiss at the door – on the cheek. Just because I slept with him once doesn't mean I want to do it again. Although kissing him puts my hormones in overdrive. I want the bad boy so badly, and I want to believe that he's not my type. He's too hot. He's too popular. He's too cocky. But his lips… They're perfect. He's a great kisser, too. He's slow and sweet and he knows exactly how to keep me wanting more of his kisses. Sigh.

I am totally judging myself for enjoying those kisses in the doorway.

He tortures me with Dustin's disgusting menagerie, and how do I reward him? A kiss and a date. I need psychological help or something. An incomprehensible magnetism draws me to Jayce. It isn't just his eyes or his physique –

and it's definitely not his teasing during physics. What the hell is it?

I can't understand where the urge to kiss him and give in to his desires comes from. He's demented. Beautiful. Angry. Caring. And it's all so fucking complicated for a girl who has never had a real relationship.

Boring girls are supposed to end up with guys like B.J. – guys who sit around on the internet, not guys who spend their time fighting and working up a sweat. I keep trying to convince myself that Jayce is wrong for me, but the harder I try, the harder it gets to silence the little voice inside me that knows how well we fit together like two weird ass puzzle pieces.

I need time to think. I was serious about not wanting to repeat the past. We find ourselves attracted to the same people, don't we? I don't want to end up pressed against a wall with some guy's hands around my neck. I know Jayce is aggressive… out of control… I know what he's capable of, and his anger terrifies me.

I'd rather be alone.

Jayce refuses to let me walk back to campus without accompaniment, even if I point out that he's been the biggest threat to my safety since my meeting with the dean. B.J. has pulled nothing and I've barely seen him since my meeting. He might not have received an expulsion, but he's playing it safe and keeping his distance.

Jayce insists on driving me back to campus in Dustin's truck. I almost refuse to get into the vehicle, but Jayce plays some old school 50 Cent, and it makes the truck seem slightly less like a terrifying terror palace. There's still a nasty box of crickets in the back seat of the truck, but after what Jayce and Dustin put me through, it will take a lot more than boxed crickets to rattle me.

When I disappear into my dorm building, the truck's engine purrs and Jayce disappears back toward Pesthouse. There's a weird, tight knot in my chest as he leaves. It's not like I wanted him to stay. Or climb into bed with me.

The dorms are still quiet, except for a few bands of fellow first year girls back early from the party scene. I text Raven about her meet up with her secret admirer, but she doesn't text me back right away, which makes me think she's having a secret hookup in the library with this mysterious "secret admirer".

I know how badly she wants a guy to treat her right, so I hope we're all wrong about her catfishing situation.

My finger hovers over Kya's name – I could text her to hang out – but remember that she's probably with Cole. They can't get enough of each other and he's been dropping hints he'll propose over the summer.

They're in love and it's hard not to want something like what they have. Jayce isn't like Cole, though. I don't think he does commitment like that. When have I ever seen him with a girlfriend? He likes the mental challenge of chasing me, and now that he has me, I'm sure he'll switch it up. Bad boys don't change and Jayce is one of the worst. I'm just the latest object of his affection that he wants to conquer. Sigh.

When I unlock my bedroom door, all my overthinking about the relationship gushes out of my head because I have a new fucking problem on my hands and it's a big one.

I unlock my bedroom and shriek in surprise and utter dismay. I expect to open my bedroom door and find a mess. Nothing new about that – but this is beyond my mess. There's pain all over every raw inch of my bedroom. Thick, red paint. I screech again and stumble backward, my door swinging and then slamming shut.

Shit. I need to call someone. My screams attract another freshman girl who lives on my hall – not my ex-roomie, thank goodness. I think her name is Jaleda.

As she comes running toward me, I send out an "SOS" message to our black girl crew group chat.

"What's wrong?" Jaleda says, rushing out of her bedroom in a cute flannel pajama set. She's one of the few freshman girls on the hall who spends the weekends catching up on beauty sleep. She's so pretty, it's not like she even needs it.

"It's my room," I explain. I lean forward and thrust the door open again. "Look. Someone vandalized it."

"Oh shit," Jaleda says. "Okay, girl. You hang here. I'll get the damn dean. I've been up here all night, and I didn't hear a thing, but the front door has cameras. They'll get who did this."

I don't know her well, but I appreciate her calm voice and her "I'll get shit handled" tone. Jaleda pulls her phone out of her pajama pocket and everything descends into chaos. The dean arrives first, armed with two "independent investigators" chosen by the faculty. Since this is the third time I've come to the attention of the dean, they're convinced I'm both the victim and someone's target with little effort.

It takes a little time to get in touch with my friends, but they rush over as soon as they can with a full support team. Cole drops off Kya after picking up Raven from the library and he steps into the freshman girls' dorm with them.. (Raven's secret admirer never showed, but Kya found her already engrossed in a new romance novel.)

Cole stops inside my bedroom for a minute to survey the damage, ignoring the whispers and giggles of every girl on my hall as he walks through. Cole gets so much attention from women that I don't even think he notices. He only has eyes for one woman, my good friend Kya Ambrose.

Cole also seems unconcerned about the paint everywhere as he steps through the door to my bedroom. He also thankfully ignores the general messiness of my place and the clothing piles all over the floor. Once he enters my bedroom, he steps into a puddle of paint with his sneakers.

"Son of a fucking bitch," he mutters under his breath. Then he exchanges a private couples' look with Kya, who shrugs.

"It really wasn't you," he mumbles, raising a curious eyebrow at Kya.

"I told you," Kya says. "Makeba, did you see anyone?" I shake my head. The deans and investigators eye Cole with curiosity, but he ignores everyone except me, Kya, and Raven.

His eyes are steel and this time Cole mutters something about talking to the boys before leaving Kya behind with us. I want to ask him what he means, but I have too many personal problems to interrupt a hockey boy on the warpath. I hope he doesn't get Jayce all fired up. I don't want him punching anyone in the face or getting into anything reckless.

"Don't worry, honey," Kya says, touching my forearm gently. "Cole's going to help."

I nod, but I'm shaken. Not only did I miss going home for spring break, but I'll have to explain to my parents that my on-campus job won't cover the costs of replacing all my stuff. I hate asking them for money. They already sacrifice so much for me and, at my age, I should be more independent. Fuck. Whoever did this knows exactly how to hit me where it'll hurt. Thankfully, my friends won't leave me to sort this on my own.

As the dean questions me about my whereabouts and attempts to establish a timeline for the vandalism, Kya butts in to tell the dean that something like this happened before. I don't remember what she's talking about until she reminds me of the incident at Pesthouse last semester.

Last semester, someone spilled red paint all over Cole's bedroom during his "arrangement" with Kya. He blamed her and made her clean it up, but no one ever reported it and after everything, with her erotica getting leaked, we mostly forgot about it. The two incidents are too identical not to have a connection.

Weird…

Once the deans leave, my problems just begin. I need to assess the damage and cringe over how much this is going to cost me and my parents – mostly me.

Most of my possessions are either destroyed or partially destroyed. Great. I don't know how I might explain to my parents that I need a new laptop or a new physics text-book or new pairs of winter boots. My friends and other girls in my dorm, including Jaleda and her roommate, help clean my room, but the sun is already up by the time we complete the arduous task of hauling everything in trash bags or struggling to salvage my few remaining possessions.

I still can't sleep there until an official cleaning crew assesses the damage. The dean promised the repairs could be done by Monday. Sigh. That means more crashing in Raven and Kya's room.

They don't seem to mind, but they have a new 'mess management plan' for me, which I tried to pay attention to, but mostly lose sight of, especially when Raven informs me that some of these tasks need to get done daily. Once we get our old sleeping arrangement from last semester back together, we fall asleep quickly and wake up late in the morning. There's a pit in my stomach the moment I wake up.

I didn't take time to respond to everything that happened the night before, but there's an urgent email from the dean sitting in my inbox and several unpleasant reminders of the night before surrounding me. Our dean wants to meet with me to continue the investigation and let me know that the school will waive cleaning fees out of courtesy. Gee, thanks.

There's even a text from Jayce.

I heard what happened. I'm handling it.

Then he sends me $500 via text message.

If you need more, I've got you.

I don't know how to respond to either of his messages. I thank him from the money, but only after I try to refuse it several times and Jayce swats me down. And handling what exactly? We don't even know who did this. Who would target me and Cole Seabrook? We couldn't be less connected to each other, except for Kya. Who connects the four of us?

I'm sitting up staring at the text from Jayce when Raven stirs and seems to read my mind. She yawns and pushes up her eye mask as she watches me scroll on my phone.

"I solved it," Raven says.

"Solved it?" I'm not sure if she's talking about the plot in one of her books or the incident that just happened.

"It was B.J." Raven says. "You know that, right?"

Raven moves her arm around my waist, pulling me into a tight hug.

"Huh?"

"The red paint. It has to be," Raven says.

Has she been getting into mysteries too in her free time?

"Why would he do something like this? We've barely talked."

Raven has his motive all worked out.

"To punish you for getting him into trouble."

"But the last person this happened to was Cole," I explain to Raven. "How the hell is that connected?"

"Kya's stories. Duh. That's probably how he got them," Raven says. "We have all the clues."

Shit. Now my heart leaps into my throat. She's probably right, which makes this a definite escalation from his other behavior. I've barely seen him and Raven has been ignoring him for ages. Apparently, he's been seething, and he's taken his rage to a whole new level.

We need to message the dean about this suspect right away. I wonder if she's known this since last night or if she just pieced it together, but I don't have time to ask before Kya makes a loud, frustrated grunt. It's just the way she normally wakes up.

Our conversation wakes Kya, who normally craves her beauty sleep over all things, except this morning, when she's fully in private investigator mode. She throws off her sleep mask and yawns.

"What we talking about?" Kya mumbles.

"B.J. did the paint thing. It has to be him. I've been getting into mysteries lately and there's this whole theory. Occam's Razor."

Kya nods. "The simplest theory fits. Fair enough."

She yawns and searches her bed for her silk scarf, which went flying during the night

Is that what Jayce meant when he said he was handling it? And what about Cole's behavior last night? I know Jayce has no control over his anger. I don't want him to hurt anyone... even if it's B.J. He could get in trouble for kicking B.J.'s ass, and that's not what I want.

"Yeah," I mumble.

"Where were you last night?" Raven asks. "I was in the library. I thought you were coming back here. How did someone get in?"

Shit. I have to explain. It's a long story. It starts with a kidnapping and probably should end with a blue-tongued skink wrapping its somewhat sticky tongue around my toes. Instead, it ends with my confession that I agreed to go on a date with Jayce Clutterbuck. A proper date. I expect my friends to chew me out, yell or just say something. I mean, something must be wrong with me, right?

Jayce is hot. There's no question, but he's a complete asshole and hangs out with the most obnoxious group of guys on this campus. How could he be right in the head with Dustin Rathbone as a best friend? I question everything about Jayce and freaking the hell out as I make my confession to my homegirls.

We just don't fit together. Yeah, something is definitely wrong with me. Kya's pressing her hand to my forehead to see if I have a fever (ironic, considering we did the same to her when she started seeing Cole) and Raven's ignoring both of us and texting some guy. At least she doesn't seem too perturbed about the date news, unlike Kya.

"You're fine," Kya says, sounding surprised. "But honey, Jayce tortured you. For a long time. How are you sure this isn't a trap or Stockholm Syndrome?"

Kya's asking too many complicated questions and the words catch in my throat.

"I don't know."

"Are you scared to go?" Kya asks, searching my pupils for evidence of whatever she's trying to find.

I shake my head. Jayce has always had limits with me. I'm not sure if I'm trying to convince Kya, or to convince myself.

"Jayce is mostly harmless. Mostly. Not completely. I don't know. I think he got revenge out of his system. He was different last night, and it didn't feel like a trick."

Kya nods understandingly. I'm happy she wants to support me, even if it's the last thing I expect.

"If he tries anything, I'll kill him," Kya warns. "Or I'll make Cole kill him."

Weirdly enough, I believe her, although it might take some convincing to get Cole to kill one of his best friends.

"I don't know how he convinced me, but I guess I'm going with it. I'm dating another white boy…"

"It might have been the spiders running up and down your butt cheeks getting in your head," Raven says, chiming in just when we all think she isn't listening.

Right. Jayce tortured me with spiders. He held me captive. How could getting into his car and letting him drive me to a second location/date possibly go wrong?

At least Raven's comment makes us all laugh, even if talking about spiders makes my stomach remember the gross itching from the nasty ass tarantula hairs. I need pretzels to calm myself and I reach for the bag I keep tucked away in my bed. Raven brushes away the crumbs as I chew on a few sticks.

I can't hide my nerves from my friends, but their support makes me think this isn't the worst idea. Raven tried to warn me about B.J. She was right and she's never once held it against me. I swear, these girls are my angels.

"It's one date," Kya says. "Even if he's an idiot… maybe you'll have a good time."

She pauses for a moment.

"Do you want your rape whistle back?" Kya asks, reaching into her tote bag. I can't believe she still has that thing, but I trust Jayce enough not to need it and shake my head.

"Are you sure?"

I shrug. "He got me back good, but… I can handle Jayce. I tied him up, remember?"

"Girl, he made a lizard lick your toes," Raven says. "He's still a potential threat."

"Yellow alert," Kya agrees. "But not red!"

Is that where the bar is these days? Hovering somewhere over Satan's dinner table in hell?

Kya might be right, but I can't stop myself from thinking about our date.

The cynical part of me expects Jayce to spend as little effort as possible. I'm not your ex, Makeba. Jayce is nothing like B.J. He's right. Jayce is rough around the edges with a well-formed body and, unlike damn B.J. he's not a coward.

I just don't want to get caught looking like a fool again. Before we head to bed, we reach out to the dean about our suspicions.

We don't know what will happen to B.J., but I'll probably find out on Monday. The administration hates working weekends. Until they sort this B.J. thing out, I just need to focus on this date with Jayce. That should be easy.

Our girl crew convenes on Sunday morning before my date. Kya and Raven come armed with copious amounts of coffee, emergency pretzels for me, which I graze on like a starved giraffe, and dating advice. I don't know if I'm ready for this. I never felt this weird pressure to look good around B.J. I thought that was normal. I thought that was what I wanted.

I hate that I actually care about how I look when I see Jayce Clutterbuck. If he doesn't like me in my hoodie, he doesn't deserve me in my... whatever this look is. I twirl around, unsure if this is the best outfit for my first date. I'm no expert on dating, though.

"I look weird..." I grumble.

I don't really like wearing anything other than a pair of jeans and a hoodie. Kya insists I dress up.

"I don't want to impress Jayce," I remind her. "I don't like him."

I swear I see Kya and Raven exchange sneaky glances. Ugh. They're so onto me. Why is it that when I'm with Jayce together, I forget all the stupid reasons we aren't supposed to like each other and I actually enjoy spending time with him? I'm so corny, it's embarrassing. I have no business liking a guy like Jayce.

I'm still mad at him for unleashing Dustin's nasty pets over my half-naked body, but I don't have time to plan any super crazy revenge. The only thing I can think of is listening for something on the date that I could use against Mr. Clutterbuck. He'll have his guard down, especially if I don't put on a black hoodie over this outfit Kya picked.

"You look amazing," Raven says. "You have perfect skin, Makeba. That's probably why he's crushing."

"He's not crushing. He's trying to piss me off."

Okay, my friends are definitely exchanging sneaky glances now.

"I can see those sneaky glances, you know."

Kya sighs. "We can't help it, okay? It's obvious that Jayce is basically obsessed with you. Even Cole thinks so."

"He's not obsessed with me. He's obsessed with torturing me."

"You had sex," Raven blurts out. "And now he's obsessed."

"He is not–

"It's your magical Jamaican heritage," Raven teases, interrupting again. "Portmore pussy."

I roll my eyes. "Girl, I never tried your Instagram love spell. My ancestors are busy working on my physics grades instead. And I've never even been to Portmore."

(It's where my dad's from.)

"But they're working," Raven says gleefully. "They're working to get you Jayce."

"I don't want Jayce."

"Exactly," Kya replies, suddenly getting all agreeable. "You want information. Go in there like Nancy Drew if you have to. Whatever makes you feel like a strong, confident, powerful, full-bodied black woman."

Kya likes using long lists of synonyms to describe women. We're lucky she stuck with a few, although I don't know what she means by full-bodied.

"Right. I don't even know what he has planned. What if I'm overdressed?"

I'm wearing a long black skirt with pleats and Doc Martens (my friends tried to change my mind but I refuse to wear heels). Raven helps pull my braids behind my head and plaits them together in one thick braid.

Kya gave me a merino blend Prada turtleneck, which I tucked into the skirt. I threw a belt over it to add some shape. I think I look okay. Maybe a little fancy, but at least I'll still be comfortable.

It's getting warmer, but it can still get colder in the evenings, so she also lends me a black wool coat from Dolce & Gabbana. It feels a little weird.

Jayce knows I'm not the kind of girl who wears designer stuff, but Kya has all the least tacky designer clothes I've seen, so maybe he won't notice that I suddenly look expensive. I don't want Jayce to think I'm trying too hard or that I'm trying at all. He's the one forcing me to go on this date. I can't have a crush on him.

I won't need the coat for long because it ought to warm up throughout the day.

I twirl around in the mirror. Damn. I look nice. I should put effort into my outfits every day…

"Are you sure this is not too fancy?"

"It's a date. You're totally covered up… but you look cute! Come on… get excited!" Kya cheers, clapping her hands. Since getting with Cole, she's suddenly pro-romance. Raven's gone all cynical, and she's totally engrossed in this "Brett" guy she's been messaging on social media, this secret admirer who never showed. I keep trying to convince her he's a catfish, but she insists that he's just shy.

I smooth the skirt again and grumble, "It's a date with Jayce Clutterbuck. I've had more exciting fillings."

"You're just nervous," Raven chimes in, taking a break from her Brett-sesh. "I would be. Jayce is hot."

Kya glares at her and then shakes her head.

"You guys think Jayce is hot?" I ask them. I can always tell when they've been having secret conversations. They've certainly had time considering how long I spent in Pest-house before Jayce released me back to my dorm room last night before the paint incident.

Raven stammers something, but I can tell she's lying.

"I mean... he's conventionally good looking, you know?" Kya says, struggling to be diplomatic.

"His ass is perfect," Raven blurts out. "There, I said it."

He has one of those sexy hockey player bubble butts you want to squeeze or take a bite of. I enjoyed digging my nails into it. I bite my lower lip and try to push the thought of Jayce's well-formed ass out of my head.

"I think you have a butt obsession," I mutter bitterly.

"I don't." Raven argues with me, but she definitely has a butt obsession.

"Whatever. He's not that hot."

"You've seen him naked," Kya mutters. "I've only seen him shirtless."

I don't know why it makes me feel weird that she's seen him shirtless. He's probably always walking into Cole's room shirtless. Jayce is one of those guys allergic to wearing a shirt in his own home. I mean… I don't mind that part of being around him. But that's not the point.

"I mean… he's fine… I guess…"

"Makeba, stop playing," Raven says. The alarm on my phone rings.

"He's going to be here soon."

As soon as I say the words, Jayce texts me. He's outside the freshman dorms in his car.

"Shit. He's here."

"Text us if he acts crazy."

"Or if he tries kidnapping you again," Kya says. "I had Cole threaten them within an inch of their lives this morning."

"Thanks."

I hope Cole's threats don't just piss him off more, but I trust Kya knows what she's doing. I walk outside with my little purse and Jayce has the top down on his convertible and he hops out with this big grin on his face. Oh. My. God. What is he wearing? A lime green button down, those hot salmon shorts, white boys love, boat shoes and his hair… it's a mane of golden brown hair with a slight curl at the end. I feel tongue-tied as he jogs over to me lightly, towering over me.

He's dressed like this is a real date. He's dressed better than I've ever seen him dress to go to one of our classes, where he usually wears sweatpants and a hockey jersey. And he's smiling. That's also pretty rare for Jayce Clutterbuck last I checked. I can't believe he's so dressed up.

"Damn," he says. "You look amazing."

"Thanks. You're all dressed up."

"It's a date, chica. I don't go on dates."

"Aren't you some type of campus ladies' man?"

Jayce chuckles. "Maybe. But I don't go on dates unless I like someone."

I roll my eyes.

"Come on, Jayce. I agreed to go on this date with you, but you don't have to lay it on thick. Where are we going?"

"You'll see."

He puts his arm over my shoulder and leads me to the other side of the convertible. I thank the heavens that I'm not wearing a wig or I would be terrified of the damn thing flying off. I don't think Jayce knows anything about dating a black woman, but he's like an excited puppy already, as he holds the door open for me.

"I got some music I think you'll like."

He hurries to the other side and starts the engine. Then the music.

"Is this the music you think I'll like?"

Jayce turns red. "Sorry. Dustin's DMX mix. My bad."

"I don't mind DMX, but… don't assume."

Jayce snickers. "Whatever, chica. Wasn't my real choice. Excited?"

"Do I seem excited?"

Jayce grins. So I'm doing a horrible job at hiding my true feelings. Crap. I don't want him to think he has a hold on me.

"Yah."

I roll my eyes. "Jayce… I don't know why you insist on torturing me like this."

"Makeba, when a guy likes a girl very much…"

Unfortunately, Jayce launches into a very rough description of the birds and the bees, rife with inaccuracies. For a man who understands how to make a woman orgasm, his technical grasp of reproduction lacks a disturbing amount of detail.

"Are you done yet?" I ask when he's finally done and we're driving down one of the state highways out of our college's small town.

"Yup. Now you know exactly how babies are made."

"Yeah. Except eggs don't chase the sperm down, begging to make him a baby daddy."

"We'll never know."

"We know, Jayce. We know."

Jayce grins and turns up the music he actually chose for me, which I'm too embarrassed to tell him I like. How does this white boy know anything about Erykah Badu? How did he guess she was my favorite singer? On the rare occasions when I tidy my bedroom, it's all because of Ms. Badu.

The wind doesn't mess up my hair, but Jayce's silky white boy hair whips around his face. He bops his head to the song, and he's not even off beat. He glances over at me and grins.

"Come on, Makeba… this is my jam."

"Tyrone is your jam?"

"Hell yeah. I saw you writing the lyrics in the margins of your physics notes."

"While you were copying off me, probably."

He doesn't bother with an apology. See? The moral fiber of a cupcake.

"Hey, chica. Your notes are pretty good."

"Thanks… now where the hell are we going?"

The longer I'm in a car with Jayce, the more I freak out about our date and whatever might 'happen' between us. I have to remind myself that he's only doing this to torture me. Nothing will 'happen' between us. One stupid date can't change everything. Right?

"Patience, chica. We're almost there."

"Are you sure you're going the right direction? There's no civilization out here."

Rural Massachusetts scares me sometimes. No subway. No patty shops. There are only trees out here. I wanted to come out to the country for college to get away from the bad parts of New York — crazy guys spitting on the train, the mixed tape street hustle and the harsh city grind. When I get too far away from civilization, though, I worry.

Jayce offers a reassuring pat on the thigh. I don't push his hand off.

"I've got this, chica."

"I got you something," he says. "But you'll find out when we get there."

"Oh-kay."

"My step-dad's a judge, by the way. I don't think I ever mentioned it."

"You didn't."

I don't know what the hell that has to do with anything, so I mutter a stupid response. Was that supposed to be a hint?

"Cool."

Then he's quiet. If I didn't know any better, I would say Jayce was lost in thought. We pull into the parking lot of a building that looks almost run down with a sign out front.

Nashua Indoor Gun Range.

"A gun range?"

Jayce stops the car and turns to me with a grin.

"Scared?"

This was exactly what I was worried about. Now I'm definitely worried about being overdressed. I roll my eyes.

"I ain't afraid of shit." Yeah, nothing scary about a heavy hunk of metal designed to kill. Nope, nothing at all. I still don't want to show Jayce any weakness, especially when he's grinning like this. He's so damn proud of himself.

"You look great, chica. I can't wait to see you holding a 12-gauge." He leans over and kisses my cheek. My skin grows warm. I'm nervous, and I don't know what to say except his name. This is it. I've fallen headfirst into a weird white boy's fantasy.

"Jayce…"

His grin doesn't let up. "Trust me, chica. You'll love this."

Jayce hops out of the convertible and rushes around the grab the door for me. I'm almost too stunned to get out of the car. A gun. He wants me to hold a gun. Where I grew up, girls like me were told to keep our heads down and avoid guns. If you wanted any hope of a better life, the warnings came like hail on a tin roof – don't touch guns, don't look at guns, avoid the bad boys who carry them and if you hear gunshots, scatter like a cup of dried lentils dropped on tiles.

Jayce grins.

"Come on. I promise you'll love this."

"I just can't believe this is where you want to take me for a date."

Jayce puts his hand in mine and practically drags me out of the convertible. Before I can protest again, he puts his hands on my hips and pulls me against him.

"Hey," He whispers. "If you're not into it, we can leave. I just wanted you to know that I will protect you and sometimes the best way to do that is teaching you how to protect yourself."

"I've never held a gun."

"Good thing you have me, then."

My skepticism amuses him.

"You'll love this shit. Trust me."

He's like a puppy as he drags me to the entrance and I break every rule I ever set for myself by entering the gun range. I expect to hear war-zone levels of gunfire, but it's dead silent.

"I rented the whole place out," Jayce says. "For us." Us. Hearing him say the word drives me wild.

Whoa. This place is huge. I want to ask if he's serious when a gentleman with a trucker hat emerges with a broad smile on his face.

"Welcome! Clutterbuck. Good to see you again."

"Cheers, Ty. This is Makeba."

"Makeba. Nice to meet you."

The white guy shakes my hand and I wonder if he thinks I'm a freak for being here. I warm up when Ty explains what we're going to do. A gun safety course, some lessons and then Jayce will take me to shoot targets for a while. I nod nervously, but I'm in too deep. I have no choice but to get into things – and listen carefully. Jayce sits patiently through the gun safety course with me, although it's obvious he already knows this stuff. I can't even imagine what type of horrifying white boy arsenal he secretly possesses.

At first, I'm terrified, but as Ty explains the parts of a gun, how to hold it and all those safety features, I find myself enraptured by the horrifying piece of metal, hewn to kill, murder, maim and worse.

Self-defense. That's what Ty focuses on, and that's what I want to hear about the most. He tells stories of his former students who have used guns to defend themselves against intruders, crazy ex-husbands, and he makes me feel like less of an idiot for not knowing any of this stuff. As for Jayce... He just can't wait until we get to shoot.

After Ty's lesson, he asks what gun I want to try and I blank out.

"I-I don't know any guns."

Jayce takes the lead. "Something simple, Ty. Basic pistol."

Ty grabs a basic pistol, enough ammo for us to mess around with, and takes us to an open lane with a target shaped like a turkey a safe distance away. Ty shows me how to set up my stance, my grip, and all that stuff. Then he shoots. He hits dead center with relative ease. There's no way I'll be able to do that…

Jayce takes the pistol next and fires three times. He's pretty good – but not as good as Ty.

"Your turn," Jayce says, handing the gun to me. My throat tightens. Fear courses through me. Ty leaves the next part up to Jayce. He's already demonstrated, it's go time.

"Relax," Jayce whispers. "You can do this. Imagine that fucker coming after you again. He thinks you're weak. He thinks you're powerless. He thinks you need a man to protect you. What are you going to do?"

Here goes fucking nothing.

I fire. I want to scream because of how powerful it feels. It just seems like a just response. But the lump in my throat just dissipates and instead of screaming, I feel this rush. Adrenaline courses through every inch of me. I remove my ear muffs and look at where I hit the target.

"Pretty good for a first time," Ty comments. "I'll leave y'all to it."

He leaves us a bunch of ammo and finally… we're alone. I set the gun down safely and Jayce grins.

"How was that?"

"Terrifying. Exhilarating. Weird."

He leans forward and kisses me slowly, taking my lower lip between his and sucking on it before letting me go. Fuck. Why does he have to kiss me like this while adrenaline floods my body, making me feel so goofy and unhinged in his grasp? I'm never in control around Jayce, and I don't know why I like it so damned much.

"Try again," Jayce says. "We're not leaving here until you hit that center."

"Challenge accepted, Clutterbuck."

I'm comfortable with the pistol and I at least try the 12-gauge shotgun before our time expires. I don't want to leave. At all. I enjoy holding the gun and knowing what to do with it. All the weapons are heavier than I expected, but once I get used to the weight, I think I could spend a lot of my time here…

"We need to do this again," I whisper to Jayce, surprising myself by using the word we.

"Ha. Knew you would like it," he whispers back, kissing my cheek and then moving to my lips again. He acts like he can't get enough of kissing me. He prefers kissing to almost anything else.

Jayce pauses once we've said goodbye to Ty and we're standing outside in front of the convertible. I don't know why he's still, but I stop too. I want to stand still with him here and soak in this entire experience. I'm no dating expert, and this definitely isn't what I expected, but I can't help this exhilaration. I don't want to help it either. I want to dive right in and forget being a "boring" black girl for a second. I don't always have to run away from that adrenaline rush, do I? There's not always danger lurking behind every corner.

Jayce touches my face and my heart won't stop pushing its way out of my chest. I just feel way too good around him. He holds my face up so I'm looking at him and I don't want to look away. For once, I feel like I have permission to gaze at his face and take in his cheekbones, the soft spread of stubble that he can't ever quite keep up with, and then those eyes. The yellowish-brown ring around the green on his iris gleams as he stands close to me. I can see words catching in his throat, but he works the lump out and sighs. Please don't stop touching my face.

"You lit up when you held that pistol," he whispers. "You don't know how fucking hot you looked."

He kisses me, gripping my face with both hands and pressing me against the convertible door. Fuck. Kissing him feels amazing. I yield to it. I grab his face back, sinking my hands into the stubble and parting his lips with mine. I don't have his experience, but Jayce responds to my kissing. I put my hand on his chest and he doesn't push me off. He makes a low growl in his throat that makes me wish I'd put my hand on his chest under that preppy white boy shirt.

"Fuck," he growls as he pulls away. "Wait 'til you see what I got you."

Then he gives me that sketchy Jayce smile again, and I get nervous.

"It had better not be a snake."

"Ha ha. Nope. Come here."

Jayce scurries around to the trunk and pops it open. I reluctantly follow him, wrapping my arms around myself protectively.

"A dirty blanket?" I grumble, unimpressed.

Jayce yanks the blanket back and reveals his gift…

"Surprise!"

"Jayce! Is that even legal?"

"I told you. My step-dad's a judge." He says that like it explains everything. Jayce takes the gun and safely puts it in my hand, closing my fingers around it. He reaches into the box in the back of his car for a card with my picture on it and Commonwealth of Massachusetts printed on the top. I have to squint to read the rest.

Jayce continues, "Here's your license to carry, which you just earned today… and your very own pistol. 9mm Glock 19, just like what you used in there."

"We can't have these on campus. What I am supposed to do with this?"

"I know," Jayce says, winking at me. He breaks every rule anyway. "Keep it hidden. Try not to use it. But if anyone fucks with you, Makeba Winston… you'll be safe."

"Do you really think B.J.'s going to try something else? I talked to the dean about the paint thing by the way. So there's no need for you to handle it."

Jayce's face reddens suspiciously.

"Jayce?" I ask him.

"Uh huh," he says. "Glad you like the gun. We'd better get going."

"Where exactly are we going?"

"Somewhere really fucking special."

"This isn't the end of the date?"

Jayce chuckles. "Don't think so, chica. I'm not done with you yet."

I feel weird when he says that, but it's a good type of weird. I don't want to be done either, but I don't know how long first dates are supposed to last. Jayce won't let go of my hand as we stand in front of his trunk.

"It's so fucking hard to keep my hands off you," he whispers before leaning in and kissing my neck. There's that rush again and this time, I can't blame the guns. It's just Jayce's lips rubbing against my neck and turning me into a stupid puddle of goo.

When he pulls away from the neck kiss, I want him to come back for more. Instead, he takes the pistol out of the trunk and hands it to me after a quick safety check.

"Stick it in your purse, babe," he whispers. "Come on."

There's another soft kiss on my cheek and I put the Glock in my handbag. I don't know what my friends would say if they could see me, but I'm definitely not telling them about the gun. It's just in case, right? I know I won't have to use it, but I appreciate Jayce wants to keep me safe.

"So, where are we going?" I ask again, hoping I can wear him down. Jayce just grins.

17

APPLES & ORANGES

JAYCE

I'm starving. And even if a gun range might be a little unconventional for a first date, watching Makeba hold a firearm has done something fucked up to my appetite. I sneak check my phone in the parking lot at our lunch time date spot.

We took care of it.

Perfect. Well, maybe not perfect once Makeba finds out what I did. But I know I did the right thing. *We all did the right thing.* The best thing you can do when you have a fucking problem is handle it. Makeba notices my moment of distraction and I could kick myself for taking my attention off her for even a second.

"All good?" She asks. Her New York accent makes everything that comes out of her mouth sound like music.

I lean over and put my arm around Makeba.

"Uh huh. Hungry?"

I don't have to ask. If there's one thing Makeba and I have in common for sure, it's our tummy lust for tasty foods. She's going to love the rest of our date.

"I'm starving."

I put my arm around her, and she sinks into the crook. I like that she's tall and strong, with a nice musculature and curves in the right places. But when she's in the crook of my arm, she feels tiny — like she's mine to protect. By the end of our date, she'll know that I can and will do anything to protect her.

I'll kill if I have to. Hopefully, it didn't come to that.

"I'm tempted to starve you a little more," I tease her, wrapping one of those sexy braids around my finger. "Revenge for the Cheerios."

My stomach produces a low rumble, as if remembering the depth of starvation all on its own. Makeba laughs loudly, and the sound makes me soar.

"White boy, stop playing," she teases, poking me in the abs.

White boy. Is it bad that I like her calling me that? It makes me feel like this dumb, boring thing about me — being white—is something between us–something that draws her to me. Makeba's different from all the chicks in my hometown, but maybe she thinks I'm different too.

We both like each other's difference.

"Come on, black girl. Let's eat," I tease, fully prepared for her to poke my stomach again or maybe even slap me. Instead, she gives me one of those side glances and a sharply intoned warning.

"Jayce…"

"Just messing with ya," I whisper, fighting the urge to smother her with more kisses. I don't want to scare her off.

I want to hold her tighter as we walk into the restaurant. Fuck it, there's a part of me that just wants to screw the restaurant and eat her pussy for lunch. But I know Makeba needs food, and she thinks I haven't noticed her secret pretzels in the car (which she dusted all over my leather seats). She's starving.

I put my arm around her hips as we walk together. I know the gun talk makes her nervous, but I also know a woman has a right to defend herself, and if that asshole B.J. or anyone else messes with Makeba, I want her to be safe. I still don't want to scare her off.

"Like the gun?"

"I feel like a gangster," she says, in a positive tone, that makes me think she's agreeing. "But…"

Shit. I hope I didn't fuck up already. I have a habit of screwing up with Makeba and I want to leave those screw ups well in the past.

"What?"

"I just hope I don't have to use it."

"You won't," I whisper. "I'm never going to let anyone hurt you again. I promise."

She offers me a smile and a little more closeness. Trust. I want her to trust me, but I know I have a long road ahead. I suddenly feel like an idiot for pushing Makeba so far with the tarantulas and the lizard. I can't even imagine where I got such a dumb idea. When we enter the restaurant, Makeba slips her hand into mine and I can feel her excitement through her fingertips. Good. I want her to like it here.

The hostess takes us to our secluded booth. Makeba seems nervous as she slides into the booth. It's probably my fault. I can't stop fucking staring at her and I don't want to stop. I just want to keep watching, staring, wanting her. It's like I can't believe I really have her here and it fucks with me that she's really mine for the day.

I'm not letting her out of my sight until nightfall.

"I'm getting a burger," I announce without looking at the menu. "Guns. Red meat. That's my kind of date."

"Pew pew," Makeba mutters, her finger running over the menu items. Fuck, she's perfect. It's messing with my head because I know once today ends, she's going to go back to her girl crew and they'll remind her that I'm a fucked up bastard who puts my fists through guys' heads and tied her up a couple times. I run my tongue over my lips. I don't just want sex anymore, and I don't even know what to do with these new feelings.

I can't stop staring at her, wondering what she's going to eat.

"I'm getting a burger too. I think," Makeba mutters, blissfully unaware of how hot she looks and what effect her sweet outfit has on me. I'm already hard under the table. I feel like a fucking high school kid again. She's barely showing an inch of skin, but there's something about her sleek, respectable outfit that gets me rock fucking hard.

"Go ahead," I grin. "I like a woman who can eat."

She smiles back and my cock goes rogue in my trousers. Fuck, Jayce. Focus.

"Then you won't mind that I dropped a bunch of pretzels on the floor of your car," Makeba mutters.

She's even adorable when she's making a huge fucking mess. I grin.

"Nope. Wouldn't bother me at all."

I want lunch to slow down so I can have more time with her, but time just slips through my fingers whenever Makeba's around. She keeps me on my toes, she keeps me laughing and we talk like we're fucking old friends throughout lunch. I never thought we could just talk like this without the insults and the secret plots against each other.

I'm a Boston guy, born and raised in Mass, and I consider all things Massachusetts superior to New York — an opinion I probably should have kept to myself if I knew what was good for me. When we finally stop arguing about which city has the better people, museums, restaurants and sports teams, I ask her about where she grew up. Much better than fighting. I need to stop fighting everyone — especially her.

I ask her stuff about the New York City she grew up in, and nod as she tells me stories about her Jamaican parents, imitating their accents perfectly in so many of her stories that I can't help but laugh. She sounds close to her family. It's weird because I'm not close to my step-dad. He'll pull through when I need a favor, but that's about it. I'm as good as my accomplishments in the Clutterbuck household, and good old 'dad' never fails to remind me that I'm a fuckup.

I don't feel like a fuck up with Makeba for once. I hope I don't change that soon.

I want a family of my own someday – the family I would have had if mom wasn't dead. After lunch, Makeba wants to walk around the orchard outside the restaurant. It's technically closed until fall, but laden with apples anyway.

"The trees here are weird," the hostess remarks as she

gives us permission to wander the orchards and pick whatever we want.

The hostess talks Makeba's her ear off about apple picking and the history of the orchard before we even get out the door, and now Makeba's totally nerding out about a bunch of rotten apples. She's so fucking hot when she nerds out.

Her excited bouncing does nothing for my raging erection, which I struggle to hide in my pants as I take Makeba's hand and lead her toward the main path between the trees. The orchard wasn't a part of my plan, but I'm in no position to deny Makeba what she wants.

I'd do anything to spend more time with her, so we head out back to the orchard and Makeba gleams.

"He said we could eat… anything…" she whispers. "Infinite apples, Jayce. We should get a sack."

Does anyone she knows walk around carrying sacks? I grin and kiss her forehead.

"Calm down, chica. I don't want you picking up anything with worms in it. Let's walk around for a bit and find you the perfect apple— no worms. Just one."

"I want a million," she whispers mischievously.

I grab her hand and she tries to pull away for a moment, but I squeeze her tightly and pull her close to me. Mine. And she's not going fucking anywhere. I relax once we're amongst the trees and there's enough shade that I won't get a sunburn. She doesn't seem to care. Eventually, she breaks free from my hand and squeals with delight as she runs through the rows of trees.

"Jayce, it smells amazing out here! I love it…" She spins around, her skirt flailing around her until she stops it and smooths it down. Her smile is fucking gorgeous.

Just watching her smile makes me feel so fucking happy, like I finally stopped screwing up for once. She eventually scampers back over to me, wielding an apple.

"Look! I found it… the perfect one."

She holds it up to my face, and she's right. It's perfect. I do what any sane man would do. I lean over and take a huge bite out of her apple.

"Jayce! You bit the perfect apple!"

Wasn't that the point? Mm… Delicious. I take another bite.

"You're eating it!" She squeals, but she keeps holding it up while I crane my head around the chomp down.

"Uh huh."

"Jayce!"

She pulls the apple away as I lunge forward and bonks me on the head. Ow. I thought she said I got hit in the head too much. Mixed messages, chica. After bonking me on the head, she giggles at my reaction. Oh yeah?

"Watch it, chica. I'm gonna get you back if you bonk me again."

"Oh yeah?"

"Oh yeah."

She bonks me on the head with the apple, giggling fiercely.

"Jayce, fetch."

She flings the half-eaten apple across the orchard. As I look in the direction she threw it in, she screams, "Sucker!" lifts her skirt a bit so she can run, and she takes off fast. Fuck... Why is it so easy for me to forget that Makeba's anything but easy? I accept that she fooled me and take off after her.

"I'm coming!"

Makeba's laugh makes me feel light. I chase after her as fast as I can, but she's fast and willing to dart around the trees and toss apples into my way, so I nearly slip as I chase her.

"You'll never catch me!"

"Wanna bet?"

She weaves around and turns the corner. I know I can catch her if I try. A part of me wants to let her get away and let her win so that I can watch her smile and laugh again. I thought torturing her was fun, but watching Makeba play is ten times better. Another part of me wants to catch her and pin her to the ground amongst the apples – for obvious reasons.

I listen to the darker part of me and push myself. I weave around a tree, fake her out, and then run at her. She screams my name, but it's too late. I have her in my arms.

"Gotcha…"

Makeba shrieks and wraps her legs around me. Her instincts get me hard as her thighs' grip my torso and her braid whips around as I spin her.

"Jayce! You're spinning me."

"Yup. That's what happens when bad girls get caught."

She shrieks again and I pin her up against the nearest Macintosh tree. Makeba gasps as her back hits the bark. My cock stiffens more. Fuck. I want to take her here. Now. And I don't want anything or anything to stop me – especially not decency. I run my tongue over my lips, desire coursing through me and I freeze in the moment. How far will she let me go?

Makeba's skirt, and presumably her panties are the only thing stopping me. Just thinking about the fact that she might not even be wearing panties gets me hotter.

"Are you wearing panties underneath that?" I whisper.

She crinkles her face like I've been too forward, but she wriggles her hips. A part of her enjoys this teasing.

"What kind of question is that?" She says, her fingers raking through my hair. I love how her hands feel. I want her to touch me more. I need to feel Makeba — now.

"Sorry," I whisper. Before she can get too pissed, I kiss her. I kiss her because I want to. After a day of shooting and eating and running around in the spring sun, the only thing I want to do is press my lips to Makeba's. I want to say 'yes' to everything I'm feeling. In some ways, I already have said yes. I want to date her. I want to fuck her. I want to be with her – and I don't want anything or anyone else coming between us.

Those days are over. I just want her in my arms and nothing else.

She kisses back enthusiastically, which encourages me to slide my hand onto her thigh beneath that long skirt. She doesn't stop me. Perfect. Touching her thigh gets me stiffer and I press my hips against her sex, eagerly awaiting her anticipatory moan. I don't know what it is about her modest clothes that gets me so rock hard.

It just makes uncovering what's underneath those clothes even better knowing she doesn't put it all on display and knowing that there are parts of her she only keeps for someone special — and I'm that someone special. I grip her thigh tighter and ease my hips forward to pin her firmly to the tree I want to fuck her against.

Fuck, she's so smoking hot when I kiss her. I spread her lips and press my tongue into her mouth, exploring her. She tastes delicious. Sweet. I love how full her lips are and the way they taste.

"You taste like apples," she whispers when I pull away. Then she presses her thumb to my lip and wipes some of the juice off before sticking that sexy finger into her own mouth. I fucking want her so bad.

"I want you," I whisper.

"I can feel that," she whispers back. My cock lurches against the front of my pants. He wants out. But this time, that's not exactly what I mean. I have to ignore my pounding heart and just get straight to the fucking point with her. I have to say exactly the words I mean and risk her turning me down — and this time, I can't tie her to the bed and humiliate her if she rejects me.

I run my fingers over her braids, moving her decorative beads along the length of one.

"I mean..." I murmur, my voice catching nervously. "I want you to be my girlfriend."

I know it's not what she expects when her dark eyes widen. Fuck. Is she going to say no?

"Jayce..."

"Stop," I whisper. "I'm serious. You never take me seriously, Makeba, and I get it. I've been a dick. I tortured you. But that night... maybe it was your first time with a guy, but it was my first time feeling something real with a woman. Ever."

She resists me — as usual.

"I don't believe that."

I grab her hips tighter. I'll do whatever I have to and show her I'm different. She made me different.

"I don't give a fuck what you believe. It's true."

I bend my lips to her neck and taste her. Her bruises finally healed, but I still remember where each one was the first time she revealed them. I kiss each spot repeatedly until she knows what I'm doing and her body responds with goose flesh. She moans my name again and her long fingers sink deeper into my hair. Yes.

"If you're mine, I'll protect you," I whisper. "I promise."

My hands travel under her skirt and I ease my fingers past her underwear, slowly massaging her flower open. She whimpers, but she doesn't respond to my question.

"Say yes, Makeba," I murmur, pushing my fingers inside her slowly. "Just say yes. I want you. Give me a chance."

Just one date. I should have known I couldn't handle that. I want her too badly and I'm in the habit of going after things I want. I can't just wait — I need her.

I thrust my fingers in deeper and she moans, "Yes..."

Fuck. I finally have her.

My heart wants to burst from my chest, but I have to make her cum first. I move my hands a little and then thrust deep again. She moans and then seems to come to her senses. Her thighs tighten around my torso, but she pushes against my chest, wriggling like she wants to get free. I don't let go of her and I don't move my fingers from her perfect cunt. She's juicy and wet. I love touching the place I'm about to put my cock, feeling how ready she is and pushing her over the edge a few times before I take her.

"Someone could see us," she whimpers half-heartedly.

I don't care if anyone sees us. I'm an animal when I want her and my lust vanquishes all common sense. That poor hostess would lose it if she saw us. I soothe Makeba with a kiss.

"I'll tell them to leave."

"We are outside," she says firmly. "People can't just leave."

"Listen, the waiter's cool," I whisper. "And I really don't want to take my fingers out of your cunt."

I press my thumb against her clit, and instead of opening her mouth to protest, Makeba moans. Yes. My fingers work her to a slow orgasm against the tree and my entire body tenses as I pull my fingers from her sweet ass pussy. I keep holding her with one hand as I lick my fingers clean.

"Want to taste?" I tease her as I suck my index and middle finger together. Her cunt tastes amazing.

"No thanks," she gasps. One step at a time. Soon, I'll have her tasting herself regularly and liking it.

"Too bad."

I slip my fingers into her mouth and Makeba scowls at first, like she's going to bite me, and then her lips soften around my fingers. Those lips. Damn. I fucking need those lips. I kiss her and before I know it, I'm on my knees and pressing my tongue against her panties beneath that skirt. I planned on fucking her until she came loud enough to bring the waiter out, but my urges take on a different slant. I push her panties to the side and let my tongue get to work on her soft, dark outer lips.

I tease the surrounding juices with my fingers and breathe in her scent before my lips and tongue work her at a faster pace. She gets wetter and juicier as she approaches a climax and I grab her hips as I push two fingers deep inside her to make her cum. When I pull away from her, Makeba's face is stunned.

"You have no control over your sexual urges," she gasps.

"Yeah. I know."

"We are outside!"

"I know."

Then she kisses me. She fucking likes it. I've never had her kiss me this fiercely. I will eat her pussy daily if this is what it takes to get her lips fiercely pressed against mine. She can taste herself on my lips and on her tongue, and it drives her wild.

"Let's go to my dorm," she whispers. "Please. Not out here, white boy."

When have I ever been able to resist her? I nod and reluctantly set her down. She takes another apple from the tree we were pressed against.

"Here," she whispers. "Not perfect. But ours."

She lifts it and we both take a bite at the same time. Makeba laughs as juice trickles down both our lips. Her laughter makes me laugh too and I take another bite like a wild dog, making her laugh even harder. I toss the apple aside and take her in my arms again.

We kiss the apple juice away for a few more minutes before we end up in the convertible again. Back to campus. Back to a fucking bed where I can finally slide between Makeba's legs and sleep with her again.

When my car gets to the campus gates with the big fucking "Laguna Grove" sign hanging over the wrought iron, we both know something's wrong. Well, I certainly hoped the mess would disappear by the time we got back. Fuck. She'll want an explanation and I don't know if I'm ready to give one yet.

Blue and red flashing lights reflect off the wrought iron and when I turn into the student lot behind the freshman dorms, my throat tightens.

Fuck. That was quick.

"I wonder what happened," Makeba muses.

She doesn't suspect my involvement, which makes me feel like an asshole. I know Makeba. She won't like that I'm keeping anything from her — especially not about this. Still, there's no telling how she'll react once she knows the truth.

I jerk the car to a stop. I know I have to tell her, but this wasn't exactly how I planned on doing it.

"Why did you stop the car?"

"I have a confession to make," I sigh, glancing over at her.

She looks at me and then Makeba glances at the police cars. Fuck. She's quick.

"Are you getting arrested?"

She's close, but not quite there. No one out here really wants to be the person who arrests Judge Clutterbuck's stepson. Every cop, lawyer, judge and public official in this part of Massachusetts knows my step-dad. Power. Privilege. Maybe I have those things like Makeba says. Today, I'm using my power, my privilege, everything I have to protect her. Not just protect her, but make sure that some slimy asshole never gets the better of her again. The gun was only one part of it.

"No. Not getting arrested."

Yeah, this isn't the answer she wants, but it's true. I'll stay out of jail, especially because I kept my hands clean. Makeba's not ready to let this go yet. Fuck. Why didn't I think about how this could affect our date?

"Jayce! What's going on?"

"Cole, Dustin, and a few guys on the team had a little chat with your ex over the Kya thing."

I know she's pissed. *I don't care. I did what I had to do.*

"A chat that called over an ambulance and several cop cars?!"

"I solved a problem. And just in case I didn't solve it, you have a little problem solver in the back that you're going to take back to your bedroom with me."

"What did you do to him? I don't believe for one second that this was a chat."

Yeah, she's right. It wasn't a chat, but believe me, it was exactly what that little fucker needed. I regret not turning my car around and dragging her away from this. I don't want her to see anything she doesn't need to.

The anger in her voice makes my fury rise. Why the fuck does she care what we did to that sniveling bastard? Whatever he got from us... he deserved. I promised to keep Makeba safe, and that's exactly what I'm doing. That's exactly what all of us are doing — keeping our women safe.

"You have nothing to worry about anymore. That's all you need to know."

"I need to know what happened," she insists.

My hand darts to her thigh, and I squeeze.

"No," I growl. "It was a mistake to bring you here. We're going to Pesthouse. I'm not finished with you yet..."

18

HE PUT A TITLE ON IT

MAKEBA

I'm Jayce Clutterbuck's girlfriend. It's official and it still feels weird sometimes, even if Jayce puts more effort into being a boyfriend than B.J.

Our feelings blossomed unexpectedly and then the day in the apple orchard made everything so much more intense. I can't get enough of him and he can't get enough of me.

I still freak out that the feelings between us are... *mutual.*

I can't even see apples without thinking of the way he pushed his fingers inside me or the way his tongue teased my lower lips. We're officially together. *He belongs to me.*

Our campus is too small for secrets and the first three weeks of dating Jayce, everyone knows. Girls who definitely didn't know my name before approach me constantly and try their damndest to fish for information.

Maybe everyone could have let the Jayce thing go if the B.J. situation hadn't spiraled out of hand.

The sirens. The ambulance. *Jayce nearly had him killed.*

Unfortunately for B.J., despite the brutal attack, the deans already chose to expel him over the red paint incident. The hockey boys are safe from any consequences. According to Cole, B.J left the situation with three broken ribs, a fat lip and a hard lesson.

The deans found the proof they needed that B.J. orchestrated the paint attacks, and considering the previous incidents with me, B.J. lost his spot at Laguna Grove. He was too cocky for his own good. I hate that I'm relieved.

What kind of message does it send to Jayce for me to celebrate his worst trait when it's turned against my enemies? This isn't helping him curb his violence in the slightest. I don't know how to talk to him about that. He insists he did the right thing and I'm not sure that I didn't. I guess there's still the tiniest part of me that needs to learn how to stand up for myself. And there's still a part of Jayce that needs to suppress his urges. He doesn't get in trouble for the B.J. thing, but that's only because of his step-dad stepping in to protect Jayce's hockey career.

I want us to get away for a while.

I grin as I stare at Jayce's message. Get away from what? Where could we even go? We still have five more weeks before final exams and then... summer. Last time I checked, Jayce has hockey stuff over the summer. If he doesn't get recruited before then, he'll spend all summer aiming for a minor or major league contract. I don't really think there's room in there for 'getting away'.

What are you thinking?

I wait for him to respond, sample a few pretzels and *try* working on the cleaning routine checklist Raven and Kya gave me to help me get my messiness under control.

I'm outside your door.

Damn it, Jayce...

I open my bedroom door and there he is, holding a bouquet of white roses and *chocolates*. My stomach grumbles. Then I get suspicious. Sure, since we started dating, everything between us has been normal, but you never know when a white boy will whip out his leather leash and tie you to the bed.

"What's all this for?"

"Hello sexy boyfriend, aren't I glad to see you," he says in a mocking tone.

I roll my eyes.

"You brought flowers. And chocolate. Thanks."

I hate that I sound so dumbfounded, like I'm not used to treatment like this. I don't want to come off as desperate, but Jayce doesn't seem to notice.

"Yup."

"Um... why?"

"It's Monday."

"I know that."

"M for Makeba. M for Monday."

I don't know how Jayce makes sense of things, but he's not trying to kidnap me again and he's standing in my threshold politely waiting for him to let me in.

"You can come in. And thanks for the flowers."

"Take them, chica."

He leans over and kisses me on the cheek. He just shaved his beard off and his cheeks smell like aftershave. Mmmm. I want more than a kiss on the cheek, so I clutch the flowers and kiss him back. *Hard.* I rake my fingers through his beard and Jayce chuckles.

"Fuck. I should bring flowers every day."

"I wouldn't mind."

"The place looks clean."

I give him a good side-eye. Boy, don't be commenting on my cleanliness.

"I said come in."

He finally enters my room and then I notice… Jayce is acting weird. He's acting all hesitant and suspicious. Hm. I invite him to take a seat on my bed and set the flowers up on my dresser. My room immediately smells like fresh roses, but nothing can compare to fresh chocolate. Actually, even stale chocolate is pretty good once you melt it in your mouth a little bit.

"Summer," Jayce says. "I want to take you somewhere."

"I'm broke, Jayce. I can't go anywhere."

"Don't give me that broke shit."

"What do you want me to give you?" I grumble, getting a few ideas about punching him in the shoulders or chest.

"Your 'yes'."

"I thought you already got that?"

"My step-dad's leaving for work. He's spending the summer and most of the fall in London and if we want… we can take his place in Boston for the summer. He's got a nice brownstone in Cambridge…"

"Seriously?"

"We could play house. See how it goes."

My face falls. "You've seen my bedroom. If you're looking for a wifey... I don't cook. I don't clean."

Jayce laughs. "We have housekeepers for that. And restaurants. Trust me, you do *plenty* of *wifey* things."

Jayce sounds hilariously white saying the word 'wifey', but I let it slide. It cracks me up how hilariously white he is and how blissfully unaware of how funny he sounds to me.

"So you want me to move in with you for the summer?"

"Yup. I'll have hockey but you can do... I dunno. Hang around the house naked with your tits out and a bow on your ass."

"That's your fantasy?"

"Or a costume. Sexy nurse?"

I roll my eyes. "I'll have to get a job. I'm still broke."

"Fine. Then get a job. I just want to be with you. *Please.*"

He wants my yes. I've said no to Jayce so many times that it's almost instinctive. This just feels like a huge jump. We've spent more time hating each other than we have dating. Can I really agree to spending my entire summer living in a rich people house with Jayce? I bite my lower lip, wondering what he'll expect of me in that situation.

"I want to say yes."

"Then fucking do it, chica. I want to take you to a Red Sox game."

"Boy, I'm a Yankees fan. Don't play."

"I have *never* heard you talk about sports."

"Yeah, well I'm loyal to New York teams. You learned something new today."

Jayce laughs. "Fine, Yankees fan. I'll take you to a Red Sox game and you can boo them. If anyone fucks with you… I'll clean the floor with them."

"Comforting."

"You're welcome."

Jayce hops off my bed and grabs one of my chocolates. My heart beats nervously as I worry he's going to eat it. Mercifully, he pops the chocolate into my mouth. He knows I'm greedy. Don't be going after my food, white boy. I close my eyes and savor the tasty high-end chocolate. I'm starting to think Jayce's taste in food makes up for anything I could possibly hate about him.

"Fine," I say, totally weakened by the sweet cocoa flavor. "I'm saying yes."

"Fuck yeah."

"But I don't need a man paying my bills. I'll get a job and I'll contribute."

"Whatever you say, chica. Come here."

He coaxes me closer with his hand on my hips and something about the way he grabs me feels so serious. I can't hold his intense gaze for long. It's too powerful and Jayce knows it. His fingers clasp around my waist and he kisses my forehead, easing me into things. He's still so gentle with me, as if every time we meet it's still my first time.

"Look at me," he whispers. I fight the terror of what I feel for him. I know he has this deep dark side, but I still can't bring myself to run. I just keep diving deeper and deeper with Jayce. When he gets all serious, I can't help worrying that it's all an illusion about to fall apart. My throat catches, but I'm looking and meeting his fierce brown gaze with my own wide eyes.

"It's too soon," he whispers. "I know it. But I know what I feel. I love you, Makeba."

Okay, now I'm freaking out. He notices because his hands grip me harder. He won't let me go even if I try.

"Don't say anything," he whispers. "These are my words for you. I love you. I want you with me this summer and I'm not sorry about what I did to your ex. He deserved it. If anyone lays a finger on you... I'll put them in the fucking ground."

Jayce doesn't need to make threats like that. I don't need him to put anyone in the ground for me or do anything crazy that he wants to do. But I know he's serious. His grasp on me tightens. He gets like this when he can't control himself. When he wants me. I move my body against his, feeling his firm chest and letting my hands roam over him the way he allows his to roam over my hips and cup my ass.

"I want you," he whispers.

"I want you too."

I *more* than want him. I think I love Jayce too. But he's right, it's too soon. He's the impulsive one. That's not really my thing. But I let the words dance over me and tease me alive. When Jayce kisses me, I melt. *He loves me.* I spent so long wasting time chasing after B.J. And he gave me so little. Jayce wants to give me everything, but I'm too scared to let him in and too scared to chase him. I want to give in. I want to give him my heart right here, but I just can't.

I grab his cheeks, my thumbs running over his new sprinkling of stubble, and I kiss him back slowly. We stumble backward against my desk and I slide my ass onto the wood, pushing aside my books as Jayce positions himself between my legs. It's easy to lose myself kissing him. He's a delicious kisser and it only makes it better that I'm not supposed to want him this badly. A guy like Jayce isn't supposed to make every inch of me feel absolutely fucking alive. I rake my fingers through his hair, thanking the heavens that he hasn't cut it yet and he juts his hips forward. His stiffness pushes against his pants resting against my thighs. I bite my lip and inch my hips forward. Fuck. It's hot with blood and eager for me. Jayce gets hard the second our lips touch and once he's ready for sex, almost nothing can stop him.

My heart pulses nervously as his hands move up my hips and he slips one under my hoodie to find the hook of my bra. *Oops.*

"You aren't wearing a bra," he whispers.

"Nope."

He responds by running his fingers over my nipples and pinching until I squeal.

"Fuck," He whispers. "I love your tits."

"Uh huh."

I can't form a proper response with his fingers rubbing against my nipples and driving me wild. When he pushes me close to the edge teasing one nipple awake, he moves to the other one until I'm squirming and panting on the edge of my desk, yearning for much more than this teasing. Jayce removes his hands from beneath my hoodie and chuckles.

"They're so soft," he whispers. He plants his lips against mine and his hands move to the top of my thighs. I don't need psychic powers to determine what he wants next. My breath catches as his hands run up my thighs and hook into the waistband of my yoga pants.

"I want these on the fucking floor," he says.

I squirm and ease myself out of the tight pants. Jayce's hands rub my bare thighs the moment they're exposed.

"Fuck," he whispers. "Look at this. Our skin…"

He runs his hand over my thigh and I notice how pale he is. He makes my skin look almost purple, he's so white. He curls his fingers into a claw shape and runs them gently over my thighs. His cock jumps in his pants.

"I love the contrast," he whispers. "You're so dark... *I love it.*"

He leans forward to kiss my neck, sending a shiver from my thighs to my lips and then straight to my sex. I scoot my butt forward, nearly falling off the desk. I just want to be close to him. Jayce catches me.

"Careful," he whispers. "Don't fall off until I fuck you."

He stops my lips before I can protest. I wrap my thighs around him to stabilize my position and Jayce keeps stroking my bare thighs until it feels like painful teasing. When he's ready, his hands edge toward my underwear and he slides a finger past my panties without warning. His thick fingers feel so damn good inside me. I buck forward and he pushes them deeper. *Damn.*

I'm soaking wet and Jayce loves it. He swirls his fingers around inside me as I moan and then pulls both fingers out and licks them clean. He always sends a shiver straight through me when he does that. I wrap my arms around Jayce's broad shoulders and ease my hips forward as he uses his fingers to make me cum hard. We're both gasping and panting together when he pushes me to an intense finish. I've never felt him this hard before and my stomach tightens in a nervous knot at the thought of taking him again.

His dick is just so big.

"You're ready for me," he whispers, kissing my neck as he slowly undoes his belt and pants. My thighs tremble as I hold him close, urging him to hurry with my heels pressing against his buttocks. Once he bares his cock, I don't think I can maintain control for long. *I need him.*

"Condom," I whisper.

"No," Jayce whispers back, like it's not up for discussion. "I want to feel you."

"What about pregnancy?"

His cheeks darken. I know Jayce is crazy, but he can't be 'knock up a freshman' crazy. He bites his lower lip and the next words appear to pain him.

"You're right," he grumbles. "But soon. I want to feel you. Soon."

I nod as he reaches for a condom and eases it around his large cock. I whimper as I feel the large head nudging me open. Jayce cups my ass as he slides into me slowly. Today, he's gentle.

"I love you," He whispers, kissing me as he thrusts the head past my opening. Pleasure spreads through me as he holds my waist and pushes deeper. Jayce's thick staff stretches and fills me as he moves his hips forward. Loud moans escape my lips and Jayce stops them with lusty kisses as he buries his cock in me to the hilt. Fuck. His dick feels amazing. I feel pinned to the desk with that big dick spreading my thighs lewdly and the pleasure from having his shaft massage every inch of my walls drives me wild.

I grab his shoulders and move against him with slow gyrations. Jayce lifts me off the desk and holds me up so we can move together. It doesn't take me long to cum with our bodies intertwined like that. As I cum, Jayce moves me over to the bed and we fall into my sheets together, crunching an empty bag of pretzels as we land on the mattress together. *Oops.*

"You're so fucking soft," he growls as he presses me into my pillow. I moan as his cock hits a sweet spot between my legs and I feel another climax coming fast.

"Harder," I gasp. "Harder…"

Even without much experience, my body seems to know what it wants from Jayce and I tangle my fingers in his hair as I beg for him to make love to me exactly the way he wants to.

Jayce tosses the pretzel baggie out of the way and holds my hips against his as he pumps into me. The more we make love, the harder it gets for him to hold back. I cry out as his movements grow faster and he pushes me over the edge into a more mind-blowing climax. After three more orgasms, Jayce finally flips me over.

I tense up instantly. His tongue has definitely been places it shouldn't and I worry he's going to put my dick somewhere it doesn't belong. Jayce presses his body on top of mine, ignorant to my concerns as he fondles my ass cheeks and kisses my neck, pushing my braids out of the way as his tongue tickles my ear lobes.

He still hasn't cum yet.

"I can last forever with you," he murmurs.

My thighs tighten and Jayce attempts to slide his hands up my leg.

"What's wrong, babe?" He whispers.

I wriggle my ass against him, unsure of how to put it into words. Jayce unceremoniously slips his finger between my butt cheeks, pressing it against my backdoor. *Fuck.*

"Jayce…"

"Is that what you want?" He whispers.

"No!"

"Oh," he whispers. "Okay. That's fine."

"Really?"

"Yeah," he murmurs. "We've had a lot of firsts. Spread your legs. I want your pretty black pussy."

My throat knots again. I've spoken to him about his comments but I can't help how wet I am or how badly I want him between my legs, no matter what unique ways he has of phrasing things.

"Come on," he whispers. "Open up for me."

I spread my legs slightly and Jayce uses the smallest opening to probe the head of his cock against my entrance again. I'm swollen from our lovemaking but still eager for more of him. I wriggle and push my hips back, taking more of his shaft between my legs. We groan together as Jayce pushes the rest of the way in, keeping his whole length between my legs. His crotch forms a smooth cup around my ass and the weight of his muscular 6'4" body feels so dominating and strong.

I lean into his masculine strength, moving my hips against his enormous cock and holy fuck, it feels amazing. Jayce moves slowly, easing into me from behind and covering my body with eager kisses until we both came together. Jayce edges his hips forward and groans as he orgasms. His cock pulses between my legs, sending a shiver of plea-sure through me. Jayce refuses to roll off me right away. He pushes hair from my face and kisses me until his cock softens. *I want to pull him closer.*

When he finally slides from between my legs, Jayce pulls me against his chest. I slide my fingers through his chest hair and find a spot for my head that smells deliciously like him. I don't know when I started appreciating how he smelled so much. I want to stay wrapped up in Jayce's arms forever. I want to say the three little words that spilled from his lips so easily. I just wasn't sure if I was ready…

Not yet. Not until you're sure.

But why can't I be sure? Yes, we had off to a rocky start, but that all seems so far in the past. *Jayce is right here.* His chest moves beneath my fingers and I sense him stirring for round two. I know I should feel safe with him. He's done everything in his power to protect me. B.J.'s gone, I have a gun and more importantly, I have Jayce.

So why do I still feel like everything will go wrong?

19

SECOND-TO-LAST GAME

JAYCE

Our second-to-last game of the season happens four weeks before summer vacation. Makeba keeps me well supplied with weed — I don't know where she gets it — and then she joins me in these meditations to help with my anger... those freaky breathing exercises are pretty chill too, especially since I get an awesome reward after. Eating pussy.

Yup, Makeba and I are in a pretty chill place and our last game starts off with a packed rink. Everyone at Laguna Grove wants our season to end in victory. It's my job to get out there and prove to Makeba I'm not the unhinged douche bag she thinks I am. I can fight my urges... and only hit a guy if he hits first.

During our pre-game skate, I see Makeba in the stands with Kya and a few of their other friends. She's wearing my jersey. My chest throbs with pride and a real desire not to fuck things up. If I screw up with Makeba, I'll never forgive my dumb ass. I want to prove to her I'm not that guy. I don't want to be the asshole that always screws things up. I hate being that person.

I made Makeba Winston a promise before this game: no fights. It's going to be hard to calm down, but I think because of her I can do anything. She understands me and my fucked up head. Cole's finally back and Tuck gives me a chance to start on the ice. It feels good to play with all my brothers again. Dustin. Cole. The rest of the team. I don't know where the fuck I would be without them.

Probably not in the college league playoffs. We're in the semifinals and playing teams stacked with guys who have straight tickets to the majors like Cole does. We're in the semifinals with the Darien Drones from Connecticut — a bunch of preppy rich fuckers who we ought to crush easily. I'm big enough to kill half the guys on their team, but they have a few stars.

The only problem is my agreement not to "crush" or "kill" anyone. It's going to be hard. I've skated with some of these guys and I have problems with a few of them. Derek. Seth. Oliver. They're bigger assholes than anyone at Laguna Grove. And they deserve a fucking fist through the ribs.

Near the end of our pre-skate, Cole gives me a pep talk between shooting drills and passing drills. I don't need a pep talk this time. I have plenty of motivation to keep my head on my shoulders sitting in the stands. She looks so fucking cute in that hoodie and jeans. It's funny how badly I used to give a shit about my reputation, how I worried what people would say. I guess we live in a different world at Laguna Grove, because nothing changes for me — I just have the girl I want and that shit makes me pretty fucking happy.

Every hockey game starts with a fast-paced rush for control. Our offense has been consistent this season. Our defense has been our biggest problem. Me. I've been the biggest problem. Well, Tuck Murphy doesn't have to worry about me fucking up his game this time. I'm on my shit.

A tall full-bearded player on the Drones checks Cole hard against the boards and steals control of the puck five minutes into the game. Until then, we're good at keeping even control, but this gigantic motherfucker and his Duck Dynasty beard rattle the fuck out of Cole and he skates smoothly past Adam, pushing the puck into my territory. I reach for the puck only to have fucking Seth pushing up on my left folder and beating me to it.

That motherfucker. I chase after him and hit him as hard as I can — legally this time. I grab the puck and I don't hear the whistle. No penalty. Fuck yeah. The Laguna Grove crowd goes crazy as I pass the puck back up the ice to Rathbone, who sinks it into the net. Seven minutes in and we score the first goal. Fuck yes.

Rathbone collects his glory and we stop to listen to Coach for a minute before we get back after it.

First goal of the game goes to the Laguna Grove Vipers, scored by Dustin Rathbone #13.

The crowd goes wild again at the announcement, but the background noise blurs as Seth skates around me, marking me for the puck. He's just about the only other guy in our college league who plays as dirty as I do. I can't fight back. Even if he kicks the shit out of me. I bite my lower lip as Seth misses a pass, intercepted by Kane, and bounced up the boards back to Cole. With Seabrook handling the puck, the crowd preemptively goes wild.

Cole zips around to tip in a corner shot and misses. Fuck. I can't see shit with Seth's large body constantly skating in front of mine. I dart around the fucker, but Seth follows me, sticking to my ass like wet toilet paper. When I miss the puck because of his big ass in the way, I consider putting my stick out to trip the motherfucker, but I feel Tuck's eyes on me and Makeba's and I can't bring myself to disappoint either of them. I can't fuck up. I can't hit him even if I want to so fucking badly. That fucker Derek gets the puck back to my turf.

As the puck gets closer to Barkov, I rush to defend the net. Marc Kane and Adam Foote form a strong force to stop the puck, but it's not enough. Seth flicks it past Kane and I lunge for it to smack it out of the way, missing Derek in my blind spot. I hear the Drones' crowd cheering before I process what happened. They fucking scored.

The second goal of the game, tying things between the Darien Drones and the Laguna Grove Vipers, goes to Derek Perfetti #19 on the Darien Drones.

Sweat drips down my neck. My jersey and every inch of me soak through with sweat as I skate slowly to the bench. Tuck pulls the first string out. I want to be out there. I want to stop this.

"You can all still win this. Jayce, I need your eyes open. Minds... clear. Cole? We need you out there in a few minutes. Rest. Drink water. Benji, you're in. Five minutes. Check your blind spot. I want you boys to get out there and make this work," Tuck says, his encouraging voice lifting us to new heights of confidence. He's right. We can win this.

He pulls me aside before the buzzer starts.

"You did good, but I can see them pushing you, Jayce. Don't break. Don't crack. I don't want to see you in that fucking box."

"Yes, coach."

He pulls me closer by the jersey and glances furtively to his left.

"Don't look yet, but to your left... that's Dylan Ward. He's an agent looking to help a couple major league teams in New York fill in some spots. He's watching you, but that attention could easily go to someone else. Don't screw up, Jayce."

"I won't."

"Good."

The pressure constricts. I know I can't screw up now, but it gets harder to control my anger the more my muscles hurt. It just gets easier to throw a punch than calm myself down. The rest of the first period passes painfully. We keep the score tied, which isn't great, but it's better than giving the Drones an advantage. Tuck gets us together during the break and then I'm ready to head on the ice again.

The second period, Cole scores another goal, followed by another goal by the Duck Dynasty beard motherfucker on the Drones' team. I make it through the period without kicking the shit out of Seth, but fucking hell, it gets harder as time goes on. I want to punch his fucking lights out every time he skates in front of me. Dylan be damned.

But Makeba. I can't disappoint her. I cast a glance in her direction from the bench. I shouldn't let her distract me, but I can't help it. She's glowing with excitement. I've never seen her give this much of a fuck at hockey games. It's incredible. She gives me strength I didn't know I had. Tuck doesn't start me in the third. He'll need the first string in the last five minutes of the game when we need to fight the Drones with every ounce of our mental strength to win. To dominate.

Benji scores in the third period. 3-2. We can hold this. We can beat this. I'm right to keep my team in high regard. We keep the score at 3-2 until we're close to the end and I'm on the ice again, dripping in sweat, heart pumping with desire for glory. I know we can win this and I don't give a fuck what happens — I won't break.

Drones take possession of the puck first, quickly sorted by me and Marc Kane, who throws the puck up to Cole from my pass. Cole passes to Dustin, and we score again. Four minutes left. The Drones know we're going to win this and it's starting to fuck with them. Derek shoves Cole into the boards so hard that he has a nosebleed and has to leave the ice. Three minutes left. We're down the best man we have on offense, so if we're going to win this, our defense needs to be tight.

I can't lose control.

Rage and desire fuel the Drones. Their offense takes control and Seth hits me like he's trying to fucking kill me when the puck slides against my stick. I throw a swift pass to Kane to get the puck out of there. The puck makes it, but it's too late for me and I miss a hard fist swinging toward my face. Fuck. Seth's fist connects with my cheek and my head hits the boards so fucking hard I see stars.

I can't hold myself back. I swing madly and I know I miss. His arm wraps around my neck and I hear screaming. It's the crowd or the teams… another fist connects with my head and it's fucking lights out Clutterbuck. I don't remember another fucking thing until I wake up — far away from the ice.

"What happened?"

I'm on a stretcher. Fuck. Tuck hovers over me. I see his mouth moving, but I can't hear any of the words coming out of it. First responders swarm me and I try to push the hive of them away, but nothing works. They keep hooking me up to things and then they stick me in the back of a damned ambulance. Is this really necessary?

I try saying something to Tuck, but instead of words, random grunts erupt from my mouth. Shit.

He says something and this time, I can make out the words. "We won."

Fuck yeah.

I lose consciousness again and wake up in the local hospital — alone. At least I think I'm alone until I hear Judge Clutterbuck's voice from the other side of the room. Fuck.

"You're awake, finally."

I grunt. Dad. I'm not in the mood to talk to the Judge. I'm never in the mood to talk to the judge, especially since his idea of a conversation involves telling me all the thousands of ways I fucked up. I hear his expensive loafers on the tiled floor and close my eyes again. I want to make him disappear.

"Replacing one fuck up with another out there," he says. "At least you won."

I'm too tired to argue with him. We won. He's at least right about one thing: it's good that we won. If there's any news about Dylan Ward and what he thought about the game, I doubt my step-dad will be the one to bring me the good news.

"Dad…"

"There's an African American woman standing outside the hospital who claims to be your girlfriend," he scoffs. "Who is she really?"

"My girlfriend."

Suddenly, the energy to argue returns. I think. I try to sit up but… I can't move. I can't move my neck. I can't move anything. What the fuck happened to me out there?

"You have a neck injury," Judge Clutterbuck grunts. "They say you might be able to move your neck in a few days, but until then, you're shit out of luck, kid. Did you say that African American girl is your girlfriend? I didn't know you dated these kinds of people. Honestly."

"What kinds of people might that be?" I growl hoarsely. Was he always like this? I hear rattling at the door and then someone flings the door open. With the curtain around my bed, I can't tell who it is. Judging by the look on my step-dad's face, it definitely isn't a nurse. Makeba flings the curtain back and shrieks my name. "Jayce!"

"Excuse me, you aren't permitted in here," my step-dad says to her in a sharp voice.

Makeba puts her hands on her hips and frowns at him.

"Says who? I waited outside for four hours. He's awake. I'm seeing him."

My step-dad gapes at Makeba.

"Why you listen here–

"Excuse me?" Makeba interrupts. "Listen, Judge Clutter-buck. I know you're Jayce's step-dad, but I am his girlfriend and I want to make sure he's okay. Lord knows what you're doing here since you obviously don't give a shit about him."

"How dare you talk to me like that?"

"I said what I said. I've been to 80% of Jayce's hockey games this season and I haven't seen you at a single one. Cole's mom comes to all his games, and she's a hairdresser who lives hours away. What's your excuse?"

"You have no right to question me. I'm calling security."

Makeba's brows pinch together fiercely and she pops her hip.

"Go on ahead, Judge. Go on."

My step-dad stomps out of the room. I want to ask Makeba if she's crazy. Haven't I told her what my step-dad does to people who piss him off? She's unbothered by that and touching my forearm. Fuck. I don't want her to stop touching my arm.

"What were you thinking?"

"We needed a few minutes alone. Raven's giving the nurse the slip and Kya's flirting with security. Cole said you broke your neck."

"Is that what happened?"

"I don't know," Makeba says. "But they think you'll be fine soon. They just need you in here to make sure it doesn't get worse. I just had to see you and make sure they weren't lying."

"Right. And you had to piss off my step-dad too," I mutter.

Makeba grins.

"I'm not afraid of him. I think."

"I've never heard anyone tell him off like that."

Makeba shrugs it off. She's so fucking cool and humble. I know they'll probably kick her out of here soon, but I want to drag her into this bed and keep her next to me. Too bad I can barely move.

"I probably should thank him for the firearm license... after he cools down."

"Definitely wait until he cools down."

"I can't stay long," Makeba says. "But I wanted to tell you... I'm proud of you, Jayce. I know this isn't how you wanted the game to end, but you killed it out there. It made me realize... I can't wait another second before I say this to you."

"Say what?"

She inhales sharply and then exhales just as dramatically.

"I love you."

"Really?"

"Yes. Really. Absolutely. I love you and when I saw you fall on the ice… I thought I'd never get the chance to tell you again. So I'm saying it now."

We both hear Judge Clutterbuck's footsteps furiously approaching from the end of the hall. Shit. We don't have a lot of time.

"I'll come back when your step-dad isn't here, but I've got to get back to campus, okay? You need rest."

Before she darts off, I try to grab her. My fingers brush her forearm lightly and her attention snaps back to me.

"Kiss me before you go," I whisper.

She kisses me. Her lips are soft and the perfect reward for victory on the ice. It almost makes up for the fact that I'm stranded in this hospital bed while she scampers away to an after-party that will surely rock Laguna Grove's campus all night long.

"Good bye," I murmur.

Fuck. I don't want her to go.

"I'll be back tomorrow. Visiting hours open at 7:30 a.m." Makeba says. "I'll be there. I promise."

20

PARTYIN' PESTHOUSE

MAKEBA

Kya, Raven, and I sneak out the back of the hospital, sprinting toward our getaway vehicle. Kya's dad just got her a new car in anticipation of her summer move to Boston. We'll be in the same city for the summer, but it won't be the same without Raven. We pile into Kya's new white Audi. I sit in the front and Raven spreads out in the back.

"How was he?" Raven asks, shutting her book.

My heart catches. Talking about it out loud makes it more real. I hate feeling like I could lose Jayce. I don't want that to be an option.

"Alive. He looks… hurt."

At 6'4", I've never seen Jayce looking weak or anything like it. I hope he's really better in a few days like they promise. I hope there are no complications. I know I shouldn't worry about him, but I can't help it. Jayce is tough as nails. He has to make it out okay.

Kya tries to lift my spirits. "According to Tuck, Dylan Ward was pleased with what he saw. If he can get back into skating before the final game... that's it. He'll be in the majors. You have to trust that he can pull through."

I nod. I don't want to be pessimistic about Jayce's prospects and I definitely don't want to be pessimistic about our summer together. He'll get better. He has to.

"Brett says we're going to meet up soon," Raven says. "He won't chicken out this time. That might make you feel better."

"Honey, Brett is a catfish," Kya says. "Trust me. My mom is an expert at catfishing my dad's mistresses."

I know Raven will only argue with Kya, even if Kya is definitely an expert in that department. Brett has her completely twisted up in knots with his mind games. I hope he is really so I can give him a good kick in the nuts.

"He's just shy!" Raven exclaims.

"If he was just shy, he would have sent you a voice note."

"He lost his voice," Raven answers weakly, even if she knows that doesn't make a lick of sense.

"Why don't we try finding you a real guy tonight," Kya says. "With a heartbeat."

"Damn. Do you think my standards are that low?" Raven grumbles.

I point out what Kya was probably just about to say. "Your standards are book boyfriends. They're impossible."

"I want a black king," Raven says. "I've decided. I can date white guys in my books, but now it's time for me to shift my focus and get serious. Maybe that's why I don't have a boyfriend. I'm not taking this seriously."

"Did your Instagram witch tell you that?" I ask Raven.

"No. She said that my moon was transiting Jupiter and that if I'm not careful, a Capricorn is going to tank my GPA."

Kya takes a left toward Pesthouse.

"Does that mean something specific?" Kya probes. "The moon in Jupiter thing. No comment on the GPA."

"Yes," Raven says. "It means that my destiny lies in getting in touch with my true self. My black identity. That means white boys are off the table if I want to reach spiritual enlightenment and keep a 4.0."

"Whoa. I thought she was selling foot rubs. Now she's selling spiritual enlightenment and study advice?"

Raven rolls her eyes. "She's a very talented woman. Her oils got Makeba a boyfriend with a big dick."

"I never said Jayce had a big dick," I blurt out. I don't know why. It's just my instinct to throw anyone who might mention it off the trail.

Kya gives Raven a look in the rearview mirror.

"Honey, you limp for two days every time he spends the night in your room. He's either packing or he's doing something else freaky that stops you from walking properly."

"I do not limp!"

"Yes, you do. Jayce has that big white dick," Raven says, reaching around to poke me in the side.

"Oh my God! Why are we talking about this?"

"We're just finally giving you shit for ending up with the white boy from your physics class," Kya teases. "I had to suffer the tribunal. It's your turn to suffer."

"Haven't I suffered enough? Jayce is basically dead, y'all."

"He's just slightly paralyzed," Raven offers her best form of comfort. "He'll bounce back. White men never die."

"I don't think you can prove that…"

"Have faith," Kya says. "And tonight, we'll find Raven a living and breathing man, okay? It'll take your mind off Jayce. He wouldn't want you to worry."

"Yeah, he'd want to put a tarantula in her coochie," Raven teases.

We shriek with laughter and then tease each other and mess around until we get to Pesthouse. We can hear the music a block away. The white people at Laguna Grove are going crazy. Scratch that, everybody's going crazy.

There's been something in the air lately. Since I started going out with Jayce and Kya started dating Cole, the Pesthouse parties have been looking a little more... diverse. It's nice to not feel like we're the only black people in a pit of beasts.

Kya slides her new car into a spot next to Cole's car. We're finally getting together for a much needed girls' night. Now that my room is finally free from red paint, we're also having a little sleepover in my dorm together. I've got plenty of space without a roommate, and I don't want to be alone while Jayce is in the hospital, in case I get a call to head over there in the middle of the night or something.

We walk in together through the back entrance and a thick fog of beer sweat greets us once we enter. Raven gags, Kya wrinkles her nose and I suddenly feel like coming here was a mistake. This place is way too crowded. My friends work diligently to pick my mood up. Kya drags me to the drinks with Raven and then we get on the dance floor. That's when the good stuff happens. Nothing can improve your mood like dancing, can it?

I turn down a couple guys who want to dance with me, but Raven attracts attention from a younger guy on the hockey team – the Canadian. Their dirty dancing gets a little too dirty when Raven pulls away and he disappears into the crowd to search for the next victim of his off-beat hip thrusting. At least he was cute.

"I didn't see his face," Raven says. "Was he hot?"

He was definitely hot, but maybe not Raven's type since she prefers getting catfished to real life men. She makes no effort to trace the Canadian, though. It's girls' night.

We dance until our feet hurt and drink a little, sober up some and then drink a little more. Kya has the keys to the kingdom and we don't even have to stand in line to get a shitty pump of foamy beer from a keg. We make "cocktails" with Gatorade and borrowed liquor and then more cocktails with some OJ Kya steals from Dustin's fridge. She had to move the frozen mice aside to get to it, but she's a hero for robbing Dustin Rathbone.

After having our drinks, we find some of the other girls in our dorm and dance with them. Jaleda comes to the party with a few of her friends and two black guys on the basketball team. We talk to them until they wander away to get some more beer. Tonight feels different from any other night at Laguna Grove. We're finally fitting in with people at this university and ⅔ of our clique has a boyfriend. Without a boyfriend, Raven's still happy as hell. She gets her grind on with several more guys before the night is through and a couple of them act way too thirsty. She's just having fun though, and not interested in taking it further with any of her party suitors.

We keep dancing and drinking until we can't anymore and together, we head back to Kya's Audi to drive back to campus. Kya stayed sober for the end of the party so she could drive us safely. Thank goodness, because I'm almost too tipsy to stand. Raven and I cuddle each other in the back seat while we all loudly sing Higher by Rihanna as the song blares from Kya's car stereo. The good sis has incredible speakers and we miss every single note in our singalong and most of the lyrics. Raven murmurs, "I love Rihanna. I want to get pregnant like Rihanna."

"Knocked up by a white boy," I mutter. "Isn't that one of your romance books?"

"Shut up," Raven says, resting her head on my shoulder. "Bestie."

"We're all besties. I love you besties."

"You're both drunk," Kya calls back to us. "But I love y'all too."

It's the best night we've had at Laguna Grove in ages, and I can't imagine it getting any better. Kya parks at the freshman lot and we have a trek back to the dorms where we try to recreate Shakira and Rihanna's duet with three voices while none of us can even remember the lyrics. We're a mess of laughs and tears by the time we return to my bedroom. I wouldn't trade our boring black girl crew for anything in the world.

And you know what? Maybe we're not so boring. Maybe we're just finding our legs in this crazy world that feels like it wasn't built for us to be seen or loved. Even if we don't find romance, we have each other–other strong black women to lean on and love us through the hardest times.

I still feel a little quickening of my heart as I unlock my bedroom door. I'm still not mentally free from B.J.'s hold on me. He hasn't been on campus in a while, but I still feel like he'll pop out of the dang bushes and wring my neck or put a roach on my pillow. At least I've had fewer nightmares about hands around my neck, even if it's a slight comfort.

Kya and Raven settle into their sleeping bags on the floor and I climb into bed with what feels like an empty package of mini-pretzels. Oops... I try to toss the bag into the bin, yelling, "Le Bron!"

Unfortunately, I miss the shot (something Le Bron doesn't need to know).

Kya yawns. "In my house, say anything other than Dwayne Ambrose and you get your allowance cut."

"You got pretzel dust on the floor," Raven says, snuggling deeper into her sleeping bag.

"I'll get those in the morning," I grumble. "Thanks for a great night, ladies."

"You deserve it," Kya says.

"Amen," Raven adds. "You're stronger than you think, Makeba. We admire you."

"Amen!" Kya says.

My chest fills with warmth as I snuggle into bed for some much needed sleep. Nothing can break us apart.

THUMP. THUMP. THUMP.

. . .

The sound comes from the other end of the hall, but the distinct noise of boots hitting hardwood zaps me out of sleep. It's early… Considering how late we were out last night, it's way too early. There are two more thumps and then quiet. I sit up and look at my watch. It's only 7 in the damn morning. I should be up right now anyway, I guess. I'm supposed to see Jayce early today. But the boots sound… weird. Different.

Who the hell is walking up and down the girls' dorm this early in the morning making a ruckus?

I'm about to swing my legs over the bed to check when I hear another distinct sound.

Rifle fire.

I freeze and blood rushes past my ears. I recognize the adrenaline rush from the range. The rifle fire wakes Raven next. Kya keeps sleeping peacefully. Raven presses her finger to her lips and then pushes Kya awake.

"Cole, no butt sex…" Kya murmurs in her sleep before Raven gets her properly awake.

"Sh," Raven whispers. "Did you hear that?"

Kya holds her tongue. Thank goodness, but it doesn't stop us from hearing more gunshots and then a shriek. It's more like an existential wail.

"Is someone shooting in our fucking dorm?" Kya breathes.

Technically, someone is shooting up my dorm, but I had to invite my best friends over and now... we're all going to get killed.

"It sounds like an automatic weapon," I whisper. "We need to call 911 and barricade the door."

We've been through drills, but honestly, the drills are stupid and nothing prepares me for the real thing. Adrenaline surges in me and I feel this powerful desire to run along with a frigidity in my muscles that refuses to move me. You can't afford not to move quick.

Raven tiptoes to the door and pushes a chair under it, pushing the locks twice. We hear a door fly open and then gunfire. No screams, just the sound of a body hitting the floor. Raven freezes at the door. She needs to step away from it, but she can't move. I hop out of bed and drag her by the hand away from it. Kya's already stepping into the closet with her cellphone. I see her fingers hit three numbers. Okay, she's calling and probably someone else is calling. Everyone must be awake right now, but you can't hear anything except the boots on the floor. My heart feels like it's in my throat.

We're going to be okay.

"We're going to fucking die," Raven hisses. "What's going on?"

"Sh," I whisper. "We won't die."

We can't die here. This isn't how Makeba Winston's story ends. It doesn't end with fingers wrapped around my neck or bullet holes in my chest. Makeba Winston's story doesn't end with me cowering in a closet or under a bed.

Well, I'll still need to get under my bed. With Raven and Kya watching me in utter confusion, I drag the little safe from its hiding spot under my bed and press my thumb to the opening. Blood courses through me so fast that I can't hear anything except my heartbeat. I can't feel anything except the urge to do something fast even if it's stupid.

Thump. Thump. Thump.

The boots get closer. Kya steps out of the closet and mouths, "They're coming."

Raven's texting furiously on her phone. She swipes a couple times and her expression transforms into one so horrific that a chill shoots straight down my spine.

"Holy shit," she whispers. "It's him…"

I don't have time to stop and see what she's talking about because I have my Glock out and everyone's attention – especially Kya's. She's made her stance on guns clearer than a freshly cleaned windowpane.

"Since when do you have a fucking gun!? What the fuck, Makeba?"

"Sh," I whisper. "I've got this."

"You've got this?!"

"Yeah."

"It's him!" Raven repeats. "Look at this. He's fucking streaming it!"

We're all shaking as we crowd around Raven. The hand on my gun is the only part of me that's steady. I've only practiced a few times. I don't know what the hell I plan to do with my gun, but I know I'll probably need to use it. I glance down at her phone and then my hand shakes.

It's B.J.

He's back.

And he's already killed three girls on my floor. Including Jaleda's roommate. He's clearly paused his rampage, not just because I can't hear his boots anymore, but because of the stream. Raven doesn't have the sound on but he's talking to the camera and I can make out some words from lip reading.

Bitches.

Sluts.

Revenge.

Fuck.

"That's it," I hiss. "I'm not waiting for the cops. I'm going out there."

Kya grips my forearm like an angry grocery store lobster. "Are you fucking crazy?"

"Girl, I guess."

I load my gun and step closer to the door, tiptoeing so anyone standing nearby couldn't hear my footsteps. Raven's trying to piece together B.J.'s location from the stream.

"He's three doors down," she hisses. "And facing the opposite way but once you step out, he'll see you."

"We have to do something!"

"We have to wait for the police!"

I already waited for everyone else to solve my B.J. problem. It never works. If I don't face this fucking white devil myself, he'll kill me and, even worse, he might kill my best friends.

He already killed Jaleda's roommate, the sweet girl who helped me when she didn't even know me. Her roomie didn't deserve to die at the hands of an assault rifle in her dorm room, the one place she ought to have been safe.

"Guys, I'll be fine."

I don't even believe that.

"I love you," I whisper. "Just know that, okay? I love you guys."

"Makeba, stop!" Kya hisses. "You're going to get yourself killed."

I'm the only one here who can actually do something. I've let B.J. get away with plenty and I've let people fight my battles. This is what Jayce prepared me for, right? I may not be the most experienced person with a gun, but since when does B.J. shoot? His dumb video games aren't anything like holding a real gun. Thanks to Jayce, I know exactly what that feels like.

"Barricade the door once I'm gone and don't open it until the cops get here," I say with more confidence than I feel.

"I love you," I add.

"Don't," Kya whispers, but I can't listen to her. I can't let B.J. take another woman's life when I have a firearm. I have to defend myself.

I move the chair and unlock the door, stepping into the hallway. My dorm room door slams shut behind me slowly – but not slowly enough. The loud slam echoes through the hallway and B.J. drops his stupid phone. Ignore the bodies. Ignore the bodies. I raise the Glock and forget everything. I forget my fear, my boyfriend, my friends. He whips around, holding his rifle in the air before recognizing me. His cheeks turn peach and the baseball cap on his coppery hair makes him look so much like a kid that a moment of hesitation floods me.

You can't hesitate when you're in a real life active shooter situation. You hesitate and you're dead meat.

Ty's words echo. B.J. raises his gun and puts his finger on the trigger. But he hesitates. I don't. There's just one definitive gunshot. Bile rises in my stomach, but I can't let my vision blur and I can't lose my concentration. One shot isn't enough. B.J. pulls the trigger and the gun jams. My fucking lucky day. I shoot again and this time, I don't hit his shoulder. I hit the chest of his bullet-proof vest. Fuck.

I know I won't get so lucky. I have 15 rounds and I've only used two. Shit. I don't want to shoot a man dead where he stands, but my body reacts before my head. I fire four more times before B.J. stumbles backward and drops his rifle. I point my gun to his legs and squelch the building nausea as I shoot his leg.

I am so going to jail for this. My gun hand falls to my side and I can't hold back the bile any longer. I throw up and heaving, drop to my knees. B.J. doesn't move. He's still. I killed him. I killed my ex-boyfriend.

I don't know how long I kneel there in pained silence. I hear sirens and in the rush of adrenaline and the mess I'm tied up in, I assume they're coming for me to take me away. I want to run towards B.J. and make sure he's okay. I want to make sure I only hurt him and didn't kill him. I want to apologize. I'm not a cold-blooded killer.

But it's too late for me to do anything for B.J. The cops grab me first when they burst into the hallway. I'm holding a gun, after all, and B.J.'s the one on the ground. I give up my weapon and put my hands in the air. This is it.

21

FRESH WOUNDS & OLD ACHES

JAYCE

I can move my neck–slightly, but it works. I can tilt to the left and the right and I want to get the fuck out of bed. Makeba. I need to see her. Where the hell is she?

I'm just glad I healed up quick, even if I can't crane my neck too far or do too much, I can at least get out of this stupid fucking bed and see my girl. I saw the look on her face when she left. I don't want her to think I'm weak, or too fucked up to keep shit going between us. The urge to see her grips me each passing minute.

Where the fuck is the nurse? It's 7:30 a.m. and I can't get Makeba out of my head. I think about her girls' night and the Pesthouse party I missed, and I bet she had a damn good time – so good that she's late to see me. Unless she got too drunk and something happened to her.

Fuck. She has me in a vice grip. I can't spend a second without thinking about her or worrying about her. I don't even care about my damn neck. I want my phone so I can text my girlfriend.

The only problem I have right now is that I'm not the guy with her, wrapping my arms around her waist and letting her dirty dance on me with that perfect ass.

Ah, well. I chalk it up to the game. Sometimes you get a gnarly injury that keeps you miles away from the perfect woman with the perfect ass – my girl. There's something about having her in my life that changes me, you know? It's not that I can't live without her or anything, it's more than that. I don't want to live without Makeba in my life. I just have to hope I can walk and move my fucking neck again. I have to hope that I can play the game.

Makeba. I can't get her off my mind. I can't stop wondering what she's doing or if she's safe. I can't exactly look after her from this stupid bed, can I? Because of my head injury, the doc wants me off my phone, but I don't think I can spend another minute without hearing Makeba's voice.

"NURSE!" I screech. "NURSE!"

They fucking hate me here. I don't know why.

A blond nurse comes in with gritted teeth. I guess she drew the short straw.

"I need a phone."

"Your father has your phone. Perhaps some water?"

"Perhaps… my cell phone. Get him in here."

"Mr. Clutterbuck–

"Damn it, Tina… I can't TAKE THIS anymore."

She scowls at me and storms off. Great. Am I getting a cellphone or not? I wait for Tina to hurry back with my phone or my step-dad, but no one comes for another half hour. Christ. Is anyone around here going to give a shit that I haven't seen my cell phone since the game? Makeba could be out there texting me or something. It's important…

When the next nurse comes in, she comes in with my scowling step-dad. I still hate seeing him angry. Like this day couldn't turn into any more of a fucking shit show.

"What do you want?" I grumble. "And where's my phone?"

"He hasn't heard the news?"

The nurse shakes her head. I know that look on his face. He gave me that look the day mom died – the day he realized he was stuck with her little shit of a kid for the rest of his life. I'll never forget that look of disappointment on his face and I hate that I have to see that look in his eye again.

"How's the neck?"

"I don't know. I haven't seen anyone."

My step-dad glowers at the nurse. I know that look too. He's going to get his way or by fucking God, this place will burn.

"Get a goddamn doctor in here to look after my son."

His son? Judge Clutterbuck only refers to me as his son when he's about to fuck my life up. I suddenly want to walk out of this bed and head out of here. I don't need the good Judge's fist coming towards my head. He notices my wariness of him. Not fear. It's been a long time since I've been afraid of my step-dad.

"So," he says gruffly. "I heard they're looking at you for the majors."

"Yeah. So they say. Mind getting my phone for me?"

"They gave it to me yesterday. You'll get it in a minute."

"Dad!"

He ignores me calling him dad, which he usually eats right up. Fuck. What's his problem?

He says, "I have news about your girlfriend."

I don't like my step-dad's tone. In his defense, I never like his fucking tone.

"What news?" I need to text her.

"She's with the cops right now."

"What? Why is she with the cops?"

I shift my body and ignore the searing pain in my neck. No permanent head injuries, but I still feel like utter shit and naturally, my step-dad makes it ten times worse. He's the one I really want to deck in the face. We haven't had that type of relationship in years, but there's a part of me that still wants revenge for the way he treated me as a kid. Maybe one day I'll completely forgive him, but not yet.

Judge Clutterbuck loves holding information over my head. I just hope he doesn't piss me off. I'm not in the mood and if Makeba's in trouble, I need to get the fuck out of here. Before my step-dad can answer my fucking question, the damn doctor enters the room. The last thing I need is another barrier to Makeba.

"Hello, Mr. Clutterbuck..."

"Doc, when can I get the fuck out of here?"

"Jayce..." my step-dad warns.

"Well, Mr. Clutterbuck, we wanted to run a few more tests–

"Later. I need to leave," I interrupt.

Groaning, I pull myself out of bed. I expect my step-dad to step in and side with the doc. Instead, he sides with me.

"Listen, doctor. Jayce seems fine. He's a tough kid, and he wants to get out of here."

"He suffered a neck injury and–

"Hey, the kid says he's fine. This place is costing me an arm and a leg, anyway. Get him discharged. Now."

When my step-dad speaks, people listen. He never expected to end up with a shit head kid like me – a kid who never listened. It excuses nothing he did, but we got stuck together and neither of us liked it. Maybe one day we can completely heal the shit that's gone down between us.

When the doctor scampers off to get a nurse to handle the discharge, the good judge turns his gaze to me.

"So," he says. "Are we good?"

I don't know what he's talking about. A lifetime of hitting me in the face or putting his hands around his neck?

"I don't know what you mean."

My neck is sore, but I don't give a crap. I'm dragging my folded clothes off the chair on the side of my bed and getting ready to see Makeba.

"I mean... listen, I got your girlfriend out of trouble. You promised me you weren't going to do anything stupid with that firearm license and you broke that promise. I'm choosing to let that go. You're welcome."

Fuck. What the hell did Makeba do and why the fuck won't my step-dad stop speaking in tongues?

"Yeah. Let's just get out of here, dad."

His face softens, which is very rare for my step-dad. It always unnerves me when he acts like he's going to get all sensitive. We don't have that type of relationship.

"Dad?"

Fuck. Are we really going to do this again? I'm an adult. We both know how fucked up things have been between us and they're always going to be fucked up. There's nothing we can do about the past, is there? He hit me until he couldn't anymore and that's always going to be between us, creating tension too thick to cut.

"Yeah. Whatever. Don't make a big deal out of it."

"She's going to be okay," he says. "That's all you need to know."

"Right."

"And one last thing..." He gets red and uncomfortable. The judge is only an inch taller than me now and his hair turned grey halfway through highschool. I've never seen him look contrite before.

"What?"

We don't have that type of relationship. I don't know if now we're going to start.

"I was hard on you, kid. You didn't deserve the half."

Hard on me? That doesn't begin to describe it.

"Understatement of the century."

For a minute, he almost looks ashamed.

"You turned out to be a good kid, anyway. That's probably your mother in you. It sure as shit isn't me."

I appreciate the apology, but there's still a part of me that wants to brush it off. At least there's hope for us one day.

"I don't even remember what she looked like. Now, can we stop the sentimental crap and get out of here?"

I'll yield an inch to the judge when I'm completely free from him. Until then, I still need to keep him at arm's length.

After my discharge, my step-dad takes me to the police station. He offers to come in, but I don't need him to handle anything. I still don't know what's going on. All I know is that Makeba fired her weapon and somehow, my step-dad took care of shit for her. I still need to see her. I give him an awkward goodbye and try to hide how much my neck and back still hurt as I rush in to see her.

When I get in through the front door, Kya and Raven are the first two people I see. Where the fuck is she?

Kya power-walks toward me with an angry expression on her face.

"Jayce! Oh my God, we were just going to send Cole to get you. Why aren't you answering your phone?"

"Step-dad came. Just got it back. He took me straight over here. What's going on?"

Kya explains everything and then explains what happened to Makeba.

"She nearly killed B.J. but she wasn't hurt and thanks to your step-dad, she won't get in trouble with the school for the firearm. What were you thinking, giving her a damn gun?"

It's just like Kya to sprinkle a moral lecture into her good tidings.

"I was thinking she needed to defend herself. Looks like it worked out."

"She's traumatized," Kya says. "The cops are finishing up questioning."

"Why did she shoot him? What the hell happened?"

I inspect the girls for signs of damage. They're alive, but they don't look so good. The school has gone into full lockdown mode and they could only leave because of the police escort. Raven's eyes are puffy and Kya's scowl is even deeper than normal. They still seem shell-shocked. Fuck. Kya's not as talkative as usual, either, so this shit is serious. I hope Cole gets his ass over here soon to look after his girl.

"B.J. came back," Raven says, her voice choking. "I never thought he was this type of person. I never would have guessed."

"Honey, this isn't your fault," Kya whispers, putting her arm around Raven's shoulders. Then she turns her attention back to me.

"B.J. killed three girls in our dorm. He's going to prison for a long time. He came to our dorms looking for revenge and I know she blames herself. Talk to her, Jayce."

"That's exactly what I came here to do. Where is she?"

I don't have to wait long for Makeba to emerge. The cops refuse to let me in the room to talk to her until they're done questioning. Apparently, my step-dad didn't just get her out of trouble, he brought her one of the best lawyers in Boston. Dustin Rathbone's dad – James Rathbone IV. Mr. Rathbone pats her on the back as he walks out of the station and my little jailbird perks up when she sees me.

"Jayce! I did it!"

"See?" Kya whispers. "She's traumatized."

She doesn't seem too traumatized. She sprints towards me and I do what any man would do. I pick her up and kiss her and spin her around, clutching her body against mine. Some asshole nearly shot her, and I wasn't even there. I don't want to let her go. It just feels like a mistake. But because of my back and neck and my face reddening from the pain, I have to set her on her feet. She keeps her arms around my neck and I refuse to let go of those hips.

"What the fuck went down?"

"Pew pew," Makeba says, her grin falling away. "But he survived, don't worry. And... honestly... it hasn't all hit me yet."

But it will. And there might be nightmares and trouble keeping track of things and all the other things that come with an event like this. The important thing is that Makeba Winston doesn't have to be alone.

"Are you safe? Were you hurt?"

I run my fingers over her cheek. Fuck, her skin is smooth. Everything about her is smooth and perfect. Even now.

"No. I'm fine," she whispers. "But I was so scared at first... Then I thought of you. It's not just that you protected me, Jayce. You taught me how to protect myself. And I realized something."

"That you're a pretty good shot for a first timer?"

"No, stupid... I love you, Jayce Clutterbuck and you are definitely the best boyfriend I've ever had. Hear me? I love you. And I'm not afraid to say it anymore."

She smiles and waits for my answer, but words won't do this justice. I need to feel her and touch her and pull her close to me. I run my hands over her butt and pull her body against mine. Her plump breasts press against my chest and I give her a deep kiss. My neck aches as I bend my head to kiss her, but every bit of pain is worth her soft lips pressed against mine. I grab her cheeks and keep kissing her until we need to breathe.

"I love you too," I whisper. "And I am so fucking happy that you're alive."

"What about your neck? Is that fine?"

"Hurts like hell, but I can handle it, chica."

Kya clears her throat.

"Not be a party pooper, but this place smells like pee. Can we head back to campus yet?"

She's right. This place smells like a drunk tank. I slip my hand into Makeba's and pull her tightly against me. I'm never letting her out of my sight again.

22

A BRIEF PICTURE OF THE FUTURE: THE SUMMER IN BOSTON

MAKEBA

July

Laguna Grove shuts down early for the summer. The hockey boys play their last game away from campus and they win. Some people think the other teams let them win because the entire world knows about the school shooting that shocked the country. Nothing like this has ever happened at a fancy private school like Laguna Grove, and B.J.'s wealthy background appears to confuse commentators. Massachusetts has strict gun laws. This isn't supposed to happen here, but it happened.

B.J.'s behind bars, but he's basically famous for what he's done. I hate that. He doesn't deserve any attention for pulling a gun on innocent women.

For the first two weeks of summer, I barely look at my phone or check the news. Jayce and I move into his stepdad's brownstone together, which means I have to explain to my parents that I'm spending my summer with my white boyfriend.

They take it pretty well. My mom asks if he comes from a good family, which is subjective really, and my dad asks if he has a job, which is more complicated to explain. Jamaican parents hear you say "aspiring professional athlete" and think what you actually mean is "brokey mcpoverty".

Eventually they come around, but they want to meet Jayce to give him a once over – and probably question him to death. He's excited to meet them, but our plan is to head over there just before school starts up again in September. Until then, it's just us in our fancy Cambridge brownstone.

Thankfully, it doesn't take me long to get a job in Boston. I'm an intern at an agency that reunites separated immigrant families. The job can get sad sometimes, but there's nothing better than seeing the looks on the kids' faces when they realize they're going to see their parents again. If Jayce gets to work in Boston, I'd love to come and work at a place like this – if Jayce will let me work. He constantly describes this fantasy of keeping me home all day dressed in sexy outfits when he's playing for the majors. I roll my eyes when he jokes about a sexy cat costume. I've spent plenty of time wearing a leash around

Jayce for a lifetime. I won't add cat ears to the mix and indulge him.

Jayce plays hockey all day, every day and at night. He's normally too tired for anything except a couple hours of sex. I don't mind! We cuddle all night and he makes me breakfast every morning without fail. When he's done with physical therapy, his schedule will ease up and we can spend even more time rolling around in bed together or enjoying walks around Cambridge. Boston lacks a bit of diversity, but I love the city in the summer. There's always something going on and I have friends here to spend time with when Jayce gets busy.

Because of Cole's training, Kya's in Boston with him, which means I get to see her when I get off work and on the weekends we take a fitness class together. Hanging out with athletes all the time has that effect on you. Cole and Jayce are physically perfect and they work out all the time. It wouldn't hurt to try to keep up so at least I can go on Jayce's Sunday run outdoors with him.

Kya wants to lose a few pounds because of Cole's rookie season media appearance, but I just want to get stronger. There's only one person we really miss .. Our best friend Raven Rose. We need her to feel like our group is complete and finally, we arrange something.

Raven spends the first four weeks of the summer with her parents before she flies to Boston to spend the rest of the summer staying with me and Jayce. There's plenty of space in the brownstone and by the time she gets here, I only have a couple more weeks left in my internship. Jayce insists we have housekeeping so that I don't have to worry about it and he hires her for a deep clean the day before Raven comes, refusing to let me pay. The crazy thing is, I'm getting a little less messy. Jayce is pretty neat, and he's a good influence in that regard (although he's a bad influence in nearly every other department).

The day Raven arrives, Jayce and Cole are at practice. Cole's with the majors, but Jayce still needs to heal from his injuries, so he's at a major league training camp that will allow him to get everything together. Kya comes over in the morning with all the ingredients we need to make freshly baked goods for Raven's arrival.

"Jayce's step-dad might be an asshole," Kya says. "But this kitchen is amazing. This oven... Honey, I never want to cook in our apartment again."

We start with banana bread and we don't stop until we have enough comfort food to supply a dorm. Raven texts us when her taxi is about to pull up and we rush outside to meet her. It's been so long and we can't wait. Raven has fresh braids down to her waist and a white and red floral sundress that makes her copper skin pop in the summer sun.

"I'm here!"

We usher her inside and Kya prepares our snacks in the living room while I show Raven to the guest room. We get her all settled in and in the living room, we toast to our friendship and slice up the banana bread with a side of chocolate chip cookies. Raven seems like she has something on the tip of her tongue to tell us. Kya notices right away.

"So. You've been all mysterious on the group chat. What's going on?"

"I'm talking to Brett again," Raven blurts out. "But... I realized you guys are right. I think he's a catfish."

"Finally," Kya says. "Honey, it's not your fault. Men are weird."

"Here's the thing though," she says. "I thought it was B.J. at first, but it isn't. B.J.'s behind bars and I'm still talking to Brett. I know it's a fake profile, but... I already told him so much about myself. I kinda want to find out who it is."

"Are you enlisting our help?" Kya asks through a mouthful of chocolate chips.

Raven nods.

"Do we have a list of suspects?"

"No idea," Raven says. "Seriously. It's weird. But I have this suspicion it's someone who goes to our school."

"Maybe one of those poetry weirdos," Kya says. "I stopped by your class once and someone was clicking. How is that poetry?"

Raven shrugs. "I don't know, but while I'm here, I want to investigate. Brett claims he lives in Boston."

"Do you believe him?"

"No. But I still want to sort this out."

"We'll help," I say. "We've got our black girl crew. We can handle anything."

"Cheers!" Kya says. "To finding Raven's stalker before we get back to campus."

"Cheers!"

"Hey!" Raven says once we clink glasses again. "I never said he was a stalker."

Kya shrugs. "I don't know, honey… he seems like a stalker."

I wonder if Kya's right…

23

VARSITY PROPERTY

September
Laguna Grove College
Raven Rose's Sophomore Year

DUSTIN

I'm broken. 6 years ago, I had to choose whether I would let *the bad shit* destroy me or whether I would claw my way out of that weak fucking mess and find myself again. I know who I am. *Dustin Rathbone. Strength.* That's what life is all about, separating the strong from the weak. I won't ever let someone make me feel weak again. I will never give up control to anyone again.

6 years ago, I chose strength. I chose the ice. Skating saved me when nothing else could. I chose my brothers over letting the pain snap me in pieces and I made it to a top tier hockey college. I'm living my dream and I'm finally at peace with what happened. *Finally.*

After high school, I found my real brothers— the Vipers— this perfect outlet for my outrage. I had healing to do. I found myself in punches and hard checks. I found women, each one more gorgeous than the last. In six years, nothing could change me. Nothing could give me purpose... *until her.*

I'll never forget the first time I saw her walking into the English department with a pair of thick black glasses and a stack of books cradled precariously in her grasp. *Nerd.* That was my first thought. My second thought was less of a thought and more of a physical reaction. *Hard.* She never knew I was watching.

She still doesn't know I'm watching — or how long I've been watching. I don't want to stop. I want to keep her. To own her. *Soon.*

I promised myself I wouldn't let it get this far. I promised myself I'd stop after finding her online, after the lies, the hiding, the secrets, the fake identities, the fishing for information I could use.

I promised myself I'd confess the truth. But I can't stop. I enjoy living in the shadows and I don't want to come out. It's safe in the shadows. It's where monsters like me belong. It's where we feel safe.

I surround myself with monsters — creatures like me — snakes, spiders, cockroaches, skinks. Creatures that were never meant to fit in. I can fake it well enough. I've practiced the facial expressions, the reactions I'm supposed to have. I've practiced emotions hundreds of times so that I can fit in, get chicks, make my friends think I'm normal. *I know I'm far from normal.*

I haven't really *felt* anything in six years — not since before I turned eighteen. I'm dead inside and the only thing that brings me any pleasure is causing someone else's pain. That's why I need to keep my distance from her. I know I'll only hurt her because I desperately *want* to hurt her. Letting her in to my fucked up life would destroy my angel.

Every day, I fight this urge to break her and every day I know I get closer to losing the battle.

I want her.

She's nothing like the women I used to try to fix my shit. She's not my hot thirty-year-old neighbor with her collection of XL dildos and a traveling husband. She's not a pair of drunken sorority chicks with low self-esteem. She's nothing like any of the himbos I've used to salve my pain.

I'm losing control around her. I don't know what I'll do next. I just know that I've already gone too far and if I let myself take another step towards her, I'm going to fuck her up. I'm going to ruin her life.

Raven Rose.

After watching her read for an hour, I approach her window from my hiding spot. *Fuck. I've already burned through two joints.* I'm properly toasted and relaxed enough that all my inhibitions have vanished. It's easy to lose myself watching her. Now, I'm close enough to see her, close enough to feel my heart race as I watch, but hidden just enough that she can't see me watching. She'll never know.

I unlock my phone and message her from Brett's profile. *Brett.* She has no clue that Brett McClure doesn't exist — that it's me, hiding behind a profile, collecting her secrets and using them to my own advantage. *I don't know what compels me to be like this.*

Brett: I'm still sorry I didn't show up. I was nervous.

She waits a few seconds before looking at her phone. I don't want to wait. I've been patient, damn it. I want her to do something. I want her to *respond.* Discomfort surges through me. She's only reading. Why can't she put down that book and *pay attention to me.*

Eventually, she can't ignore the powerful tug of her cell-phone. None of us can, really.

Raven: You let me down again. I'm done, Brett.

. . .

Something catches in my throat. This is the third time she's tried to end our friendship. It's my fault. I keep chickening out. This time, my finger hovers over the keys and I consider my words carefully. If I do this, I'll commit to setting my plan in motion. I'm great at plans.

Brett: I understand. I won't contact you again.

She blocks my account. Fuck. What was I thinking? I won't contact her again?

It's a fucking lie and I know it. Raven won't know that. I may leave Brett McClure behind, but I'm definitely contacting her again. *I want her.* Once she sets her phone down, she strips her hoodie off. My breath catches. She wasn't wearing anything under that hoodie. *No bra.* Her tits are gorgeous. I hope she doesn't walk over and close the blinds, ruining my fucking view.

If her roommate comes in, I'm going to lose it. Hopefully her roommate Kya's back at the hockey house straddling my teammate. *Lucky guy.*

I want my own woman. I want her.

Raven... She turns away from the window to grab a t-shirt, denying me a view of her breasts. *Her tits turn me on so much.* I told my teammate Jayce Clutterbuck I was on the hunt, and I meant it. Raven's my prey and she doesn't even know it yet. I've toyed with her slowly. Teased her. I finally have all the information I need to seal the deal when I finally get my hands on her. I've spent a long time preparing for this.

Hunting women is like hunting anything else. You need patience. Raven turns around bare-breasted and I nearly cum in my pants. Her nipples are large and dark against her dark-copper skin. *She glows.* My cock tents my forest green *Laguna Grove* sweatpants and the urge to touch myself heightens. I just want her to touch her tits. Play with them a little. I want to put my tongue in places she'd never let me go. She doesn't have a clue what she does to me. She doesn't have a clue that she's broken my brain and pulled this out of me. My tongue teases my lower lip and I keep wishing she'll do something unexpected like touch her tits or push her hands into her panties and play with herself for me. My cock wants to burst.

She slips into that t-shirt and my little show ends. *Fuck.*

She cracks open a book and it's like the world vanishes to her. Seriously. I stand outside her window for 35 minutes before she gets up again, just watching the way she twirls those braids around her finger or how her tongue grazes her lower lip when she gets to a good part in her story. It's Friday night and she's just here... in her bed... reading. She fascinates me.

I don't think there are any chicks like this at Laguna Grove. When she returns to her bed, I notice she has something in her hand. What the fuck is that? I lean in, but I still can't make it out. I'll have to get closer to the window if I want to see, but that means I risk getting caught.

When has she ever caught me? I've done this as often as I could this semester. We're still in hockey preseason and there's nothing better to do than to hunt down the ones that got away. *Raven.* It's been a year since we first met – 377 days exactly. I've had other women in my bed since then – lots of other women. But there's one fantasy I can't get out of my head. Maybe it's how she looked that first night when she walked into Pesthouse with her friends. *Young. Happy. Pure.*

She reminds me that I used to be innocent. *She reminds me that I used to be weak.* I want to have her. I want to break that innocence. I don't even have a good reason why. There's something about her that gets my cock going, that makes me want to climb through that fucking window and take the woman I've been watching for such a long time. She climbs into her bed and that book opens right back up.

Christ. Is she just going to read that thing all night? I don't know how she can stand it.

I can't help myself. I shuffle closer to the window. I know I'm taking it too far. I know what I'll do if I keep going with this fantasy. *I know she doesn't lock her windows.* My breath catches as I nearly trip. Luckily, I'm not that much of a stupid fuck. I lean against her window and... oh. She slides her hand holding *that thing* between her thighs and it's pretty obvious what it is. I'm so close to the window that my breath fogs up the glass. I don't even care that she might notice. *That thing is a vibrator.*

A fucking vibrator. She's reading a book and using a vibrator. This chick loves reading so much she's literally flicking the bean to words. I can't stop myself. My hand slides into my pants and grips my hard cock. *Fuck.* He feels even bigger than normal today. Her back arches slightly as she gets that thing in a good spot and then she squirms…

I barely stroke myself before I cum *hard.* Fuck. All she did was *squirm* in her bed with a piece of plastic between her legs and I lose control. I can't handle being near her. I'm too fucked up.

The worst part is, this isn't the first time this has happened. Not the vibrator thing. Sometimes it's just the way she holds her pencil while scribbling her homework. Sometimes it's those nerdy fucking glasses. I keep telling myself I'll stop doing this. I haven't had sex with a woman since July. I *can't* have sex with anyone else when I can stand here and touch myself thinking about her.

I'm broken.

I don't know how much longer I can stand this. I don't know how much longer I can go without feeling her skin beneath mine. If this is me holding back, I'm totally fucked when I let go with her. *I'm going to break her too.* Maybe I *have* already broken her. I don't know. All I know is that I need to clean myself up and prepare for phase 2 of my plan, which doesn't involve cumming in my pants while staring at a woman through a piece of glass.

My plan involves cumming inside Raven.

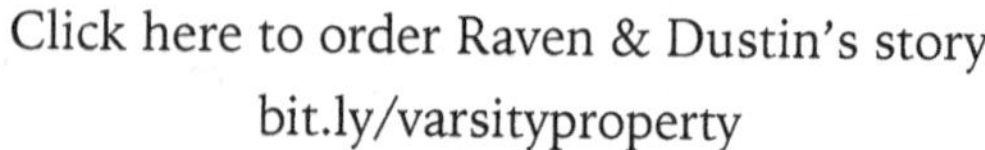

Click here to order Raven & Dustin's story
bit.ly/varsityproperty

Click here to get an update when the next book
comes out
bit.ly/textjamila

ABOUT JAMILA JASPER

The hotter and darker the romance, the better.

That's the Jamila Jasper promise.

If you enjoy sizzling multicultural romance stories that dare to *go there* you'll enjoy any Jamila Jasper title you pick up.

Open-minded readers who appreciate **shamelessly sexy romance novels** featuring black women of all shapes and sizes paired with smokin' hot white men are welcome.

Sign up for her e-mail list here to receive one of these FREE hot stories, exclusive offers and an update of Jamila's publication schedule:
bit.ly/jamilajasperromance

Get text message updates on new books:
https://slkt.io/gxzM

EXTREMELY IMPORTANT LINKS

ALL BOOKS BY JAMILA JASPER

https://linktr.ee/JamilaJasper

SIGN UP FOR EMAIL UPDATES

Bit.ly/jamilajasperromance

SOCIAL MEDIA LINKS

https://www.jamilajasperromance.com/

GET MERCH

https://www.redbubble.com/people/jamilajasper/shop

GET FREEBIE (VIA TEXT)

https://slkt.io/qMk8

READ SERIAL (NEW CHAPTERS WEEKLY)

www.patreon.com/jamilajasper

JAMILA JASPER

Diverse Romance For Black Women

MORE JAMILA JASPER
ROMANCE

Pick your poison...

Delicious interracial romance novels for all tastes. Long novels, short stories, audiobooks and more.

Hit the link to experience my full catalog.

FULL CATALOG BY JAMILA JASPER:
https://linktr.ee/JamilaJasper

PATREON

13 SEASONS OF SERIAL CHAPTERS

NEW preview chapters published WEEKLY on my Patreon.

Read all 6 seasons of *Unfuckable* (Ben & Libby's story)...

UNFUCKABLE

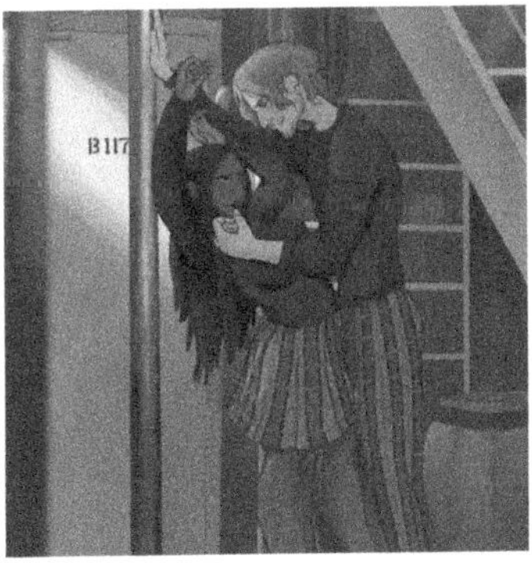

For a small monthly fee, you get exclusive access to over 375 chapters of my first completed bwwm dark and spicy serial romance, as well as the spin-off serial...

DESPICABLE

The second serial, despicable has 300 chapters available for all Patreon subscribers to access instantly and... we officially have a **third completed spin-off bwwm romance series.**

And yes you get access to all of this at the $5/month tier with more benefits at more pricey tiers.

The third serial is about Clover + Thomas. Thomas has a shocking connection to a character in the second serial and Clover is an all-new African American female lead.

POWERLESS

This series has three *very long* "seasons" of chapters, the length of five full-length novels all-together.

You will probably have over three months of binge-reading before catching up to current content, making this one of the most 'bang for your buck' author Patreon subscriptions out there.

Don't take my word for it.
Check the post history:
www.patreon.com/jamilajasper

PATREON HAS MORE THAN THE ONGOING SERIAL...

INSTANT ACCESS

- NEW merchandise tiers with t-shirts, totes, mugs, stickers and MORE!

- **<u>FREE paperback</u>** with all new tiers
- **<u>FREE short story audiobooks</u>** and audiobook samples when they're ready
- #FirstDraftLeaks of Prologues and first chapters **weeks** before I hit publish
- Behind the scenes notes
- Polls and story contribution
- Comments & LIVELY community discussion with likeminded interracial romance readers.

LEARN MORE ABOUT SUPPORTING A DIVERSE ROMANCE AUTHOR

www.patreon.com/jamilajasper

THANK YOU KINDLY

Thank you to all my readers, new and old for your support with this new year.

I look forward to making 2023 an INCREDIBLE year for interracial romance novels. I want to thank you all for joining along on the journey.

www.patreon.com/jamilajasper

Thank you to my most supportive readers — my Patreon subscribers!:

Martha

Nikki Valentina

xjkpop

Valeria

BlkBae

SweetS

Msteeq

Rhonda

Darrah

Killa

Shavon

Misty

India

Kassandra

Imani

Nala

Chantell

Benvinda

Roger

Lexi B

Zapphire

Vbrooks

Tasha G

Kiera

Valencia

Stacy

YANITZA

Texansgurl76

Emma

Tinette

Jenny

Mariah

Nale

Tanisha

Trenita

Shelle

dulcemaria413

Shanice

Letarsha

Tania

Neeka

Julia

Linda

Lisa

Jiannie

Jillian

Tameka

Asia

Scarlette

Olwyn

R W

Fayefaefee

Brianna

Tiffany

Katie

Diamond

Kera

Tia

Love Reading

Dominique

Sheria

Jennifer

Georgette

Monique

Wendolyn

King Turtlc22

Jessica

Nic M.

JustChill

DJC

Atira

TheeLastHokage

Yvonne

Chrissy

Janelle

Rian

LaRonda

LaRonda

Deanna

dlawson382

Jasmine

Haley

Belinda

Sercee

Yvonne

Jadelock

Farah

Tamiya

Quin

J.Payton

Geek Girl

Ashley

Rubi

Pilar

Sandra

Jurnee

Anni

Shannet

Joneesa

GlitzyHydra

Amanda

Barbara

Brianna

Jamica

Lyons

MARY ANN

Marketia

SarahD

LoverofHawaiiHearts

ceblue

Yolanda

MonaGirl Lewis

Dianna

Mary

amna

Nysha

fayola

Ty

Abria

Shyra

Andi-Mariee

Jamila

Naee's World

KEISHA

Jennett

Fredericka

Candece

Chante

Pholuv

Lydia A

Sabrina

JM

Jackie

Mo

Natrilly83

Ashaunte

Tolu

Margaret

Wendolyn

Lori

Dionne

ZLB

Kristina

Nicol

ELBERT

A. Harris

Jesi

Brenda

Desiree

Angela

Frances

LaShan

Only1ToniD

Debbie T.

Tiffanie

April L

shawnte

Kay

Lisema

Yvonne F

Natasha

Colleen

Julia

Amy

Jacklyn

Shyan R

Kiana B

Pearl

Javonda

Sheron

Maxine

Dash

Alicia

margaret

Love2Read

Juliette

Monica

Sandhya

MaryC

Trinity

Brittany

June

Ashleigh

Nene

Nene

Deborah

Nikki M

Dee

TyKira

Kimmey

Laytoya

Shel W

Arlene

Judith

Mary

Shanida

Rachel

Damzel

Ahnjala

Kenya

momo

BJ

Akeshia

Melissa

Tiffany

sherbear

Nini J

Curtresa

REGGIE A.

Ashley

Mia

Tink138110

Phia

Sharon

Charlotte

Assiatu C

Regina

Romanda

Catherine

Gaynor

BF

Perpetua

Tasha G

Henri Ann

sara

skkent

Rosalyn

Danielle

Deborah J

Kirsten

ANA

Taylor R.

Charlene

Louanna

Michelle

Tamika

Lauren

RoHyde

Natasha

Shekynah

Cassie

AnnaBooms

Keitheena

Nick R

Gennifer M

Rayna

Anton

Jaleda

Kimvodkna

JaTonn

Jazmine

Anoushka

Raynischa

Audrey

Valeria

Courtney

Donna

Patrisha

Jenetha

LaKisha J.

Ayana

Taylor

Christy

Monica

FreyaJo

GRACE

Kisha

Christine

Alexandra

Amber

Natasha

Stephanie

LaKisha

kristylove7

Cynthea

DENICE

Latoya

monifacd .

Doneishia

Mariah

Gerry

Yolanda T

Yolanda P

Susan D

Phyllis H

Alisa K

Daveena K

Desiree S

Kimberly B

Robin B

Gary S

Stephanie MG

Georgette A

Kathy

Marty

JanetDaniels

Megan

Shelle

Delores

Janet

Lydia

Phyllis

Freda

Charlott R

<u>Join the Patreon Community.</u>